'...der most enjoyable ... An author who never takes himself that seriously, and for whom any fictional murder can frequently form part of the entertainment industry'
COLIN DEXTER, *The Oldie*

'A crime novel in the traditional style, with delightful little touches of humour and vignettes of a small town and its bitchy inhabitants'
Sunday Telegraph

'With a smidge of adultery thrown in, some wise observations about stagnant marriages, disillusioned lovers and the importance of friendship, and, of course, plenty of whiffy red herrings, it all makes for a highly enjoyable read'
Daily Mail

'This is lovely stuff, as comforting – and as unputdownable – as a Sussex cream tea. More please'
Brighton Evening Argus

'Crime writing just like in the good old days, and perfect entertainment'
Guardian

THE WITNESS AT THE WEDDING

Simon Brett worked as a producer in radio and television before taking up writing full time. As well as the Mrs Pargeter novels and the Charles Paris detective series, he is the author of the radio and television series *After Henry*, the radio series *No Commitments* and *Smelling of Roses* and the bestselling *How to Be a Little Sod*. His novel *A Shock to the System* was filmed, starring Michael Caine.

Married with three grown-up children, he lives in an Agatha Christie-style village on the South Downs.

The Witness at the Wedding is the sixth novel in the Fethering Mysteries series. The ninth, *Blood at the Bookies*, is available now.

By the same author

SIMON
BRETT

THE WITNESS AT THE WEDDING

A FETHERING MYSTERY

PAN BOOKS

First published 2005 by Macmillan

First published in paperback 2006 by Pan Books
an imprint of Pan Macmillan, a division of Macmillan Publishers Limited
Pan Macmillan, 20 New Wharf Road, London N1 9RR
Basingstoke and Oxford
Associated companies throughout the world
www.panmacmillan.com

ISBN 978-0-330-51964-9

1 3 5 7 9 8 6 4 2

A CIP catalogue record for this book is available from
the British Library.

Printed and bound in Great Britain by
CPI Mackays, Chatham ME5 8TD

Visit **www.panmacmillan.com** to read more about all our books and to buy
them. You will also find features, author interviews and news of any author
events, and you can sign up for e-newsletters so that you're always first to hear
about our new releases.

To Jack,
with thanks for a really good idea
(*which sadly didn't make it into the book*)

Chapter One

'Oh, I didn't tell you there's a history of murder in my fiancée's family, did I?'

The speaker was Stephen, Carole Seddon's son, and as soon as he'd said the words, she wished he hadn't. Everything had been going well up until that point. Carole was entertaining Stephen and Gaby on her own ground, over lunch in the Crown and Anchor pub in Fethering, and discussion of the wedding arrangements had been harmonious, even at times exciting.

But Gaby hadn't liked the mention of murder. The bubbliness of her personality had been instantly punctured, and she looked pained as she turned to her fiancé and said, 'You're exaggerating. I don't think local gossip qualifies as a "history of murder".'

To give him his due, he did back off very quickly, aware that he had crossed a threshold into forbidden territory. Carole was again surprised by her son's sensitivity. In Gaby's company Stephen displayed sides of his personality whose existence his mother had never suspected . . . or, Carole thought ruefully, had never taken the trouble to explore. She still didn't

1

ever feel quite at ease with her son, still a little guilty for her lack of instinctive maternal feelings, for her part in the break-up of the marriage to his father David.

And as she looked across at him, she was again struck by how like Stephen was to a distorted image from her own mirror. He had the same earnest and potentially cold pale blue eyes, which peered through similar rimless glasses. Though not yet as uniformly grey as her own, his hair had a patina of silver over it. His relationship with Gaby had considerably lightened his personality, but there had always been hanging about Stephen an aura of the middle-aged. Though only in his early thirties, he looked older.

'More drinks,' Carole announced, mainly to break the mood. Stephen demurred; he was driving and he'd had the half of bitter he'd rationed himself. This proper caution only served to reinforce his middle-aged image. But Gaby said she'd join Carole in another glass of Chilean Chardonnay.

The moment she moved to the bar, Carole was aware of the two heads in the alcove behind her drawing closer, of the whispered remonstrance from Gaby to Stephen. She must have been berating him further for mentioning the subject of murder. Carole felt intrigued, but knew that this was not the moment to probe further. An opportunity might arise to find out more, or it might not. Carole wouldn't be that bothered either way. With Gaby Martin about to become a fixture in her life, there would be plenty of time to find out about her family background.

She ordered two glasses of wine from Ted Crisp, the Crown and Anchor's landlord, scruffy of beard and matted of hair. He was an ex-stand-up comedian and – perhaps more unlikely – one of Carole's very few ex-lovers. The mutual consent by which the relationship had ended seemed now to have developed into a mutual agreement that no mention should ever be made of the incident by either of its participants.

'Nice day, isn't it?' Carole observed.

Ted did not take issue with this uncontroversial assertion. 'Yes, really get the smell of the sea with the windows open.'

'Have you still never been on the beach, Ted?'

He shook his shaggy head in mock-fear. 'Ooh, no. Not my element, the sea. I'm a city bloke, really.'

'Yes, but you have been living on the South Coast for some years now and the beach is less than a hundred yards away.'

'No, not for me. I find it easier to pretend the sea's not there.' He leant forward conspiratorially over the bar. 'That way I'm not at risk from mermaids.'

'What?'

'They're well known for luring men to their deaths.'

'I thought those were sirens.'

'Mermaids do it too. I should know. Had a girl-friend who was a mermaid once. Beautiful. Her vital statistics were thirty-eight – twenty-four – and a large cod.'

Carole winced. 'What a loss you were to the stand-up circuit, Ted.'

He chuckled, then nodded across to the well-rounded, bubble-haired figure leaning in towards Stephen. 'That's the famous fiancée, is it?' He had not been behind the bar when they arrived, so no introductions had been made.

Carole confirmed that it was indeed the famous fiancée.

'Looks as if she's a good thing for Stephen,' Ted observed.

'How do you mean?'

'I've seen you having lunch in here with him a few times over the years. Conversation seems to be flowing a bit more freely with the fiancée around.'

Carole neither confirmed nor denied this, but she knew it was true. The days when Stephen had come down to Fethering and picked up his mother from her house, High Tor, for dutiful lunches had never been particularly relaxing for either of them. He had always taken refuge in talking about his work, which made Carole feel guilty because she had so little understanding of what he did, and could feign so little interest in it. Gaby's appearance on the scene had certainly freed up the conversational logjam. Even without the reliable stand-by of the wedding, there never seemed to be a lack of topics for discussion when Gaby was present.

Murmuring some all-purpose response to Ted Crisp, Carole crossed back to the table. The momentary dissension between the engaged couple had evidently been smoothed over, but the firmness with which Stephen embarked on a new topic of conversation showed that Gaby's family history was not about to be probed further.

'We've absolutely decided that we're going to get married down here.'

'Down here?'

'Yes, Mother. In Fethering.'

Carole still winced inwardly at the formality of that 'Mother' – particularly as she couldn't forget that Stephen called his father 'Dad'.

'But surely Gaby's parents – I mean, it is traditional for the bride to be married where she grew up.' Carole looked at Gaby, who shrugged.

'Well, I wasn't brought up in Harlow, which is where they live now. And in fact I do have a West Sussex connection.'

'Oh?'

'My mother went to school in Worthing. I wasn't born down here, but I think she'd only just moved out of the area. I don't know. Mum's always a bit vague about that period of her life.'

'Fine. So it'll be Worthing rather than Harlow.' Carole hoped the relief didn't show in her voice. Her middle-class sensibilities would have been troubled by the idea of her son being married in Essex. Hard to disguise that kind of thing. People viewing the wedding photographs would be bound to ask where the event had happened. And, of course, it'd be on the marriage certificate for perpetuity. The genteel folk of West Sussex did not hold the county of Essex in the highest esteem.

'Yes. Besides . . .' Gaby paused, as though uncertain

whether she should proceed with the sentence. She made up her mind and went on, 'The fact is, Carole, that my parents aren't really . . . Well, it's going to be easier all round if Stephen and I make most of the arrangements.'

Carole didn't say anything, but her disquiet communicated itself, so Gaby hastened to correct any false impression. 'It's not that they aren't happy about Stephen and me getting married. They're absolutely delighted. It's just . . . well, the fact is that my mother is a terrible worrier. Organizing a wedding would be like a nightmare for her. She's just not good at that stuff. The only way she's going to enjoy the event is if she has nothing at all to do with the arrangements.'

Carole took a rather dim view of this. She hadn't got a daughter, so the situation would never arise for her, but she liked to think that in the same circumstances she would have done her duty. She might not enjoy organizing a wedding, but she knew it was part of the complex package of agreements every parent of a daughter signed up to. Still, maybe those rules didn't apply to people who lived in Essex. She tried to keep the disapproval out of her face, but clearly failed.

'I know you think that's wrong, Carole, but believe me, if my mother was in charge, a) the wedding wouldn't be at all well organized, and b) being responsible for it would probably give her a nervous breakdown.'

'Well, you know best. That sounds fine.' But Carole wasn't convinced it was fine. Also the mention of a 'nervous breakdown' raised the disturbing possibility of instability in the family of her future daughter-in-law. Carole Seddon was very old-fashioned about the concept of mental illness. She liked to think that she kept her emotions so firmly under control that she herself was in no danger of such a lapse, and tended to be judgemental towards those who did succumb. A psychologist might have reckoned that this attitude reflected her fear of losing control of her own mind, but then Carole Seddon was not a psychologist – nor indeed had she ever consulted one.

'There's also the matter of money,' said Stephen. 'Gaby's mum and dad would do anything for her, but the fact is that they haven't really got a bean . . .'

'Afraid not,' his fiancée concurred. 'They've only got Dad's pension.'

'. . . whereas we're fortunate enough to be quite well-heeled at the moment. So it was always going to be us who were going to pay for everything.'

Carole thought of her handsome civil service pension and her carefully squirrelled savings. 'I'd be very happy to help out if—'

'Not necessary, Mother. Honestly. We don't have a problem with it. A lot of our contemporaries pay for their own weddings. It's different if you marry straight out of university, when you have no money at all . . .'

'Not to mention a huge student loan these days,' Gaby added.

'Right. In those circumstances you expect the parents to stump up, but Gaby and I are . . . well, both healthily established in our careers, so it makes sense for us to foot the bills.'

'Yes, I'm sure that's fine,' said Carole, again with more conviction than she felt.

'And,' her son continued, 'on the "he who pays the piper" principle, that will also mean we can conduct the wedding in exactly the way we think fit.'

He pronounced this with an almost wolfish satisfaction, which again set alarm bells ringing for Carole. Surely they weren't going to go for some 'alternative' style of wedding? Not exchanges of vows they had written specially for the occasion, or readings from *The Road Less Travelled* or *Captain Corelli's Mandolin*, or crowning each other with garlands of wild flowers? None of that sounded terribly likely from the Stephen she knew, but Carole was coming to realize increasingly how little of her son she did know.

'And what,' she asked tentatively, 'do you "think fit"?'

'Oh, nothing outrageous,' he replied, to her considerable relief. 'Traditional, white church job, that's what we're after.' Seeing his fiancée's wry grimace, he went on. 'No, Gaby, if we're going to do it, we'll do it properly. A big number. Invite everyone we know.'

The girl looked almost pleadingly at Carole. 'A large part of me would just like to dash off to a registry office and get the deed done on the quiet.'

'No way. It's not as if we're ashamed of each other.'

'Of course not.'

'Then let's let everyone know about it. I think the most important bit of the wedding service is that "before this congregation" bit – though no doubt they've screwed that up too in the Modern English version of the service.'

Carole wasn't enough of an expert on the liturgy to pass comment. Gaby still looked dubious. Though she worked in the flamboyant world of a theatrical agency, there was a reclusive quality about the girl, an unwillingness to be put into any kind of limelight. And that tendency seemed to strengthen as the reality of the wedding approached. She jutted out her lower lip. 'I don't know. I think the playwright Ian Hay probably got it right when he described marriage as "a ghastly public confession of a strictly private intention".'

Stephen chuckled. 'It'll be all right, love. I want to show you off. I want everyone to know that I'm marrying the most wonderful woman in the world.'

Carole lowered her eyes in embarrassment. This seemed a rather effusive statement from a member of the Seddon family. The thought seemed to cause further disquiet to Gaby too.

But it enabled Stephen to move on to what was clearly another bone of contention for the engaged couple. 'Which is why, Gaby, I think we really have got to put the announcement in the paper.'

'I honestly don't think that's necessary, Steve.' Carole had never heard her son called 'Steve' by anyone but Gaby; even his school friends had stuck to the rather sedate 'Stephen'.

'We've told all our friends,' Gaby went on. 'Everyone who needs to know already knows.'

'But somehow the engagement doesn't really seem

proper unless there's been an announcement in *The Times* and the *Telegraph*.'

Carole sympathized completely with her son's response. There was a right way of doing these things. 'I agree. Really, Gaby, you'll be amazed by the reaction you get to an official engagement announcement. People you knew as a child, school friends, people you've completely forgotten about – they'll all write and congratulate you.'

Gaby grimaced without enthusiasm. 'I'm not sure that I want that. People coming out of the wood-work . . .' The idea troubled her for a moment, then she moved on in a lighter vein. 'Anyway, from what friends of mine have told me, newspaper announce-ments also mean your parents get inundated with flyers from wedding caterers, wedding video compa-nies, wedding insurance brokers . . . I can do without all that.'

'I still think we should do it,' said Stephen, with a dogged truculence that Carole remembered well from his childhood.

'All right, we'll talk about it again. Not now.'

Gaby spoke with a surprising firmness, which had the instant effect of making Stephen change the sub-ject.

'Incidentally, Mother, have you talked to Dad?'

After another little internal wince, Carole replied, 'Well, I spoke to him soon after you announced your engagement.'

'But not since then?'

'No.'

'You said you were going to.'

The reproach in Stephen's voice put Carole instantly on the defensive. 'Yes, but I didn't say when.'

'No, but you must.'

'I will.'

'It's very important that you and Dad are relaxed with each other at the wedding.'

'I can assure you,' said Carole with some asperity, 'that your father and I will be as relaxed as it is possible for us to be. But neither of us is about to pretend that the divorce didn't happen.'

'I wasn't suggesting that. I was just thinking, the more contact you've had before the event, the easier it will be for you.'

'That, Stephen, is a matter of opinion.'

'But you will try.'

'Of course I'll try!' Carole was surprised at how close she had been to putting a 'bloody' in her reply.

'I spoke to him a couple of days ago, and said that you'd be ringing him soon.'

'And I'm sure I will. But I'll do it without prompting from you, Stephen.'

'OK, fine.'

The spectre of David loomed closer in Carole's consciousness, and it was a troubling presence. There was a lot about the whole wedding business that troubled her. Not that her son was marrying Gaby Martin – that seemed a piece of unqualified good news – but the attendant details that this basic fact gave rise to. A reconciliation – at whatever level – with David was the most worrying of these. And now it had been joined by the fact that the wedding was to take place on Carole's home patch. She knew she should be pleased and flattered by the news, but all it had done was to raise her anxiety. In spite of her mental strictures about Gaby's mother's response to the idea of organizing a wedding, Carole didn't want to find herself forced into too much responsibility for the event.

As these two worries jostled for prominence, a third, which had been lurking in Carole's unconscious, rose to join them – the prospect of meeting Gaby's parents. Carole had the social skills of any middle-aged woman who'd been brought up in the right middle-class way, so she was not going to disgrace herself, but the mere thought of the encounter disturbed her. It was fear of the unknown. These two people were about to become inextricably involved with her, and that knowledge brought to Carole Seddon the familiar terror of losing control of her carefully circumscribed existence. In her Fethering retirement she had simplified everything – she had her comfortable Home Office pension, High Tor all paid for, her Labrador Gulliver to prevent her from looking like a lonely single woman. She resented anything that threatened to recomplicate her life.

As if reading her thoughts, Gaby said, 'And we really must fix a date for you to meet up with my mum and dad.'

'Yes,' Carole agreed, envying the ease of that 'mum'. Without total honesty, she went on, 'I'm really looking forward to that.'

'I'll ring them this evening and try to sort something out. Are weekends best for you, or would a week-day be as good?'

'It doesn't make a lot of difference,' replied Carole, suddenly overwhelmed by the bleakness of her social calendar.

'I'll get back to you when I've talked to them.'

'Fine.' Everything seemed to be 'fine' that lunchtime, Carole thought wryly. At least, everyone kept saying everything was fine.

'We're going to have to move soon,' Stephen announced, looking at his watch. 'Want to look at some churches.'

'I thought you'd decided that you were going to get married in Fethering.'

'*Near* Fethering. If there's a prettier church in one of the other local villages, then we'll go for that. Since Gaby isn't a resident . . .'

'And since neither of us has a shred of religion,' his fiancée contributed, anticipating his thought.

'. . . we may as well make our choice on purely aesthetic grounds.'

Gaby's face took on an expression of mock-guilt. 'And the only person who'll be offended by that will be my grandmother. Still carrying a very large candle for the Catholic Church, I'm afraid, *Grand'mère*. Still, she lives in France, and I think she'll be too frail to make it to the wedding – so, as Steve says, we'll just go for the prettiest church we can find.'

'Yes, well, fine.' Though Carole had no more religious feeling than they did, she had found her son's words a little offensive. Without buying into the belief side of the church, she felt there were still certain social niceties that should be respected.

She reached for her handbag. 'I'll settle up.'

'I'll get it, Mother.'

'No, my treat. My patch. My idea to meet here.'

'I won't hear of it.'

And he wouldn't. Before Carole had time for further remonstration, Stephen was up at the bar, wallet at the ready.

Gaby eased her body against the hard back of the settle in their alcove, wincing as she did so.

'You all right?'

'Getting a bit of pain from my back.'

'Have you had it looked at?'

'No, I'm sure it'll sort itself out. Just tension.'

'Worried about the huge step you're taking in getting married?'

It was an atypically direct question for Carole, but Gaby just laughed it off. 'No, a client at work's giving us a hard time. Actor who's just hit the big time – or may have hit the big time. He keeps talking about moving on to another agency, and my boss is on my case all the time, trying to make sure I don't allow that to happen.' She grinned weakly. 'Usual stuff.'

Carole wasn't entirely convinced by the answer. She thought her own diagnosis might be nearer the truth. Suddenly she noticed how pale and stressed Gaby looked, how different from the vivacious young woman she had first met only a few months previously at the Hopwicke Country House Hotel. Though her body retained its plumpness, Gaby's face seemed to have thinned. There were deep hollows under her eyes and the tight blonde curls had lost their lustre.

'How long has the back been bad?'

Gaby shrugged, a movement which again caused her to wince. 'Few weeks.'

'Doesn't Stephen think you should see someone?'

'I haven't told him it's hurting. I have to be strong for him.'

Carole hardly had time to register the strangeness of this remark before Gaby, almost childlike in her pleading dependency, asked, 'Why? You don't know a good back person, do you? Because we are going to be down here for a few days.'

'Well . . .' Carole Seddon couldn't quite keep the scepticism out of her tone as she replied, 'I know someone who does some *healing*.'

Chapter Two

'No, she hasn't called me,' said Jude.

'Oh, well, probably the back got better of its own accord. As backs do.'

Jude instantly picked up the implication of the last words – that all back pain was psychosomatic, and didn't affect people who had a proper control over their emotions. As Carole had. She smiled. 'A pain may have its origin in the head, but that doesn't mean the bit where it manifests itself hurts any the less.'

There was a predictable, 'Huh.'

'Don't worry, Carole. I'm not about to go into a riff on holistic medicine. I'm just saying that the physical and the mental are deeply interconnected.'

Jude's neighbour sniffed. It still sounded like mumbo-jumbo to her, and she devoutly hoped she would always continue to think of it as mumbo-jumbo. Carole Seddon had been brought up to consider the physical and the mental as totally separate, and the idea of breaking down the barrier between them she found positively frightening. Unwelcome thoughts and emotions were hard enough to control as it was, without suddenly changing the traditional rules that kept them in their proper place.

They were sitting in the front room of Jude's house, Woodside Cottage. The space was cluttered with 'things' which their owner had accumulated over many years. Very few of them had any practical use. There were ornaments, shells, bottles, drapes, chains, bangles, faded photographs in frames. Each 'thing' represented a memory for Jude, of a time of her life, of a friend or a lover. She could have told visitors the history of each, but that was not why she had them on display. They were private aides-memoires, and in fact she was rarely asked about them. People who came to Woodside Cottage seemed to accept the clutter, as just another manifestation of its owner's personality. And they were always more interested in telling Jude about their lives than in asking about hers.

Even Carole had got used to the clutter, and Carole was distrustful of 'things' – particularly 'things' that brought memories with them. She tried to exclude such 'things' completely from High Tor, hoping to keep the lid tightly closed on most of her past life.

The windows of Woodside Cottage were open that morning, and the warm June air presaged another hot summer. An 'unnaturally' hot summer, the Fethering locals would say darkly, before moving on to lugubrious talk of 'climate change' and its inevitable corollary of a man-created Armageddon. But that day there was still sufficient movement in the air to set the bamboo wind chimes tinkling. Not for the first time, Carole wondered why, though she'd have despised the sound anywhere else, she didn't find the wood-chink noise irritating in Woodside Cottage.

Jude was one of those people who carried with her a unique personal environment. Outwardly, she was a plump woman in her fifties with blonde hair gathered up into a gravity-defying structure on top of her head, but an inward serenity set her apart from other women of her age. Though her personal life had not been without its passions and disappointments, she emanated calm to everyone with whom she came in contact. It was not an effect at which she worked, it was instinctive. When they first met, Carole had felt jealous of this quality in her neighbour, but that jealousy had given way over time to a wistfulness, a recognition of how different their personalities were. For Carole, all emotional responses were hard work, the road to them fraught with misgivings and potential disasters. In low moods, she sometimes feared the only spontaneous instinct she had was for prejudice.

Evading further well-rehearsed arguments on the subject of holistic medicine, Jude moved the conversation on. 'How are the wedding plans going?'

'Fine,' replied Carole, instinctively echoing the conversation in the Crown and Anchor. Then, more dubiously. 'At least, I think everything's all right.'

'Nobody getting cold feet, I hope?'

'No, no, they still seem as besotted with each other as ever. It's just . . .'

'What?'

'After being so positive about the whole thing at the beginning, a kind of apathy seems to have set in.'

'Oh?'

'Well, they still haven't sorted out a church, or a venue for the reception, or caterers, or any of that stuff.'

'Time enough. What's the actual date?'

'Fourteenth of September. And we're into June now.'

'They've got three months. Many weddings have been sorted out in a lot less time than that.'

'I know. It's just . . . Well, it's unlike Stephen to be so dilatory. He was always terribly punctilious about forward-planning, almost obsessed with details of arrangements.'

The question crossed Jude's mind as to where he might have inherited that quality from, but she was too considerate to voice it. 'Probably just shows that being with Gaby is making him more laid-back.'

'Maybe.' But Carole wasn't convinced. 'I'd believe that, if Gaby herself was being more laid-back. But she isn't. She seems terribly tense, evasive when the subject of the wedding arrangements comes up.'

'So she's acting as a brake on Stephen?'

'Seems to be. And she's also very resistant to the idea of the engagement being announced in the papers.'

Jude shrugged. 'Surely that's up to her. Some people want every detail of their weddings plastered all over *Hello!* magazine, some just tick the box for "no publicity". There's nothing sinister about it.'

'Maybe not,' said Carole dubiously. 'But there is a right way of going about things, you know.'

That was such an archetypal Carole Seddon remark that Jude could not suppress a little smile. Then she asked tentatively, 'Have you . . . had further contact with David about the wedding?'

'No.' The reply was almost a snap. Carole had never liked the feeling of being nagged.

Instantly Jude backed off. 'Still, it'll be interesting for you to meet the rest of Gaby's family. Didn't you say she'd got some relatives in France?'

'Just her grandmother, I think.'

'Whereabouts?'

'South somewhere.'

'Ah.' Pleasing nostalgia came into Jude's brown eyes.

Carole picked up the cue. She'd never heard the details of Jude's stay in France. 'How long was it you lived there?'

'Two years. Well, just under two years.' Then, as so often, before Carole had time to ask supplementary questions, her neighbour moved on. 'Incidentally, I've got a friend coming to stay for a while.'

'Oh?' However much she tried, Carole couldn't keep the frost out of her voice. The last friend Jude had had to stay for any length of time had been an ex-lover, who had not only revived their relationship, but had also died of cancer in Woodside Cottage. Even though he had proved useful in researching the background to a murder case, Carole could still not think of Laurence Hawker without a little flicker of jealousy. She had felt excluded by Jude's absorption in him. While accepting her neighbour had many circles of friends in many different parts of the world, on their home ground in Fethering she felt a proprietorial interest. Unwillingly, she found herself asking, 'Is this another of your lovers, Jude?'

'No. By no means. A woman friend. Been through a bit of a rough time recently. Just needs to chill out for a while.'

There were two reasons for the inward wince that this prompted in Carole. First, there was the fear of someone new, someone who might unbalance the delicate microclimate that encompassed High Tor and Woodside Cottage. Second, there was the atavistic revulsion Carole felt towards expressions like 'chill out'.

'When's she coming?'

'This afternoon. She's been . . . well, she'll be free then.'

Carole did not miss the hesitation. For her its instant implication was that Jude's friend had just come out of hospital – or possibly even prison.

'What's her name?'

'Gita.'

'Gita?'

Jude smiled at the ill-hidden prejudice in the repetition of the name. Carole wasn't exactly racist. She was just one of those many middle-class English women who had very rarely encountered people of a different ethnicity from their own. Jude was amused to see the tension leave Carole's face as she said, 'It's a childhood name. Short for "Marguerite". She's always been called "Gita". Gita Millington.'

'Oh.' The name did sound vaguely familiar, but Carole couldn't think from where. 'And what's been wrong with her?'

But Jude wasn't to be drawn on that kind of detail. 'Just been under a lot of stress. Needs a break.'

Carole clearly wanted more information, but was too genteel to press the point.

'Will she be staying long?'

Jude knew that her shrug would infuriate Carole, but she was determined to say no more. Until Gita actually arrived, until it was clear what kind of state she was in, Jude wanted to keep information to the minimum.

Carole looked dissatisfied, but ceased her interrogation. With a slightly huffy, 'Well, do tell me if there's anything I can do to help while your friend's here,' she moved the conversation on. 'Stephen took Gaby to look at the local churches yesterday afternoon, so I suppose that's a step in the right direction. Though the chances of one not having another wedding already booked for the fourteenth of September is—'

She was interrupted by the phone ringing. Jude answered it and, after mouthing 'Talk of the devil', said, 'Yes, that's me. Gaby – right. Carole mentioned you, yes. Congratulations on the engagement. OK, whereabouts are you feeling the pain?'

Having fixed for Gaby to come and see her the following morning, Jude told Carole she'd better be getting on. Carole agreed that she should be getting on too.

There was shopping to be done, and Gulliver needed a walk. Jude said that a car was coming to pick her up at two. She was going to meet Gita. Resisting the appeal in Carole's pale blue eyes for more information, Jude saw her neighbour to the door, and made herself a quick lunch of bruschetta with salami, cheese and tomato.

The car was on time. It was a big expense, but a necessary one. Carole's offer of help would certainly have covered a trip to North London in her immaculate white Renault, but Jude didn't want to confuse Gita with new acquaintances. An anonymous hire-car driver was a pricey option, but the right one.

The clinic was private, housed in two adjacent West Hampstead mansions. The girl at reception was expecting her. Miss Millington was ready to leave. If Jude wouldn't mind waiting for a moment, a nurse would take her to Miss Millington. The doctor would like a word.

Gita looked pale rather than ill. A smile flickered across her lined face at the sight of Jude. Though not resisting her friend's hug, she did not return it. She was docile almost to the point of being uninterested. On heavy medication, Jude reckoned.

Gita Millington was almost her exact contemporary, but looked older. Without its usual make-up, her face seemed pulled downwards by care. Her hair had always been carefully dyed to reproduce its erstwhile dark-chocolate sheen, but enforced absence from the hairdresser now left a stripe of white along the parting.

She was dressed casually, too. Trainers and grey

jogging bottoms, a zip-up navy-blue fleece a couple of sizes too big, whose sleeves came down over her knuckles. A scruffy nylon knapsack on the floor by her chair presumably contained her other clothes. Gita, normally so soignée, seemed to have lost interest in what she looked like.

She seemed, in fact, to have lost interest in everything. Again, probably the medication.

There was a lot of it. The woman doctor, practical, efficient and seemingly determined to allow no glimpse of personality, took Jude through the various pills and doses. She concluded by asking how long Gita would be staying in Fethering.

Jude shrugged. 'As long as she wants to. There's no rush from my point of view.'

The doctor said this was good, and checked that Jude would be there a lot of the time.

'Yes. I do work, but most of my clients come to me.'

The doctor asked politely what her work was. On hearing a mention of the word 'healing', a professional disapproval of alternative medicine froze into her face, and she reiterated the importance of Gita's taking her medication regularly.

'It's all right,' said Jude. 'I'm not about to put her on a regime of St John's Wort and aromatherapy. I believe in complementary medicine. I don't think you should exclude anything that might help.'

The doctor's sniff suggested that there were a good few things *she* would exclude. She then gave Jude a list of phone numbers, and told her that she shouldn't hesitate to make contact in the event of 'another incident'.

At this, Gita spoke for the first time. Her voice sounded furry, unfamiliar to herself, as if she had not used it for a long time. 'It's all right,' she said. 'I'll be fine.'

She didn't speak again in the car on the way back. Jude chatted a bit about Fethering and the surrounding area, but soon stopped. The lack of response from Gita was not combative, though, and the atmosphere in the silent car was peaceful.

When they arrived at Woodside Cottage, Jude paid the driver – yes, it had been expensive – and led her guest inside. Was Gita hungry? No, most of all she was tired. Very tired. Would it be all right if she had a sleep?

Jude showed her the spare bedroom and the bathroom, and went downstairs to prepare a meal for later. While she was in the kitchen, the phone rang.

'Hi, it's Gaby Martin. You know, we spoke earlier about my back.'

'Yes, of course.'

'Thing is, I don't really want to waste your time.'

'I'm sure you wouldn't be wasting my time.'

'No, but coming tomorrow morning, well, I'm not sure that . . . Point is, my back actually feels better, so I think we should take a rain check on it.'

'OK. It's your back, it's your decision.'

'Sure. Sorry to mess you around.'

'No problem. And if it does get bad again, and you're in the area, just give me a call.'

'Yes. Thanks. Bye.'

Slightly odd, thought Jude. But not that odd. Backs, she knew, worked by a logic all their own.

Half an hour later she tiptoed up again to the spare room.

Gita Millington was out cold, her face more relaxed and younger in sleep. The short-sleeved nightdress revealed what the tracksuit top had hidden.

A bandage held in place a dressing over the slashes on the inside of her left wrist.

Chapter Three

'Hi, it's Gaby. I spoke to them.'

Not expecting the phone call, Carole couldn't think what her future daughter-in-law was talking about.

'My parents,' came the explanation. 'I've talked to them about us getting together.'

'Oh yes, of course.' Their lunchtime conversation in the Crown and Anchor came back.

'I suggested us meeting in London. Hope that'll be all right with you?'

'Yes, fine. Halfway.'

'Well, Harlow's a bit nearer London than Fethering, but . . .'

'It's not a problem. When did you have in mind?'

'They could do next Tuesday. Rather make it lunch, if it suits you. They're not very keen on going back on the train late.'

'Lunch on Tuesday would suit me very well,' said Carole, wondering for a moment how old Gaby's parents were. There had, of course, been talk of her father's pension. But then again, Carole herself had a pension. And she too would try to avoid late-night trains if she could.

'Haven't worked out where yet, but I'll give you a call in the next couple of days.'

'Fine,' said Carole, already starting to feel nervous at the prospect of the meeting ahead.

'I'll be there, of course, but I'm not sure whether Steve will be able to get away from work. Everything seems pretty frantic there at the moment.'

'Well, be nice to see him if he can. But if he can't, he can't.' Another potential cause for disquiet loomed up in front of Carole. 'Erm . . . will you be inviting David to the lunch?'

Gaby sounded surprised. 'I hadn't intended to. I mean, he has already met Mum and Dad.' Yes, of course he would have done, thought Carole with another pang of jealousy. 'But I could invite him, if you like?'

'No, no. No need at all,' came the hasty response. 'Well, I'll really look forward to meeting your parents. I'm sorry, I don't think you've ever mentioned what their names are.'

'Oh, haven't I? No, you're right, I probably haven't. Well, they're Marie and Howard.'

'Marie and Howard, right.'

'And they're . . .' Gaby hesitated, uncertain how to put the next bit. 'They're very . . . quiet. I mean, not flamboyant people. They live a sort of . . .' no other adjective offered itself '. . . quiet life.'

'That's fine. So do I.'

'Yes, but I mean even quieter than yours. I—' But the words wouldn't come to describe exactly what

Gaby was trying to say. 'You'll know what I mean when you meet them.'

'Fine. As I say, I'll look forward to it,' said Carole with even less conviction than she'd had when she last used the words. 'Oh, by the way, I gather you've talked to Jude.'

'Yes.'

'Good. How is the back now?'

'Much better, actually. I almost feel a bit of a fraud. It's always better in the evening. Steve and I have had a good dinner at the hotel and I'm feeling more relaxed.'

'Glad to hear it.'

'In fact, I've rung Jude, and cancelled our appointment in the morning.'

'Oh.'

'Yes.' There was a silence, as if Gaby was about to say something else.

'Well, I'd better be getting on,' said Carole. 'That is, unless there was anything else.'

'No. No . . . Well, just . . .'

'What, Gaby?'

'Carole, please be very gentle with my parents, won't you?'

Which, to Carole's way of thinking, was an extremely odd thing to say.

Carole had spent the rest of the following day putting it off. Gulliver had no idea why he had had an extra-long walk that afternoon, but he was delighted anyway. By the evening, though, Carole knew there was no escape. She'd made the decision and she had to go through with it.

Carole Seddon had an almost photographic memory for figures and especially phone numbers. She could still remember most of the numbers she had dialled regularly during her Home Office career, and at home never resorted to the use of the storing facility or quickdial on her phone. There was one number, however, to which she had never given houseroom in her mind, so she was forced to look it up in her address book.

He answered straightaway.

'David, it's Carole.'

'Ah yes. Stephen said you might be calling.'

So the stage management had been busying away on both sides of the divide. His voice, even in the few words he had spoken, opened a Pandora's box of unwelcome emotions, but Carole pressed on. This was just something that had to be done. 'I'm meeting up with Gaby's parents next Tuesday.'

'Yes . . . erm. So I gathered.'

She always forgot about the 'erm' until she heard it again. David's erm was a nervous tic. He uttered very few sentences that didn't contain at least one. Carole remembered the agony of anticipating its inevitable appearance, like waiting for the second shoe to fall. He hadn't seemed to do it when they first met, at least not so much. But when their relationship soured, as David became more nit-picking, the erm-rate increased. It was like a symptom of his fastidiousness, a necessary punctuation while he selected his next word. Carole had forgotten how much the erm had infuriated her.

'Well, I was thinking,' she soldiered on, 'if I am going to meet Marie and Howard—'

'You won't find them any problem,' David re-assured her. 'They're . . . erm . . . well, they seem to be very good people.'

Good? If ever there was a word that damned with faint praise, thought Carole. 'What are they actually like, David?'

'Well, it's . . . erm . . . They're difficult to describe. But you won't dislike them. They're not difficult or . . . erm . . ' But this erm failed in its function. David didn't seem able to find a word that encapsulated the Martins.

Carole's anxiety about the following Tuesday's encounter increased. But even that wasn't as distasteful as the task she was about to perform.

'David, we've been apart for quite a long while now . . '

'Yes,' he agreed cautiously.

'. . . and we're both grown-up people . . '

He didn't deny this.

'. . . so I'm sure we would be able to meet up now without any particular animosity.'

'Oh, yes, I'm . . . erm . . . I'm sure we could.'

Carole felt she was floundering. The breezy words she had planned to say to him didn't seem to be coming out right. She tried to get control of herself and as a result sounded too forceful when she announced, 'The point is that we're definitely going to meet on the fourteenth of September, when – for both Stephen and Gaby's sakes – we really must present as united a front as we can.'

'Oh, certainly.'

'And no petty animosities between us must be allowed to spoil their big day.'

'I couldn't . . . erm . . . agree more, Carole.'

'So I was thinking we ought to meet before then – just to talk – clear the air.'

Again the words came out too aggressively. Carole knew she sounded hectoring, the archetype, in fact, of the nagging wife. But David didn't seem fazed by her manner.

'I was . . . erm . . . going to suggest the very same thing myself,' he said.

'Good. Well, do you want to fix a time now?'

'Erm . . .'

She remembered another infuriating habit of her ex-husband's. He was very bad at making arrangements on the hoof. She had always had to plant the idea of a social engagement, then give him a little time to assimilate it. A few days later, once he had taken the suggestion on board, he would then raise the subject himself and be ready for the fine tuning of dates and times.

Wishing to give him time to go through this essential routine, and by now desperate to get off the phone, Carole said quickly, 'Think about it. Get back to me after Tuesday, when I've met the Martins.'

'Yes. I think that would be . . . erm . . . a good scheme.'

'Fine. I'll hear from you then then. Goodbye, David.'

At least, Carole thought as she put the phone down, the idea has been broached. I have re-established contact – that was always going to be the most difficult one.

But 'difficult' is a relative term. She wasn't actually looking forward to the subsequent contacts that would inevitably follow.

Chapter Four

Jude hovered by the front door. In her hand was the brightly woven African straw basket she used for shopping. She was dressed in her usual wafty style – a long Indian print skirt in burgundy tones, a voluminous amethyst silk jacket over a pale pink T-shirt. The blonde hair was held up by an insufficiency of chopstick-like wooden pins.

She looked across at the sofa. In the last forty-eight hours Gita had gained a bit more colour, but still did everything in a kind of slow-motion lethargy. She had retained the jogging bottoms, but the trainers had given place to smart grey sandals, and the tracksuit top to a well-cut loose denim shirt (whose sleeves were still long enough to hide her bandaging). There was the lightest of foundations on her face, a touch of mascara and a dash of pale lipstick. It wasn't her full working war paint, and the white central streak was still in her hair, but it was a step in the right direction.

'I was just off to the shops, Gita. Anything you need?'

This prompted a sleepy smile. 'You know there isn't anything I need.' Her speech was still a little slurred, as though the words were too big for her mouth.

'Well . . .'

'And it's very unlike you, Jude, to be so indirect.'

'Meaning?'

'Meaning that what you're really saying is: "Gita, are you sure you'll be all right on your own here while I go to the shops?"'

'All right.' Jude parroted, 'Gita, are you sure you'll be all right here on your own while I go to the shops?'

'Absolutely. My emotions are so damped down by the medication that I'd hardly react to the news of an imminent nuclear holocaust. I'm OK. You don't have to worry.' She gestured to the pile of women's magazines on the sofa beside her. 'I'll be quite all right here, reading very slowly, checking out the opposition.'

Gita was a journalist; a feature writer. A very good feature writer. Or at least she had been until recent events.

'That's good,' said Jude. 'Well, I'll have my mobile with me if . . .'

'If what?'

'If you think of anything you need at the shops.'

There was another tired, wry smile from Gita. 'Meaning: "If you suddenly feel bad and need me".'

'Well . . .'

'This is really most unlike you, Jude. Look, OK, we both know what I did, but I can assure you I'm not about to do it again.'

'No.'

'And my staying here with you – for which I am

more grateful than I can say – well, it's not going to work if you're constantly afraid of letting me out of your sight.'

'No. Right. I accept that.'

'Good. Off you go.' With a surprisingly sudden movement, Gita reached for her handbag. 'Ooh, there *is* something I want you to get at the shops.' She handed across a twenty-pound note. 'Convert that into Chilean Chardonnay, will you? My contribution to the Woodside Cottage domestic economy.'

As she took the money, Jude grinned. 'Thanks, Gita.'

Carole got the feeling that a lot of thought had gone into the choice of restaurant for her encounter with the Martins. It was pricey – probably Stephen's input – but reassuringly homely. Gaby wouldn't want her parents fazed by menus they might need to have explained to them, by flamboyant waiters or an over-trendy clientele. So she'd homed in on a restaurant that specialized in traditional English cooking for traditional English people who wouldn't respond well to it being called traditional English cuisine. So traditionally English was the food that many of the customers were Japanese and American tourists, under the illusion that their Burberry and Dunhill disguises would let them pass for the real thing. But it was the perfect venue for those in search of such delicacies as potted shrimps, roast beef and Yorkshire pudding, steak and kidney pie and bread-and-butter pudding.

As predicted, Stephen was not there, but Gaby was already installed, sitting between her parents, when Carole was led across to the table. Marie and Howard Martin could not have been less alike. She was a tiny, birdlike woman, whose tight, greying curls accentuated her resemblance to Gaby. Thick glasses and vague, blinking eyes indicated extreme myopia.

Her husband, by contrast, was huge, not fat, but very tall with a bulky body and gunmetal hair slicked back almost in the brilliantined style of the late forties. He looked like an old black-and-white photograph of a former boxer, and when he rose to greet Carole, he towered over everyone else in the room. He was a lot older than his wife, perhaps as much as eighty, and he had bulky hearing aids in both ears. Marie herself looked so washed out it was difficult to fix her age with any certainty. Still, given the fact that Gaby must be round the thirty mark, her mother couldn't be less than fifty. Might even be my age, thought Carole.

Howard Martin did not carry with him the assertiveness that might be assumed to go with his size. In fact, both he and his wife seemed paralytically nervous. Carole was nervous too, but she liked to think she wasn't showing it as much as they were.

Gaby was maintaining a professional front, but she couldn't hide her own unease. Her body language was taut and jumpy. She sat awkwardly on the edge of her seat. When she'd rung Jude she'd claimed her back was better, but Carole reckoned the problem had now returned with a vengeance.

As soon as they were all seated, Gaby suggested

drinks. The situation needed an injection of some relaxant, and alcohol was traditionally the most reliable ice-breaker.

But ordering drinks did not ease the atmosphere. Marie Martin said all she really felt like was mineral water, and Howard agreed, 'Yes, I could go along with that.' But Gaby wasn't satisfied. She was going to give them a slap-up lunch, whether they liked it or not. 'No, we'll have some wine.'

'Well, I won't,' said her mother, with self-effacing firmness.

'You prefer white, don't you, Carole?' asked Gaby as she perused the wine list.

'Yes, but if I'm the only one, I'm very happy with mineral—'

'I'm drinking too,' Gaby announced firmly. 'And Dad'll probably have a glass or two when the bottle's actually here.'

'I might at that,' Howard Martin conceded.

Gaby attracted a waiter's attention with practised ease. Her job as an actors' agent involved a lot of professional lunching, so she knew her way around restaurants. Her familiarity with the milieu seemed only to point up the discomfort of her parents. And yet why were they so ill at ease? Marie was half-French. They spent their Augusts in France. Surely they should be used to eating out? Still, Carole wasn't about to get answers to those questions. On with the social niceties.

'Well, I must tell both of you how delighted I am about the engagement.'

'Oh yes, we're very pleased too.' Marie Martin spoke cautiously, as if in danger of using the wrong word. 'It's very good news.'

'Very good news,' her husband agreed.

And that seemed to be it. Neither had anything further to add, so Carole, forced to be more than naturally fulsome, went on, 'No, I'm so pleased for Stephen – that he was lucky enough to meet Gaby.'

'Yes,' Marie agreed, and Howard nodded. Carole decided that their hesitancy had nothing to do with disapproval of the proposed union. The Martins just weren't people who were used to expressing their emotional reactions.

'The fourteenth of September doesn't seem far away now, does it?'

This elicited no response, but fortunately Gaby came to the rescue. 'No, and there's still so much to do.'

Marie seemed to take this as a cue. Hesitantly, and blushing furiously, she began. 'I would like to apologize, Carole, that Howard and I haven't offered to do more in making the arrangements for the wedding.' The way she spoke suggested that she was embarking on a prepared speech.

Carole was embarrassed at the prospect of hearing more of it. 'Not a problem,' she said. 'Stephen and Gaby have explained everything to me. Quite honestly, at their age, it makes much more sense that they should do it all themselves. Then they can have exactly the kind of day they want.'

Marie seemed not to hear this, but pressed on with

her text. 'The fact is, we're not very good at public events. We tend to keep ourselves to ourselves very much. It's not something we're proud of, but that's the way we are. So we thought it better that I should explain that to you now, so's we don't get off on the wrong foot.' That was the end of her speech. To emphasize the point, she said, 'That's all.'

'It's not a problem,' Carole reiterated. Making the statement had been such agony for Marie that it had been agony for her too. The conversation needed to be moved on as quickly as was humanly possible.

Gaby came to the immediate rescue with the menu, and some time was spent choosing what to eat. Her mother insisted that she 'didn't want much, not a big eater at lunchtime.' This was true of Carole too, but, seeing how determined Gaby was to make the meal an event, she ordered much more lavishly than she normally would. Chef's pâté, followed by Dover sole. Gaby ordered two courses as well, and Howard was persuaded to go for a prawn cocktail before his prime sirloin of beef. But his wife wouldn't be shifted from her decision to have 'just a cheese omelette – and I probably won't eat all of that.'

The ordering had used up only a few minutes, and the lunch yawned ahead of Carole. Marie and Howard didn't seem about to offer any further topics for discussion, and in their presence Gaby too was uncharacteristically subdued. Carole realized that, unless the meal was to pass in total silence, she was going to have to take on the role of conversational initiator.

'Now, I'm sorry to say,' she began boldly, 'that I know almost nothing about you. Just that you live in Harlow . . .'

'Yes, we do,' Marie agreed. 'Very nice and quiet, Harlow.'

Howard didn't take issue with this assessment. He nodded, but said nothing.

'And I do remember Gaby saying that her grand-mother lives in France . . .'

'Yes, that's my mother,' Marie acknowledged.

'The South of France, I gather.' Carole was having difficulty matching the undeniable drabness of the senior Martins with her image of the South of France – rich people with yachts.

But Gaby quickly put her right. 'It's the south-west, actually. Lot-et-Garonne. Near Villeneuve-sur-Lot.' Her French accent was impeccable. 'That's where *Grand'mère* grew up. But I doubt if she'll be able to make it over for the wedding.'

'No, *Maman* is far too frail,' her mother agreed. 'And she can hardly see at all these days. Her eyesight was always very bad.'

'Yes,' said Gaby glumly, 'and I've inherited that. Can't see a thing in the mornings till I've got my lenses in.'

'Well, *Maman* was only in her forties when she started to have to read large print books.'

'Thanks, Mum, that's really cheered me up. Something to look forward to in ten years' time. I wonder if Steve realized what he had taken on when he asked me to marry him.'

Having met the Martins, Carole was rather beginning to wonder that too.

'Still,' Gaby went on, 'I must try and get out to Villeneuve-sur-Lot before too long. Ideally with Steve – if he can get the time off work. I really want to introduce my fiancé to *Grand'mère*.'

'I'm sure she'd like to meet him,' said Marie automatically.

The chasm of silence once again gaped before them. Carole gamely bridged it. 'But that's about all I know about your family. Oh, and, of course, that you were brought up in Worthing.'

Marie Martin looked alarmed. 'How did you know that?'

'Gaby mentioned it.'

Marie's daughter received a look of pained reproach for passing on the information. Carole persevered. 'Which is of course very near where I live. Do you remember Fethering?'

'No. I don't remember anything much about the area. I didn't live there long.'

Which was a very clear ending to that subject of conversation. Carole struggled on. 'But I do feel I still know very little about you. For instance, I don't even know whether Gaby has brothers and sisters.'

'I have a brother,' said Gaby, looking at her mother, as if expecting to prompt further comment. But none came. The ball was back in Carole's court.

'As you probably know, Marie, Stephen's an only child. I sometimes think it'd have been nice to have had more, but . . . well, I had a full-time career and then . . .' Time to bite the bullet. 'I'm divorced. Did Gaby tell you that?'

'Yes, she did.'

But again Marie Martin didn't volunteer anything else. No judgement, no reaction.

'So what's your son called?' asked Carole desperately.

'Phil.'

'And is he older than Gaby?'

'Oh, no. Pascale came first.'

'I beg your pardon?'

It was Gaby, rather than her mother, who provided the explanation. 'I was christened Pascale. Changed my name when I was in my teens. You know what teenage girls are like, unhappy with everything about themselves, about their home, about their family – so I became Gaby. And it kind of stuck.'

'Not with me, it didn't,' said Marie, with more vigour than she had shown before.

'Well, I like the name. And the rest of the family have accepted the change, except for *Grand'mère* who still calls me Pascale. Anyway, all my working life I've been Gaby Martin, so that's the way I'm going to stay.' This was said defiantly, but her mother did not rise to the challenge.

'So how old is Phil?'

'He's twenty-nine. Only eighteen months younger than me.'

'It must have been hard, when they were little, having two children so close together.'

Carole had said it as an all-purpose platitude, but

Marie Martin seemed to take the comment more seriously. 'Yes,' she said. 'Yes, it was a very hard time.'

'They go so quickly, the childhood years,' Carole went on, with continuing banality.

Marie nodded, but didn't speak. Howard shadowed his wife's nod, though Carole wasn't sure that he could hear much of the conversation. His large face was impassive most of the time, only showing animation when someone looked at him or addressed a direct question. He sat still, isolated in the muffled world of his deafness.

'So what does Phil do?' asked Carole, sticking to her role as conversational initiator. 'Is he in show business like you, Gaby?'

She laughed dismissively. 'It's hardly show business. But Phil doesn't do anything like that. He works in a warehouse.'

'He's a checker,' Marie added, as if this were important.

'And is that near you, in Harlow?'

'Near Harlow. Hoddesdon.'

'Ah.'

'He's got his own flat there,' Marie volunteered, with something approaching pride. 'In Hoddesdon.'

'Well, I'll look forward to meeting him.' Carole saw a look pass between Gaby and her mother at this, but she couldn't interpret its subtext. 'I look forward to meeting all the rest of your family and friends at the wedding.'

'There aren't many others.' Gaby grimaced. 'As I say, *Grand'mère*'s unlikely to leave France.'

'Very unlikely,' her mother agreed. 'Which may be just as well.'

'Oh?' asked Carole casually.

She looked at Marie, but it was Gaby who supplied the explanation. 'Mum means Granny would disapprove of my not being married in a Catholic church.'

'Ah yes, I'd forgotten you said your family was Catholic.'

'Brought up Catholic, but none of it means anything to me now.'

'Well, it should,' Marie asserted feebly.

'Why? Why do you say that? When did you or Dad last step inside a church of any denomination?'

'I may not be very good at church-going and what have you, but at least I'm not disrespectful to the church. And, when he was younger, your father was a very devout Catholic.'

Marie Martin was now, by her standards, quite animated, and Carole intervened to avert the incipient row. 'Does this mean, Gaby, that you and Stephen have decided on the church where you are going to get married?'

'It looks like we have, yes. Most of the ones round Fethering were already booked for the fourteenth of September, but one vicar thought the wedding on that day was about to be called off.'

'Oh?'

'He sounded a bit vague, but he's going to ring us in the next week when he knows for sure.'

'And which church is this?'

'The one in Fedborough. All Souls.'

Carole knew it. She had also met the vicar, the Reverend Philip Trigwell, when she and Jude had become involved in an investigation into a human torso found in one of the town's cellars. That he should 'sound vague' about arrangements was entirely in character. She had never met a man so indecisive or so unwilling to express a firm opinion.

'Oh well, I hope it works out. All Souls' is a lovely church.'

'Yes,' Gaby agreed. 'If we've heard from the vicar by the weekend, we're going to come down on Saturday and check out some venues and caterers.'

'Maybe I'll see you again then.'

'Maybe.'

The conversation was once again becalmed. 'So,' Carole battled on, 'I now know about all your immediate family, do I?'

'Except, of course, for Uncle Robert.'

'Oh yes – Uncle Robert.' In her echo of Gaby's words, for the first time Marie Martin displayed genuine enthusiasm, and also her French origins – the 't' at the end of the name was silent.

'He's Mum's brother.'

'Always a very lively person to have around. And he's always adored Pascale. Having no children of his own, he thinks of her almost as his own daughter. You'd like him, Carole. Everyone likes my brother Robert. Don't they, Howard?'

Her husband nodded, though quite possibly he hadn't heard the question.

'Yes, Robert'll certainly be at the wedding. He's a

46

real live wire. We must get him to do a speech. He's very funny when he does public speaking – just a natural at it.'

Inwardly Carole flinched. Over the years she'd suffered from too many public speakers who were naturals at it.

'Actually, I've had a thought . . .' Now her brother had been mentioned, Marie Martin seemed quite happy to take over the conversation. 'Perhaps Robert could give you away, Pascale.'

'No.' The suggestion stung Gaby. 'Dad will give me away. It's always the father who gives the bride away. You only get someone else to do it if the father's not around.'

'Yes, I suppose you're right.' But Marie sounded disappointed. And her next words made it seem as if she was trying to convince herself. 'Your father'll do it absolutely fine.'

'It's all very exciting,' Carole observed meaninglessly. 'Everything about the wedding.'

'Yes. You will like Robert,' Marie repeated. Her brother seemed to be her prize exhibit. As a couple, the Martins might not have much to show for themselves, but they did at least have Robert. 'It'd be nice if you could meet him before the wedding.'

'Yes. I'd love that.' Unease encouraged fulsomeness in Carole.

'I know!' Her mother's sudden boldness was so out of character as to prompt a curious look from Gaby. 'We'll give an engagement party for you and Stephen.'

'Oh, I don't think we really want that.'

But Marie Martin was impervious to the warning in her daughter's eye. 'Yes, you'll love it. It'll make your dad and me feel better about not making the wedding arrangements.'

'Mum, you don't want the trouble of anything like that. It'd be a lot of hassle.'

'I'm not suggesting we do it in the flat. We'll go to one of the local hotels, and get them to cater it.'

'I really don't think—'

'There was that hotel you went to that function at, wasn't there, Howard? You remember, last Christmas.'

Her husband opted for a 'Yes', which he reckoned was a safe response to most questions.

'What was it called now?'

This he seemed to hear, because he replied that he couldn't remember.

'We'll find out when we get back home. And I'll have to sort out a date when Robert's free. But it'll be such fun.'

If it was anything like the lunch, Carole wasn't so sure about that. But further discussion of the engagement party was stopped by the arrival of a waiter with the three starters. When conversation was re-established, Marie, after her brief flurry of animation, had shrunk back into her shell.

Still, there was one topic on which Carole genuinely wanted to check the Martins' opinion, and this seemed as good an opportunity as any to broach it.

'Marie, Howard, I'm sure you've already had this discussion with your daughter – but I wondered what you thought about a newspaper announcement of the wedding?'

Alarm flickered instantly in Gaby's eyes. 'Steve and I have talked about it further, Carole, and we've decided we don't want any announcement.'

'Oh.' She wasn't going to be stopped by that. 'I just wondered, though, what your parents thought. I mean, to me, an engagement doesn't seem complete until it's been trumpeted abroad in the national press.'

Marie Martin's face had lost the little colour with which it had started the lunch. Her eyes widened as she murmured, 'No. I don't want it in the press. Nor does Howard. We don't want anything about it in the press.'

And Carole realized that what she could see in the woman's face was not just self-effacement, but fear. And that, indeed, except for the brief moment when she had proposed the idea of an engagement party, Marie Martin's predominant emotion throughout the lunch had been fear.

There was something of which she was desperately afraid.

Chapter Five

'And the phone has been ominously quiet too.'

'Gita, all your friends know you've been ill.'

'Thank you for the word "ill".' She smiled wryly. 'But I wasn't actually thinking about my friends. It's been very silent on the professional front too. No editors ringing me with offers of work.'

'Time enough for that.'

Gita grimaced. 'Not that much time. I am a freelance; I need some kind of income.'

Jude grinned. 'I would say this is very encouraging news.'

'What?'

'The fact that you're worrying about work. It shows you're getting back to normal. Come on, let me top up your wine.'

'You know, on the instructions for the pills, it says one should avoid alcohol.'

'Yes, I know it says that, but I'm afraid you've ended up in an environment where you can't avoid alcohol. You're here in Woodside Cottage with me. No escape. Social decency, apart from anything else, demands that you accept my hospitality.'

'Well . . .'

'Besides, you're not about to drive or work heavy machinery. The worst that can happen is that you feel drowsy. And if you feel drowsy, then all you have to do is fall asleep.'

'Which is what I seem to be doing most of the time, anyway.'

'Exactly. It's your body telling you it wants lots of lovely, delicious mindless sleep.'

'Hm.'

'Which can be assisted by copious draughts of alcohol.'

'In that case . . .' Gita shrugged, and held out her glass, which was topped up with Chilean Chardonnay.

'Cheers.'

There was a silence after they had both taken substantial slurps. Then Jude spoke. 'If there are people you want to see – you know, people you want to invite down here, that's fine.'

Gita gave a strained grin. 'Thanks, but I don't think I'm quite ready for that.' She looked troubled. 'There *are* people I need to see – people I *must* see – but not yet.'

'That's fine. Just go at your own pace. Don't rush yourself. There's no pressure.'

'Except, as I say, the financial pressure of making a living.'

'Don't worry about it. As I say, time enough.'

'Mm.' Gita reached out and took her friend's hand. 'I'm not going to spend every minute while I'm here saying, "Thank you, Jude." I'm going to save it up for one big eruption of gratitude when I leave. But I would just like to say it now – a little keep-you-going thank you. Thank you very much, Jude.'

'Gita, it's my pleasure.' And she meant it.

The phone rang. 'Hello?'

'Jude, I don't know if you remember me. I'm Gaby Martin.'

'Yes, of course.'

'Look, I'm going to be down in your area at the weekend. Steve and I are staying in a hotel overnight, and your Carole's cooking lunch for us on Sunday.'

'And the back's still giving you pain, is it?'

'Yes. Yes, it is.'

'Well, I can do any time on Saturday.'

'About eleven?'

'That'd be fine.'

'There's just one thing . . .'

'What?'

'Could you not tell Carole I'm coming?'

'OK. If that's what you want.'

'I don't really mind her knowing, because after all it was Carole who put me in touch with you, but I don't want Steve to find out.'

'Gaby, your secret is safe with me.'

'Thank you very much for sorting all this out, Mother.' Stephen gestured to the spread of brochures and flyers laid out over the dining-room table at High Tor.

'No problem. Glad to do it.' And Carole had been. Finding out details of potential reception venues and caterers was a nice specific project, which made her feel that she was contributing something to the on-going wedding planning. When she had worked for the Home Office, Carole Seddon had always been attracted to tasks that had a finite end.

'And you say Gaby's coming down later?'

'Yes. Had some stuff to do in London, so she stayed in her flat last night, and she's getting the train to Fethering round lunchtime.'

Stephen and Gaby were not yet fully cohabiting. She still kept on the Pimlico flat she shared with an actress friend called Jenny, but she spent much of her time – and all weekends – at Stephen's house in Fulham.

Carole indicated four brochures. 'I thought those were the most promising for what you said you wanted. They could all currently do the fourteenth of September. Two are hotels, so obviously would cater the reception themselves. The other two are just venues. Both have caterers they recommend, but equally would allow us to bring in our own caterers if we wanted to. I've rung round. We can have a look at any of the venues any time today, though the hotels would rather we avoided lunch and dinner time.'

'You have been busy, Mother. Thank you very much.'

That Saturday morning, without Gaby present as a catalyst, Stephen seemed all formality again. Carole wondered, with a pang of envy, whether he was more relaxed with his father than he was with her.

'This one at least you'll recognize.' She proffered an

elegantly printed brochure for the Hopwicke Country House Hotel, where Stephen and Gaby had stayed a few months previously, and where a murder had taken place. 'Though that'd probably be pretty pricey.'

'Money's not a problem.' It was a line Carole had longed to be able to say all her life, but never would. Money was always a problem. Even now, with her secure index-linked pension and modest outgoings – only herself and Gulliver to look after – money remained a problem. Not so much a real problem, as something about which to feel a constant undertow of anxiety. A middle-class upbringing made that unavoidable. She was surprised that Stephen hadn't inherited it.

'No,' he went on, 'my worry with the Hopwicke Country House Hotel would be whether the place'd be big enough.'

'Big enough? Why, how many guests are you proposing to invite?'

'Hundred – hundred and twenty . . .'

'Goodness. Well, you may be right. As I recall, they could only do sixty for a sit-down meal. But I suppose, if you have a buffet—'

'No, we'll have a sit-down meal.' The firmness with which he said this made Carole wonder once again exactly how her son made his living. His particular combination of finance and computers certainly seemed to be lucrative. 'Anyway, Gaby and I know the Hopwicke, so we don't need to look at that. But, if you're ready, Mother, let's go and see the other three. And you've shortlisted some potential caterers too, have you?'

Dutiful and efficient, his mother assured him that she had.

They were in his newly registered BMW on the way to a converted tithe barn near Fedborough when Carole brought up the subject of Gaby's parents. Tentatively, she tried to find out what Stephen really thought of them.

'They're fine,' he said, unhelpfully.

'Rather shy, I thought.' Carole probed.

'Yes, but nothing wrong with that.'

'Oh, no. No . . . Howard must be quite a lot older than Marie.'

'Yes. And he misses a lot because of his deafness.'

'Mm. Still, he looks very fit for his age.'

'Yes, he is, remarkably. Apparently he had cancer seven or eight years ago.'

'Really?'

'Yes, bowel cancer. Gaby told me. She was terribly worried at the time. But he had surgery and radio-therapy, and made a complete recovery.'

'He certainly looked fine, and he really tucked into his food.'

'He's in very good nick for someone pushing eighty.' Stephen sighed, almost with satisfaction. 'No, I don't see the Martins being a potential problem as in-laws. They'll keep a low profile. All the skeletons will stay firmly in the closet.'

Which, Carole thought, was rather an odd thing for her son to say.

*

Gaby had rung Stephen from her mobile on some pre-
text, but with the real purpose of ensuring that he and
his mother had left High Tor before the taxi from
Fethering Station brought her to Woodside Cottage.

Gita had gone for her first outside trip alone since
her arrival. Jude had carefully shown her the way to
the beach, naming cafes where she could stop if she
felt exhausted, saying it'd be no problem if she
returned while Gaby was still there. In fact, she had
fussed so uncharacteristically that Gita, with a wry
smile, had eventually said, 'It's all right, Jude. I'm not
about to walk into the sea with my pockets full of
stones.'

'I know. I didn't mean—'

'Yes, you did. And I know exactly why you did. But
don't worry. From my recollection of Fethering Beach,
I'd have to walk about a mile before the water got up
to my knees.' An exaggeration, but not a huge one. 'An
even less efficient way of topping myself than the last
one.'

It was said with bravado. Increasingly over the last
few days, Gita had been mentioning her suicide
attempt, daring herself to bring it out into the open.
But the words still made Jude wince.

'I'll be all right. I've got to start being on my own
sometime.'

'I know. But this girl'll only be here till about
twelve. And it's not a problem if you're back earlier
than that. You can just—'

'Jude, I will not be back earlier than that. In fact I
won't come back.'

'What?'

Gita smiled at the ill-disguised anxiety in her friend's voice. 'You come and join me. I'll buy you lunch in that pub – the Crown and Sceptre, is it?'

'Anchor.'

'Right. See you there twelve-thirtyish.'

So only Jude was there to greet Gaby. Her back was clearly bad. The girl's body was skewed, and she walked gingerly, uncertain which footfall was about to trigger another explosion of pain.

Jude had prepared the sitting room, stripping the throws off what looked like just another shapeless sofa to reveal the hard flat couch underneath. This she raised by a hydraulic mechanism to about three feet above the floor. On a small table she set out a row of bottles of oil. She lit two scented candles, and smiled inwardly at the image of Carole's reaction if she'd walked into Woodside Cottage at that moment.

There was nothing magical about Jude's preparations. Their aim was simply to induce calm and relaxation in her client.

She asked Gaby whether she'd be more comfortable standing or sitting while she asked a few questions, and the girl opted to stand. Quickly, Jude ran through the details of Gaby's medical history, scribbling notes on a file card. She started with her date of birth. Twenty-fifth of March 1974.

The girl's general health had always been remarkably good. Her eyesight was poor but was aided by strong contact lenses, and everything else worked as it should. Three years previously, she had had some stomach trouble and been worried that it might be bowel cancer. But extensive tests had ruled out the possibility and diagnosed Irritable Bowel Syndrome. A slight adjustment to her diet – the total exclusion of onions – had solved the problem almost completely. She had had very rare recurrences of the symptoms.

'Pity, though,' Gaby concluded, 'because I really like onions. Still, small price to pay.'

Jude agreed. Then she asked Gaby to remove her top, trousers and shoes, and manoeuvred her on to the bed. 'See if you can lie on your front.' With fierce intakes of breath as the pain stabbed at her, Gaby managed to achieve this.

'Do you want me to show you where it's hurting?'

'No, I think I can see that,' Jude replied.

'See? Is it inflamed?'

'No. I can see from the way your body's moving, the movements you're trying to avoid.'

'Ah.'

'Now could you just do a couple of movements for me? Stop as soon as it hurts. Can you point ahead of you with your right hand?' Gaby couldn't. The pain stopped her dead. 'Try the left hand. OK. Thank you. Now can you just try bringing your heels together?' The mere attempt brought a whimper of pain. 'OK. Stop it. Don't push yourself.'

Jude moved closer to the couch, and placed both her plump hands on the dent in the flesh at the bottom of Gaby's spine. 'That's where the pain's coming from, isn't it?'

'Well, I'm feeling it all along my arms and legs.'

'Yes. But this is where it's coming from.'

'Do you think I've slipped a disc, or trapped a nerve or . . .?'

'No.' Jude's fingertips ran lightly over the girl's lower back, as if reading some Braille message from the hurt within. 'No, it's not an injury in that way. It's just tension, and the tension is throwing you out of balance, so the way you sit and stand puts pressure on your spine.'

'Do you think it's something to do with the chair I have at the office? Because I spend most of my day on the phone.'

'Yes, Carole said you were a theatrical agent.'

'That's right.'

'I used to be an actress myself.'

'Did you, Jude?'

'You can tell how long ago it was, though, from the fact that I say "actress". All of today's young women in the theatre call themselves "actors".'

'Which I have to say I think is pretty silly. I mean, if a director's casting something, he knows whether he wants an actor or an actress for the part.'

'Of course he does.'

'And in *Spotlight* – that's the professional directory for actors—'

'I know.'

'Well, there they still have categories for "Actors" and "Actresses". If they didn't, nobody would be able to find their way around.'

'No, that's true.'

Gaby wasn't aware of the magic that was being

worked on her. Jude had the same effect on everyone she met, and nobody was ever aware of what was happening. People just found it easy to talk to her. Her presence soothed anxieties and encouraged confidences. Jude herself didn't even think of it as a skill, or a mystery, just a quality with which she had grown up.

'Now, what I'm going to do, Gaby, is put some oil on my hands and work on the centre of the pain.'

'When you say "work on", do you mean manipulate it?'

'No, I'm not an osteopath. And what's wrong with you doesn't need the attentions of an osteopath. You're just out of balance. You need to get yourself back in alignment.'

As she spoke, Jude was opening a bottle of oil on the table. A herbal aroma, redolent of Mediterranean hillsides, joined the scent from the candles. Jude poured oil on her hands, rubbed them together, and wiped the excess off with a small white towel. Then once again she stood over the girl on the couch.

'So it won't hurt?' asked Gaby.

'No. It certainly won't give you any more pain. And, hopefully, it will diminish the pain you're already suffering.' Jude put her hands again on the small of Gaby's back, and started to move her fingers. There was only the slightest of pressure, but the placing of the fingertips was very exact.

Gaby sighed, as she felt the warmth melt into her locked-up vertebrae.

'Funny,' she said drowsily. '"Out of balance." That's

what you say when someone's off their rocker. Well, not that exactly. "Unbalanced", I suppose is what you say.'

'Very sensible description. Amazing how many of our bodily metaphors actually work on the literal level. You speak of someone "being on the back foot". That's how they are physically when confronting danger. "Showing a bit of backbone", "backing off", "putting someone's back up", "putting someone's back out" – they all mean exactly what they say.'

'Mm . . .' Gaby murmured.

There was no effort in the movement of Jude's hands, but there was an intensity about her body. Though her ministrations seemed minimal, almost casual, a lot of energy was being put into her actions.

'So,' she asked lightly, 'can you think of anything specific that may have "put your back out"?'

'I don't know . . .' But the words weren't said as a deterrent. As Gaby relaxed, she seemed increasingly ready to talk.

Jude let the silence continue between them, knowing that, in her own time, Gaby would break it.

'Well, you know I'm getting married?'

'I certainly do. Living next door to Carole, there is absolutely no way I couldn't know that you were getting married. She's very excited about it.'

'Yes, so's everyone.'

Jude caught on to the wistfulness in the girl's words. 'Meaning you're not?'

'No, not meaning that at all. I'm as excited about it as anyone else. God, they're all sick to death of me at work. They can't wait till I actually am married, and then they hope I'll stop talking about it.'

Again Jude let the silence stand. She wasn't probing. If Gaby wanted to volunteer more . . .

Inevitably, Gaby did. 'I'm ecstatic about getting married. Steve's the man I've been looking for all my life. And he seems to feel the same about me, which I sometimes can't believe, but deep down I know it's true.'

'Sounds pretty good to me,' said Jude.

'Yes.' Again the slight wistfulness.

'What is it that you think attracts you and Stephen to each other?'

'I don't know. Don't like to question it too much. If you analyse things, you can spoil them.'

'Very true.'

'But I think with us – well, we have a lot of similarities in the way we were brought up – I mean, very different homes, but both homes where – well, there were always secrets – nobody quite said exactly what they meant—' Suddenly Gaby was aware of who she was talking to. She shifted her head sideways to look apologetically at Jude – a movement, incidentally, that she couldn't have performed twenty minutes earlier. 'I'm terribly sorry. Carole's your friend, isn't she?'

'Yes, she's my friend, but that doesn't mean I have any illusions about how relaxed or otherwise she is in her approach to life.' Jude's grin took the edge off her words.

Gaby grinned too as she straightened back out on

the couch. 'So Steve grew up where there was always tension between his parents.'

'Carole's never talked to me much about her marriage.'

'No. I get the feeling she has put the lid firmly down on that particular pressure cooker. But according to Steve, the atmosphere at home wasn't great, even before they started thinking about the divorce. He coped as kids do – putting his head down, getting on with his school work, trying to avoid situations in which he might be expected to take sides. And then, like me, getting the hell out of the family home at the first opportunity. So I think that inculcated a kind of . . . I was about to say deviousness, but let's call it caution, in his approach to life.'

'And where does your deviousness – or caution – come from?' asked Jude casually. 'From what Carole told me, your parents seem to be absolutely devoted to each other.'

'Yes, they are, but, you know, there were things in their past history, things that happened before they got married. My grandfather died around that time, and then *Grand'mère* had a major breakdown and . . .' The deviousness – or caution – which Gaby had been talking about asserted itself, and her words trickled away to silence.

Jude let the stillness continue, as her fingertips fluttered over the slowly unknotting muscles of the girl's lower back. She knew that, when she was ready, Gaby would again pick up the conversation.

'And I think it's that that's making me tense.'

'The baggage of the past?' Jude hazarded.

'Mm. No worries about marrying Steve.'

'Worries about having a family?'

Jude had hit a spot there. 'Slight anxiety, I suppose. The fact is, I was born quite premature and – I mean, I've been absolutely fine since, but maybe it was touch and go when I was born.'

'Have you talked to your mother about that?'

Gaby laughed at the preposterousness of the suggestion. 'You don't know my mother. I'm afraid that kind of detail doesn't get talked about in the Martin household.'

'Oh. So are you really worried about your ability to have healthy children?'

'No, not really. Well, it's another worry to add to the list, you know, when my head's full of worries, but not really a problem.' With a visible effort, the girl pulled herself together. 'No. As I say, no worries about marrying Steve. No worries about the arrangements either, really. I know we've left it late, and I'm sure there'll be various panics and crises along the way, but equally I know we'll be able to cope with them. Steve and I are both organizers by nature and profession. No, all that'll be fine. It's just . . .'

'What?'

'It's the thought of the wedding bringing back to life things that should have been long forgotten.'

'Things to do with your parents' wedding?'

'Not really. Well, things that happened round that time, I suppose, but— No, I shouldn't be talking like this. It's disloyal.'

'You can't be disloyal in the abstract, Gaby.'

'What do you mean?'

'By definition, don't you have to be being disloyal to someone?'

'Yes.' The girl didn't answer the question directly, but her next words were still revelatory. 'The fact is, my parents are fine. Well, as fine as they're ever going to be. I don't mean they're happy. I think they both find life too difficult and challenging ever to be actually happy, but they're content. They've got a small, circumscribed life which they can cope with. I don't want that put at risk.'

'And why should your wedding do that?'

'Well, it's a public thing. A lot of people will find out about it.'

'And are there people – or a person – who you don't want to find out about it?' Gaby didn't answer. 'An ex-boyfriend? An ex-fiancé?'

But no. Jude had lost her. 'That feels so good, down in my back,' said Gaby determinedly. 'Amazingly warm. Is it the oil that does that?'

'No, not the oil.'

'Well, whatever you're doing, it really seems to be working.'

'Good.'

'I feel I could leap up and play a game of squash.'

'I wouldn't advise you to do that straightaway. I'll give you some exercises to do, to keep you loose.'

'So do you think this'll cure it? The pain won't come back?'

'The pain won't come back when you've got rid of what's causing the pain.'

'But you said there wasn't any injury, nothing actually physical causing it.'

'Right,' Jude agreed. 'That's what I said.'

Chapter Six

Gita pushed the remains of the Crown and Anchor's fisherman's pie around her plate. She hadn't eaten much. For the first time since Jude had collected her from the clinic, she seemed actually depressed. Maybe the effects of the medication had decreased as her body got used to it. Maybe for the first time she was facing the reality of what she had done, the division made in her life by the suicide attempt, and the fact that she now had to face the continuity she had tried to escape.

'I must try and get some work,' she said, not for the first time.

'Don't worry. You're not on the breadline yet.'

'No. But it's not just the money. For someone like me – any freelance probably – the work's more than what you get paid. It's a kind of self-validation.'

'I know.'

'For me working means I'm functioning. It's all to do with the way I look at life. I can survive anything if I think there might be an article to be written at the end of it.'

'So are you going to . . .?'

Jude didn't need to finish the sentence. Gita replied firmly that she intended never to write anything about her suicide attempt. 'I can't stand that – journalists who only write about themselves. Television personalities who have heart attacks and then write books about heart attacks. Germaine Greer even wrote a book about her own menopause, for God's sake. I write about other people. My attitude to them is obviously coloured by my own experiences and my own judgement, but I am not the subject of my writing, and never will be.' She looked gloomily across the bar of the Crown and Anchor. 'But I've got to get something going soon. If I can re-establish myself professionally, then maybe I can start to pick up the pieces of my private life.'

'You haven't heard from . . .?'

'No. Don't expect to. Hope I never do.'

'But he did hear about your . . .?' Uncharacteristically, Jude skirted round the words. 'What happened to you?'

'I'm sure he did. We have enough mutual friends. He must've done. Which I think is the thing that makes me angriest about the whole business.'

'Oh?'

'The satisfaction that he would get from that.'

'Surely not?'

'You don't know him.'

'I've met him.'

'That's not what I said, Jude. You don't know him like I do. The idea that his walking out on a woman would have driven her to suicide he'd regard as an alternative notch on his bedpost.'

'Oh dear.'

'And I bet even now he's using it as a come-on in his chat-up routine – saying how sorry he is that the woman he lived with for years had such problems, how he tried to be supportive to her, but what can you do in the face of mental illness? And how he's been terribly wounded by the experience, but he's daring tentatively to start thinking about relationships again.' Gita took a savage sip of wine; its taste seemed no more attractive than the words in her mouth. 'The bastard!'

'On the other hand,' said Jude quietly, 'it wasn't him who you turned your anger against, was it?'

Gita shook her head. 'No. His behaviour just made me reflect on myself. If I could let someone treat me like that, what did that make me? And I thought of everything else that had gone wrong in my life: all the other men; the fact that I haven't got any children whose lives I could mess up; the fact that any looks I might have had are long gone. Oh, the same endless spiral.'

'A friend of mine, Gita, once described depression as "constipation of the mind", the way your thoughts get stuck and stale, and make you feel heavy and lethargic and incapable of anything.'

'Hm . . .'

'And he also reckoned anti-depressants acted like laxatives: freed up the flow, allowed your ideas to move again.'

'What a quaint taste in metaphors your friend had.'

'Yes.'

Gita sighed. 'At my lowest – I'm not at my lowest now – but at my lowest, the whole world seems to be a reproach to my own inadequacy. Everything I see anyone else doing I think "I can't do that". It gets quite funny sometimes – well, it would be funny if it weren't me in the middle of it all. I open a door, and I think, "I couldn't make a door. What use am I if I can't even make a door?"' She chuckled wryly. 'Sorry. That's just how I sometimes feel.'

'Not all the time, though.'

'But when I'm down there, it feels as though it's going to go on for ever. That's what's so cruel. When you're depressed, you can't imagine there will ever be a time when you're not depressed.'

'And when you're high?'

'Same story. You think you'll never be depressed again. You think you'll spend the rest of your life glorying in how wonderful you are, loving yourself.'

'That's not real love.'

'No, that's a kind of manic, mad infatuation. You should know it's the kind of feeling that can't possibly last – but, at the time, you don't.'

'Loving yourself is the secret.' Jude spoke very softly. 'When you love yourself, you can spread love to other people.'

'I know. How easy you make it sound. But how many of us have got so few hang-ups, have suffered so few bad experiences, that we really can love ourselves?'

'It's possible. You can learn.'

Gita was suddenly despondent. 'Some people can learn. I think if I was ever going to learn, I'd have done so by now before I became a shrivelled old bag.'

'You can learn.'

'Will you teach me?'

Jude suddenly realized how tired she was. Healing always drained her. Energy was finite. But she was going to need a lot more energy for the forthcoming conversation with Gita – and for the many other conversations that would follow.

'Yes,' she replied. 'Of course I'll teach you.'

Carole reckoned the afternoon had been a success. Gaby had been much more like the girl Carole had first encountered at the Hopwicke Country House Hotel. She and Stephen were affectionate – almost silly – together, which was a surprise to his mother because she had never imagined her son had a silly side. But Gaby also seemed to have lost her ambivalence about the wedding arrangements, and had thrown herself into everything with great gusto.

Of the three venues Stephen and his mother had looked at that morning, Gaby was taken first to the Fedborough tithe barn, which she loved on sight. Of fifteenth-century construction, it had been lovingly renovated by the farmer on whose land it stood, and turned into a venue for corporate events and celebrations. The barn itself formed one side of a rectangle of outbuildings, which had been converted into toilet facilities, kitchens and conference rooms. The complex huddled in the foothills of the South Downs and, if the weather was anything like decent on the fourteenth of September, would make an idyllic setting for a wedding reception.

The engaged couple made their decision instantly, and informed the farmer's wife, who had shown them round, that they would like to book the venue. Only a mile outside Fedborough, travel from All Souls' Church would not pose too much of a problem for the guests. In his negotiation of the costs Stephen then showed a toughness which surprised his mother. He also resisted the farmer's wife's pressure to employ the catering company in which she had an interest, until he had looked into other possibilities. Carole had never before seen him so assertive, and began perhaps to understand his success in his mysterious working life.

The venue sewn up, the three of them then went to visit three of Carole's shortlisted caterers. As a guide, they took the menus and price lists which the farmer's wife at the tithe barn had given them. With the caterers, Carole was interested to see that Stephen and his fiancée worked more as a double act, capping each other with ever more detailed questions. Gaby showed no signs of dilatoriness or reluctance. Her enquiries demonstrated that she had thought through all the logistical minutiae involved in making a wedding work.

At the end of the three exhaustive interviews, Stephen and Gaby had a brief discussion in his BMW and their decision was made. He rang through to the winner of the contest – who would no doubt be ecstatic because they had selected the top-of-the-range menus – and said that, subject to written confirmation, the job was theirs. Suddenly, after months of vagueness, the wedding on the fourteenth of September had become a reality.

'We must sort out invitations next,' Stephen announced.

'I can do that. There's a printer we use a lot at the agency. He'll give us a good deal.'

'And we'll have to work out who exactly we're going to invite,' said Stephen.

'You're still thinking of round the hundred and twenty mark?' asked Carole.

'Oh yes. And in fact we're lucky . . .'

'How so?'

'Well, Mother, neither of us has a large extended family – so that means most of the people we invite to the wedding will actually be people we like.'

Carole wasn't quite sure how to take that, but she didn't think he meant to be insulting. Probably better, though, that her son had pursued a career in computers and finance, rather than the diplomatic service.

'Which is actually another advantage of us making the arrangements ourselves.'

'God, yes,' Gaby agreed. 'Friends of mine have had dreadful fights when the parents wanted all the guests to be *their* friends.'

'Well,' said Carole, with a slight edge in her voice, 'I'll try and see to it that I don't interfere.'

Stephen chuckled. 'Oh, we aren't worried about

that.' And he said it so innocently that Carole felt rather gratified.

'So,' she asked, 'are you going to have all these people at the engagement party too?'

'Lord, no,' Gaby replied. 'Mum and Dad couldn't cope with those kind of numbers. Couldn't cope with many of our friends either, come to that. Some of the actors I know would be a little too exotic for Harlow. No, it'll really just be family. A chance for you and David to meet Phil . . .' She seemed for a moment about to say more about her brother, but decided against it. 'And Uncle Robert and a few others. It'll be very low key.'

'Fine,' said Carole, surprised how uncomfortable she felt at the casual coupling of her name with David's.

'But there'll be nothing low key about the wedding itself,' Stephen enthused. 'We're going to ensure that it's a day when—'

He was interrupted by the ringing of Gaby's mobile, which she immediately answered.

'Jenny? Yes, it's – what? Oh, God! Are you OK? Well, let me know when you've checked. And I'll give you a call as soon as I've worked out what I'm doing.'

She ended the call, and looked with horror at Stephen and Carole.

'My flat's been burgled.'

But the manner in which she said the words made it sound more as though she was announcing a murder.

Chapter Seven

'She's very strong-willed.' Stephen spoke with some puzzlement, as though still coming to terms with various unexpected elements in his fiancée's personality. 'I'm slowly learning not to argue when she's clear about what she wants to do.'

'You're quite strong-willed too.' Carole thought back to childhood confrontations when neither she nor her son had been willing to budge an inch.

'Yes.' He took it both as a compliment and an unarguable truth. 'That's why we're right for each other.' This too was a confident statement of fact.

They were sitting over lunch in the dining room of High Tor. Which, Carole realized, reflected a change in their relations. She couldn't remember the last time she had cooked for her son. University vacations, it must have been. When he started working, he had distanced himself. Or perhaps that had happened when she moved down to Fethering. The timing was all tied in with her divorce from David. Without either of them commenting on what was happening, Stephen had redrawn the parameters of his relationship with his mother. From that time on, they had always met on neutral ground, in pubs and restaurants, as if he was spelling out to her that the old family intimacy could never be re-established.

But the arrival of Gaby had changed that. Inviting them both to Sunday lunch at High Tor had not seemed incongruous – in fact, Carole had relished the idea and looked forward to reminding herself of her old skills with joint of beef, Yorkshire pudding and all the trimmings.

Except, of course, Gaby wasn't there. She was in Pimlico, assessing the loss and damage caused by her burglary. And that task was one which, very insistently, she had wanted to do on her own. That was the evidence of her strong will to which Stephen had referred.

Even in Gaby's absence, Carole still felt the lunch represented an advance, a changed understanding between herself and her son. She had forgotten how rewarding he was to feed, how much he relished his food, how he'd always been in thrall to her roast potatoes. Carole felt closer to Stephen than she had for years.

'And I gather the damage to the flat wasn't too bad?' she asked. Stephen had spent a long time on the phone to Gaby that morning, but not yet brought Carole up to date on the burglary.

'No. Whoever it was smashed a kitchen window to get in, and managed to immobilize the alarm. He – one assumes it was a "he" – was a real professional.'

'And have they lost a lot of stuff?'

'Hardly anything.' Rather than pleasing Stephen,

this fact seemed to trouble him. 'Not even too much of a mess. Gaby reckoned everything in the rooms she and Jenny share had been gone through, but then replaced more or less exactly where it should be.'

'They were lucky.'

'Yes . . .' But again her son didn't sound convinced. 'The thing that worries Gaby . . .' he hesitated before sharing the confidence '. . . is that whoever it was didn't even go into Jenny's room.'

'How can they be sure?'

'Jenny's a bit obsessed by security. She always keeps her door firmly locked. There had been no attempt to force it.'

'Maybe the burglar had skeleton keys, like they do in crime novels?'

'Well, if he did, he didn't use them. Nothing of Jenny's had been touched. Maybe he was just put off by the locked door.'

'Is that just Gaby and Jenny's view, or do the police agree?'

Stephen grimaced. 'They haven't informed the police.'

'What?' His words were an affront to all Carole had learnt during her long career in the Home Office. 'But they have to tell the police! There's been a break-in at their flat. Even if they haven't suffered too badly, the police might still collect evidence to tie in with other crimes.'

'I used that argument too. All the obvious arguments.' Stephen shrugged weakly. 'As I said, Gaby's very strong-willed.'

Carole shook her head in disbelief, and took a sip from the rather nice Argentinian Merlot she'd bought from Sainsbury's specially. 'But it's – well, I just don't understand. Is Gaby saying that absolutely nothing has been taken?'

'She's not sure. She hasn't had time to go through everything in proper detail. But, as of this moment, she can't see anything that's missing.'

'Which would imply – what? That the burglar lost his nerve? That he was disturbed while he was in the middle of the job?'

Stephen smiled grimly. 'Or that he was looking for something specific?'

His mother nodded thoughtfully. 'Yes. Has Gaby any idea what that something might have been?'

'Well, if she has, she's not telling me.' He didn't sound as though this was an entirely preposterous suggestion. 'There are still areas of Gaby's life, things about which she's very secretive and—' He seemed to realize that he was close to betraying confidences, and lightened his tone. 'Still, I guess that's true of all of us, isn't it?'

'Yes.' Carole knew it was certainly true of her. But if Stephen had hoped that his words would end the subject, he was mistaken. 'So had all of Gaby's belongings been turned over, or did the burglar concentrate on one specific area?'

She could see the calculation pass through her son's mind, as he assessed whether this information could be released. He concluded that it could do no harm.

'He seemed to be interested in her personal files. Those had been put back in place, but not quite in the right order. You know, things like her passport, birth certificate, address book, health insurance details, tax records, that kind of stuff.'

'But he didn't take any of them?'

'Not so far as she could tell, no.'

Carole was silent. They had both finished eating, but she resisted her normal knee-jerk reaction to clear the plates immediately. The current subject had not yet been exhausted.

'Stephen – do you remember, when you and Gaby and I met up in the Crown and Anchor a few weeks back?'

'Mm.'

'You said that there was a history of murder in her family.'

His pale face reddened and, behind their rimless glasses, his eyes blinked.

'Yes, I remember. I shouldn't have said that. Gaby really took me to task for it afterwards.'

'But you did say it, Stephen. And presumably you said it for some reason. You didn't just make it up?'

'No.' He realized he had to make some kind of explanation. 'Once again, I'm afraid I misjudged Gaby's reaction. We'd been talking about murder cases, you remember?'

'Yes.'

'And I just thought, ooh, there's this story Gaby once mentioned and . . . I didn't realize that she'd told me in confidence.'

'So what was it? One of her family got murdered?'

'No. It was a school friend of her mother's. I don't know the details. Just that it was before Marie had married Howard and it all got involved with other things—'

'Other things?'

'Other things that were happening to the family. It was a dreadful time for them, I gather. Gaby's grandfather died round then – before she was born, so she never met him. And then her grandmother – *Grand'mère* they call her – had what seems to have been a major breakdown.'

'Breakdown?' Carole echoed coldly. With her deeply neurotic mother and now a grandmother who'd had a 'breakdown', perhaps Gaby's own stability could not be guaranteed. She seemed fine, but Carole Seddon was the kind of neurotic who had a great fear of mental illness. 'Do you know any more details, Stephen?'

'No, that's it, really.'

'But you don't know the name of the girl who was murdered?' He shook his head. 'Or, come to that, who murdered her?' Another shake. 'Or, indeed, whether anyone was ever caught for the crime?'

'I do know that. Gaby said they got the man who did it.'

'But that's all she said?'

'Afraid so. Sometimes I think I'm very insensitive, Mum.' He would never know how much that carelessly dropped 'Mum' meant to her. 'I think I know Gaby, and I think I know how she'll react to things, and then I do something crass like that – mentioning this murder that she'd only told me about in confidence.'

'Don't worry. Nobody knows anything about their partner when they get married. Finding out about each other is both one of the great pleasures – and one of the great pains – of marriage.'

Stephen looked at her. She knew he wanted to ask whether she'd found that when she'd been married to his father, but fortunately Stephen's recent awareness of his own occasional insensitivity stopped the words from coming out.

'Hm.' Carole reached across to pick up his plate. 'I've made a treacle tart for pudding.'

'Ooh, my favourite.' Stephen sounded about five.

His mother paused for a moment in her clearing. 'It must be horrible for Gaby – feeling that someone's targeting her, that someone has an unhealthy interest in her.'

'Yes. She was trying to sound bouncy this morning on the phone, but it's clearly got to her.'

'And you've absolutely no idea what the reason could be? Who the intruder could be?'

'No.' Stephen was silent, again weighing up how much he should tell. Again, he came down on the side of further revelation. 'Look, I may as well tell you this, because you're going to find out sooner or later. I don't know whether it's got anything to do with the burglary, but whenever anything odd happens in Gaby's family—'

'By "odd" you mean "criminal"?'

'Possibly. The fact is that her brother – Phil – well, he's been in trouble with the police a few times.'

'What kind of stuff?'

'Nothing major. Petty theft. Stealing cars. I think he has a bit of a drug habit.' Stephen blushed again. 'I feel guilty saying this, but Gaby did say I should. She said better you know a bit about Phil before you actually meet him.'

'I see. Have you met him?'

'Yes, and he's a perfectly nice lad. A bit brash, maybe, and he looks a bit of a thug, but he's amiable enough. The story is that since he's got the warehouse job in Hoddesdon, he's a changed character, back on the straight and narrow, but . . . well, he does have this history.'

Suddenly Stephen looked very vulnerable, a sight Carole had not seen since he was a small boy. 'I'm sorry,' he said.

'What are you apologizing for?'

'Involving you in this. It's Gaby I'm marrying, not her family.'

'Oh, for heaven's sake, Stephen. It's not a problem. Gaby's adorable. She's absolutely right for you. And all families have their secrets and black sheep and what have you. I mean, Howard and Marie probably think I'm rather odd.'

'Hm . . . No, I'm sure they don't.' Carole wouldn't have minded if he'd come in a bit quicker with that reassurance.

'So . . . Gaby has a brother who's occasionally been on the wrong side of the law. That's not her fault.

82

I'm sure,' Carole went on, her confidence more for Stephen's benefit than because she felt it, 'that I'll get on fine with Phil. On the other hand, though – why on earth would he have wanted to break into his sister's flat?'

'I've no idea. I should think it's extremely unlikely that he's got anything to do with the break-in. It's just, as I say, in the Martin family, whenever something happens that's odd . . .'

'Or criminal?'

'Mm. Phil is the first suspect.'

'Which might explain why Gaby is unwilling for the police to come and inspect her flat?'

'Yes, Mum. I think it might.'

Carole had only momentary qualms about sharing with Jude what Stephen had told her. As soon as his BMW disappeared down the road, she was round at Woodside Cottage. Only after she had rung the door-bell did she remember that Jude had a guest.

But, to Carole's relief, there was no sign of Gita when Jude ushered her into the cluttered sitting room. 'Fancy a glass of wine? I've got some open in the fridge.'

'Well, I did actually have some with Stephen at lunchtime.'

'All the more reason. Come on, it's Sunday,' said Jude as she disappeared into the kitchen.

When they were both set up with a glass of white wine, Carole announced, 'What I'm saying is in confidence, but I think I should tell you, because it may be useful background – you know, if Gaby does come and see you . . .'

'What?' Jude was bemused, and about to say that of course Gaby had already been to see her, when she remembered the girl's stricture about not telling Carole. So she changed her tone and asked, 'About her back, you mean?'

Carole nodded. 'You've often said that bad backs are caused by tension.'

'Frequently, yes.'

'So I thought it might be useful for you to know what's making Gaby tense.'

Jude had her own theories about this, but she waited to hear what Carole had to say.

'The fact is, there's no problem between her and Stephen, which I must say is a relief. But there are things in her family which may be upsetting her.'

'Ah.' Jude wondered if she was about to hear more details of what had happened round the time of the Martins' marriage, the 'things' which Gaby didn't want brought 'back to life', which 'should have been long forgotten'.

She was disappointed. 'Gaby's brother apparently is a bit of a delinquent.' How characteristic of Carole to use that slightly dated word. 'He's called Phil – short for Philip, I assume. Got a police record, that kind of thing. Only for minor offences, but all the same – I think Gaby could be worried that Phil might do something to disrupt the wedding.'

'What kind of thing?'

'I don't know.'

Jude took a sip of her wine, thinking again about Gaby's words when she had been lying on the couch. 'Did Stephen say anything about the Martins' past? Was there anything unusual, you know, round the time they got married?'

'I don't think so, no. Well, apart from the murder.'

Jude's brown eyes widened. '"Apart from the murder"? That was rather casually said. What on earth do you mean?'

Carole brought her neighbour up to date with the little information she had received from her son on the subject. 'But it wasn't anything to do with their family. Just the victim was a school friend of Marie's. They got the man who did it, anyway.'

'And he wasn't a family member?'

'No, I'm sure Stephen would have told me if that were the case. But whether or not this ancient murder has anything to do with Gaby's unease, I've no idea. As is so often the case, we have insufficient information.'

Jude was torn. She felt tempted to share the tiny bit more information that she did have – the fact that Gaby had expressed anxiety about 'things' being brought back to life. But there were two strong reasons why she couldn't. The first was that she had been treating Gaby and, though Jude was not a conventional practitioner, there still existed a rule of confidentiality between patient and healer. The second, even more compelling, reason was that Gaby had expressly asked her not to tell Carole about their consultation. With exasperation, Jude asked herself how she managed to get into such situations. Her instinct in life was always to tell the complete truth, and whenever she was persuaded by someone to go against that instinct – even for the best of motives – trouble ensued.

Still, she'd given Gaby her word. She couldn't break that confidence.

Further conversation about the causes of the girl's distress was interrupted by the arrival of Gita from upstairs, where she had just woken up. Instantly, Jude could see her neighbour tightening up with jealousy. After some brittle chat about very little, Carole finished her drink and announced that she must 'be getting on'.

Seeing her out, Jude reflected, not for the first time, that Carole was not the easiest person in the world with whom to sustain a friendship.

Chapter Eight

Carole Seddon had long since stopped pretending that she hadn't got prejudices. Prejudices were unavoidable for a woman in her fifties, brought up in the middle of the English middle-class, and one of her biggest was geographical. Almost as big as the divide amongst Londoners between 'north of the river' and 'south of the river' was Carole's attitude, from 'south of London', towards places and people 'north of London'. She had been brought up and lived her working life in the outer suburbs south of the metropolis, and her ambitions had always been directed towards the English Channel. Living in Fethering, therefore, seemed entirely right and appropriate. And, though 'some very nice people' came from and lived in the North of England, they were always bound to be 'rather different' from people from the South.

In this geographical hierarchy, Essex occupied a unique position. Proximity to London might be thought to make it a special case, but not to Carole's way of thinking. Though she would never admit it if asked, her image of the county was a lifelong compilation of media stereotypes. She imagined it to be full of semi-retired East End gangsters, larcenous travellers, overpaid uncouth footballers and their wives, who, like most of the other female denizens, were blondes of voracious sexuality and minimal perception. She thought the only bathroom styles available in the county were onyx and gold, the only garden accessories were windmills and wishing wells, the only newspaper read was the *Sun*, and no vowel was ever properly pronounced. And Epping Forest existed only as a place to put murder victims in shallow graves.

There was not the slightest danger of reality softening the outline of any of these images, because Carole Seddon had never been to Essex.

But as her immaculate Renault approached the outskirts of Harlow, she saw nothing to change her ingrained perception. The fact that she had driven through the Dartford Tunnel to reach her destination served only to emphasize her feeling of being in an alien land.

Maybe when the 'new town' had first been created – the construction started in 1947 – Harlow had had some glamour. Maybe its tightly contained centre, its cement colonnades of shops, had then been state of the art, and the envy of more traditional towns. But, in common with many other examples of post-war building, Harlow had not aged well. Though some developments of that period survived to find a renaissance as 'retro-chic', the hopes of that ever happening to Harlow were so small as to be beneath statistical significance.

Perhaps the hotel Carole had chosen to stay in after

the engagement party reflected her determination not to find any glamour in Essex. Outside the immediate environs of Harlow itself, there was more comfortable accommodation on offer, and she couldn't pretend to be unaware of the fact, because Stephen and Gaby had booked into a very luxurious hotel converted from an Elizabethan mansion. But Carole had opted for a room in the identikit glassy rectangle of an international chain.

She felt a grim satisfaction as she drove into the car park, from which cement walkways led to the cement monolith itself. The hotel was one you could imagine someone checking into when contemplating suicide; if they hadn't arrived with suicidal thoughts, they would certainly have them by the time they left.

She looked forward to returning to Fethering as soon as possible the next morning. Carole Seddon didn't like being off home base. There was no practical difficulty about being away – Jude was going to feed and walk Gulliver – but Carole didn't like sleeping anywhere other than her own bed at High Tor.

She had no idea where her ex-husband was staying. When Carole had last spoken to Stephen, his father had not yet booked anywhere. Characteristically, David had been late in committing himself to a decision. Equally characteristically, he hadn't phoned her back, as promised. Carole had contemplated ringing him again before their inevitable meeting at the engagement party, but she had put it off, comforting herself with the argument that it really was his turn to ring her.

Yet somehow she wasn't surprised, as she walked through the anonymous automatic doors of the hotel, to see a man standing at the anonymous reception, giving his details to the anonymous blue-suited girl behind the counter.

'Yes, the name is . . . erm . . . Seddon. David Seddon. I have a single room booked for just the one night.'

'Of course, Mr Seddon,' said the receptionist in perfect received pronunciation, confounding at least one of Carole's preconceptions.

He hadn't seen her yet. Carole cleared her throat as she took up a position behind him. He didn't react. 'Excuse me . . .' she began.

'Won't be a moment, madam,' said the beautifully spoken girl. 'Just dealing with this gentleman.'

Still David didn't turn. He would always studiedly avoid confrontation or potential unpleasantness.

'Yes, but this gentleman was actually my husband,' Carole found herself saying.

He did turn at that. They stood awkwardly facing each other. Compounding the discomfort, the receptionist asked innocently, 'Oh, so will you be wanting a double room then?'

'No,' said David.

'No,' said Carole, with equal promptness, and then added tartly, 'I said "was". He's my ex-husband.'

'Ah.' The girl's eyes moved discreetly down to her computer keyboard.

Carole tried to think how many years had passed since she and David had seen each other. At least five, probably longer. What she was now confronted with was a middle-aged man slightly below her own height, the dominant feature of whose face was a pair of black heavy-rimmed glasses. His hair, the crown of which had been brown when they last met, was now uniformly white, and he'd had it cut short and spiky, which gave a slightly raffish air, totally at odds with his nondescript beige suit. David Seddon looked what he was, a minor civil servant in retirement.

But Carole had enough detachment to know that, as he looked at her, the same thought was probably crossing his mind. She felt she looked drab and ordinary, an increasingly neurotic middle-aged woman; a minor civil servant in retirement.

Neither of them could think what to say, but the receptionist prevented total silence. 'There's your key, Mr Seddon. Do you want any help with your bags?'

'No, I'm fine, thank you. Just got this little wheelie one.'

'Splendid. Well, I hope you enjoy your stay, Mr Seddon. And now . . . Mrs Seddon, is it?'

'Yes. Carole Seddon.'

David hovered. To go straight to his room without saying anything would have been downright rude, but he couldn't think of anything appropriate to the circumstances.

'Maybe,' Carole suggested, to ease the awkwardness, 'we could meet for a cup of tea – or a drink – you know, once we've got settled into our rooms?'

'Yes . . . erm . . . good idea. I'm sure they must have a bar here somewhere.'

'The Avalon Bar, just to the left of the lifts,' the receptionist supplied helpfully.

'Thank you so much. Well, look, Carole, I'll see you in . . . erm . . . half an hour, say?'

'That sounds fine, David.'

'And if you need to . . . erm . . . contact me –' he fingered his keycard nervously '– I'm in room number six one three.'

'Would it help if I were to see if I can put you in a room near Mr Seddon, Mrs Seddon?'

'No, it wouldn't, thank you very much,' replied Carole, with perhaps a little too much vigour. After all, the girl had only been trying to help.

And yet, after David had gone up in the lift, while the girl was taking down her details, Carole found herself reacting strangely to his words. There had been a time in their marriage when arriving at a new hotel had had a definite aphrodisiac effect on them. The thought of anything like that now was of course ridiculous, and yet Carole found the memory both disturbing and faintly titillating.

The Avalon Bar was a good place for the person contemplating suicide to have that final, nerve-bracing drink. There was nothing in there to make him change his mind. Its decor, pastel and anodyne, was reminiscent of an inadequately endowed private hospital. The only atmosphere was provided by ambient music, in which standards by the Beatles, Abba and Stevie

Wonder were filleted and garnished with swooping strings.

It was about half past five when Carole arrived in the bar. David was not yet there – no surprise. He had always been a strange mixture of meticulous planner and erratic timekeeper. Carole felt a seething within her, familiar from the many other bars and restaurants in which she had sat waiting for her husband.

At that time there wasn't much business in the Avalon Bar. Three over-large and over-loud business-men had just emerged from a day's conference and were downing lagers. A young mother's sour face tried to blackmail her husband into hurrying down his pint so that she could get their grizzling toddler to bed. A man who shouldn't have been with a younger woman tried to look as if they had all the time in the world to finish their drinks before rushing off to the room he'd booked.

The anonymous blue-suited young man behind the bar took Carole's order. She didn't feel like tea or coffee, resisted the lure of the white wine she really wanted because she was pacing herself for the engage-ment party, and so ended up with a mineral water. Even that failed to sparkle much in the Avalon Bar.

David came in after she had been sitting for about five minutes. As ever, just late enough to be infuriat-ing. She had rather hoped he might have brought something to change into for the party, but no, he was still in the beige suit, to which he had added an inappropriately bright, flowered tie. Carole was shocked how immediately and instinctively critical

93

thoughts came to her mind in David's presence, but then that attitude had had a long time to build up. They'd shared the mounting resentment of the years when their marriage was supposedly 'all right', then the petulant spats of the divorcing process. Since that time Carole had only avoided feelings of irritation by keeping an iron control over her thoughts and never letting them stray towards her ex-husband. She shouldn't have been surprised that seeing him again opened up the floodgates of annoyance.

And, trying to be fair – not an activity that came naturally to her – she was in no position to carp at David's sartorial shortcomings. She was wearing her inevitable Marks and Spencer's 'little black dress' and, though she had deliberately bought something unfashionable in the hope that it would never go out of fashion, she knew the garment was showing its age. Carole felt a sudden access of gloom at the image of the two of them – a lacklustre middle-aged couple. The balloon of superiority over the Martins, which had been inflating slowly in her mind, was punctured. She and David looked at least as drab as Howard and Marie.

Still, the evening had to be got through. And the protocol of politeness had to be observed. 'Can I get you a drink, David?'

'Erm . . .' He looked at his watch. 'I'm not sure that I've got time. When exactly does the party start?'

'Six thirty. But we don't want to arrive on the dot.'

How many times before had she said that in the course of their marriage? Neither of them had instinctive social skills; both had got nervous before parties and needed to gear themselves up beforehand in different, and mutually irritating, ways.

'Erm . . . well . . .' David was still assessing the feasibility of a drink. 'The fact is, I should be ordering a taxi.'

'Didn't you come by car?'

'No, I came on the train and got a cab from the station.'

'Ah.'

'Why? Did you come by car?'

Carole knew what reply this should have cued, but she resisted the answer. The Renault was her haven of security. Alone within its shell, she could arrive at the party venue – another hotel – park some way away, and then go through the process of make-up-tweaking, deep breathing and general psyching-up that she needed before she faced company. Even more important, with the car parked outside, she would have her escape route. If the party got too boring, or too confrontational – if she got too exasperated by the presence of David – she always had the option of slipping away early. With him relying on a lift back to their hotel, her freedom was curtailed.

But, even as she had these thoughts, she knew her position was hopeless. She would have to bite the bullet.

'Yes. So you don't need to get a taxi, David. I can give you a lift.'

'Oh, thank you, Carole. That's . . . erm . . . very kind.' He had another look at his watch. His ex-wife

felt another tug of familiar vexation. How could someone who was always so aware of time be persistently
late for everything?

'We don't need to go yet. You've got time for a
drink.'

'Yes, and of course, if you're driving, I don't have to
worry about it.'

'You wouldn't have had to worry if you'd got a taxi,'
Carole pointed out.

'No, I suppose not.' Suddenly – and unexpectedly –
decisive, he announced, 'I'm going to have a large
Scotch. Think I'll need a bit of a stiffener for the
evening ahead.'

For Carole, this was most unusual. During their
marriage, David had never drunk spirits. While he was
at the bar ordering, she wondered whether, in his
second single life, he had turned to drink. Men, she
recalled reading somewhere, were much worse at cop-
ing with divorce than women. Had David gone to
pieces since they parted? Did he have a whisky bottle
permanently on the go?

While these seemed unlikely conjectures, they did
remind Carole how little she knew of her husband's
current domestic circumstances. She had a phone
number she deliberately couldn't remember, and
indeed an address, but not one she had ever visited.

'So you have met the Martins, haven't you?' she
asked, once David was ensconced beside her with his
uncharacteristic Scotch.

'Yes. Yes, I have.'

Carole probed, 'And what did you think?'

'Well, they're . . . erm . . . They seem a very pleasant – a very quiet couple.'

'And Gaby's brother?'

'No.'

'Or the uncle they keep talking about. Uncle
Robert, is it?'

'Yes, but I haven't met him either.'

To Carole's disappointment, David seemed content
to let the conversation about the Martins end there.
But she should have remembered from their marriage
that David rarely volunteered his opinions of people.
If she'd wanted to find out what he thought, she had
always had to dig.

'I got the impression,' she began, 'when I had lunch
with them and Gaby, that Marie seemed rather . . .
frightened of something.'

'Life,' said David ponderously, 'is a rather frightening business.'

Carole tried again. 'And don't you think it's odd
that Stephen and Gaby haven't put any announcement
about the wedding in the paper?'

He shrugged. 'I would have thought that was up to
them.'

'Yes, but –' Carole persisted – 'it seemed to me that
it's Gaby and her mother who're anti the announcement.'

'So?'

'So – why are they?'

The second shrug was more irritating than the
first. 'Who knows? I don't think it's a very big deal.
Some people like to announce their forthcoming

marriages in the papers, and some . . . erm . . . don't.'

Carole wasn't getting anywhere with David. Indeed, when she came to think about it, she'd never got anywhere with David. It was amazing that their marriage had lasted as long as it did. Even more amazing, in fact, that they'd ever got married in the first place.

David looked at his watch again. 'I really think perhaps we should . . . erm . . . be getting along.'

This time she couldn't argue. She picked up her Burberry raincoat. 'Yes, we must go and face the . . .' 'Martins' was the word she used, but her tone said 'music'.

Chapter Nine

If any support were needed for Gaby's assertion that her parents should have nothing to do with the wedding planning, the engagement party provided it. The venue was another chain hotel, almost indistinguishable from the one in which Carole and David were staying, and the function room booked for the event made the Avalon Bar look sexy. Clearly all arrangements for the food and drink had been left to the hotel's banqueting manager. While Marie and Howard Martin's hearts were undoubtedly in the right place, they had very little experience of – or aptitude for – entertaining.

As Carole entered the room (the Caledonian Suite, with sad plaid on the walls), she wondered what phone calls must have been exchanged between Gaby and her mother over the event. She now knew that her son and fiancée's tastes ran to the lavish, so she wondered how they were reacting to this charmless venue. One look at the strain on Gaby's face provided the answer. The girl had not wanted to interfere. Her parents had taken the unusual step of initiating a party; advice on how to do it would only have upset them. Their daughter had to bite her lip and let the event be done their way. In both Gaby and Stephen's eyes glinted the insecure energy of people determined to make the best of a bad job.

Carole's fears of arriving on the dot had been avoided, but they arrived only just after the dot, and she was surprised to see how many people were already there. She knew about thirty had been invited, and most of them must have checked in at six thirty sharp.

Howard Martin was wearing exactly the same suit as he had done in the London restaurant, but Marie had clearly made an effort for the occasion. Perhaps a rather misguided effort, though. The print of pansies and violets on her dress drained what little colour there was in her face, and its tight high waist drew attention to the shapelessness of her body. As ever, the thick glasses blurred the features of her face. And yet she had the potential to be a pretty woman. With the sparkle of youth and energy, Gaby could look stunning, but her mother seemed deliberately to avoid making the best of herself. Again, Carole got the strong impression that Marie Martin found the world a very frightening place.

Oh well, the evening had to be got through. Although she'd arrived with him, Carole tried to look as though David had nothing to do with her, as she strode across to greet Howard and Marie. They were standing awkwardly to one side of the entrance, as though in a truncated reception line. Neither had a drink or seemed to regard their role in the proceedings as anything other than to be greeted.

Pleasantries were exchanged, and Carole was encouraged to 'have some of the nibbles'. These were being listlessly handed round on a tray by an anonymous blue-waistcoated waitress, but neither the soggy smoked salmon on soggier bread nor the desiccated vol-au-vents with unguessable fillings held much appeal. Carole was relieved to be whisked away by Gaby and Stephen to get a drink from the bar. Her son instantly blotted his copybook by saying, 'It's great to see you and Dad together again.'

There was a bit of confusion with the anonymous barman (clearly both hotels got their staff from the same anonymous employment agency). Having failed to take on board that the guests were not supposed to be paying for their drinks, he had been charging everyone. Stephen put the barman right on this detail and then felt obliged to go round to explain the situation to those who had already parted with good money for his future in-laws' hospitality. Gaby negotiated for Carole a welcome glass of white wine (slightly less welcome when she felt how warm it was to the hand), and then said, 'I must introduce you to my brother.'

Anyone who'd met Howard Martin would have known that Phil was his son. He was probably about the same height, but being more slender, seemed taller than his father. And, in spite of gelled, spiked-up hair and silver earrings, he looked like someone from an earlier generation; his face bore the pinched look of post-war austerity. He was dressed in a shiny grey suit over a black satin shirt. A silver necklace gleamed at his throat. The bottle of Becks from which he took frequent swigs looked diminished in his huge hand. Carole couldn't work out whether it was just his height, but something made Phil Martin look menacing.

Gaby introduced her. She was not overtly affectionate to her brother, but seemed at ease in his company.

'Hello, Phil. Gaby's told me lots about you,' said Carole, knowing she sounded over-effusive.

'Not everything, I hope.' Phil's voice was unvarnished Essex, unlike his sister's laid-back mediaspeak. Carole wondered whether they'd had the same education, and, if so, at what point Gaby had decided to get to work on her vowels.

'Not everything, no,' Carole replied, suddenly remembering that the young man she was speaking to had a criminal record. 'But she told me you lived in – Hoddesdon, is that right?'

'Yeah.'

'And you work in a warehouse?'

'Yeah. Checker.' His pride in the word echoed that which his mother had shown in the restaurant.

'Mm.' Carole tried to think of supplementary questions about working in a warehouse, but nothing sprang to mind. Jude, she felt sure, could instantly have elicited fascinating details about a checker's lifestyle. 'Well, we're all delighted about the wedding,' she went on uncontroversially.

'Yeah. Well, Sis has landed on her feet all right, hasn't she? I gather your son's loaded.'

Carole wasn't quite sure of the proper response to this. Phil seemed to be being a little ungracious, and that perception was not dispelled, as he went on, 'Relief all round, actually. Gab's no spring chicken. Didn't think anyone'd ever take pity on her.'

'Oh, shut up, Phil.' But Gaby spoke automatically. Her brother's words didn't seem to worry her at all.

'And you're not married yourself, are you?'

'No way. Had girlfriends, of course – don't get me wrong, nothing funny about me – but no way I'm going to get tied down.'

'Right.'

'Have too much of a good time with my mates. You know, we all got bikes. I'm saving up for a Harley.'

'Are you?' said Carole, as though she had a clue what he was talking about.

'Yeah, rather save up for a Harley than save up for a deposit on a three-bed semi.' He grunted out a laugh, as though this were rather a good joke.

'Mm.'

'Got to enjoy life while you can, don't you? You're a long time dead.'

This was not an exact reflection of Carole's own philosophy of life, but she nodded nonetheless, and scoured her brain for something else to say. She might be wrong, but she couldn't somehow envisage her son spending a lot of time with his brother-in-law in the future. She hoped this wouldn't lead to tension between Stephen and Gaby.

The potential conversational impasse was saved by the arrival of a newcomer, who received a much more affectionate greeting from Gaby than her brother had. Even before he was introduced, Carole felt certain she was meeting the famous Uncle Robert. He was a short-ish man, not much taller than his sister Marie, with soft white hair puffing out from a central bald spot. His suit was casual but well-tailored, and he carried him-self with a confidence lacking in the older generation of Martins. The huge hug that Gaby gave him demon-strated that he was very much the favourite uncle. It also emphasized the family likeness. Uncle Robert shared the energy and sparkle that Gaby radiated, but which seemed to have bypassed her mother.

'Robert, this is Steve's mum.' Carole got a frisson of referred pleasure from Gaby's use of the word.

'Carole, that's right, isn't it? I'm Robert Coleman.' Her hand was taken in a firm grasp, and his brown eyes twinkled as he looked her in the face. Unlike his sister, he anglicized his name, pronouncing its final 't'. 'Heard a lot about you from young Gabs, and it's a great pleasure to meet you.'

'You too.'

'And you're from – Gabs did tell me – South Coast somewhere, isn't it?'

'Fethering.'

'Of course. I know exactly where you mean. I grew up in Worthing.'

'That's right. Marie said you were there for a short while.'

'Yes.' He seemed to readjust his memory. 'I

suppose it was only a short time, really. But a lovely part of the world.'

'Oh yes,' Carole agreed automatically. She was sometimes guilty of ambivalent thoughts about where she lived, but it was certainly better than Harlow.

'And you're retired, is that right?'

Gaby had gone to greet new arrivals and Phil had drifted off to get another beer. David was in a knot of people around Stephen. But Carole didn't mind being isolated with Robert. He was a man who knew that one of the big ingredients of charm was appearing fascinated in the person you were with, and in everything they had to say. For Carole, being at the receiving end of this treatment was an unusual and pleasant experience.

'Yes, retired from the Home Office,' she replied.

'Ah, my old employers.' She looked at him quizzically. 'I'm an ex-copper. Did twenty-five years. Desk jobs, not on the beat.'

'Really?'

'Took early retirement at forty-five. They offered me a good package. Yours must have been an early retirement too.'

Carole didn't know whether this was just a manufactured compliment, but she didn't dislike it. 'Yes, a bit early. And, when you were in the Force, did you work . . . er . . .' she managed to avoid saying 'in this God-forsaken hole' '. . . out here?'

'Yes. First job out of Hendon Police College was in Billericay, and I spent my whole career in Essex.'

'Mm.' Carole felt she ought to say 'How nice', but

couldn't. 'And are you having a lazy retirement of golf and fishing?'

He grinned. 'Don't think that's really for me. Always like to be doing things. And, particularly since my wife died – well, I don't want to have time on my hands. I'm a JP, though, and that keeps me pretty busy.'

Carole did a quick memory check about policemen becoming Justices of the Peace. Any serving officer would be disqualified, but after two years of retirement an ex-policeman was eligible to serve on the Bench.

'Oh, I'm sure that keeps you very busy. Still, must be very helpful for the other magistrates, having someone with your specialist expertise.'

'Yes, I like to think I have some understanding of the criminal mind.'

'Always useful to have someone around who can do that. So, as an ex-policeman, what did you make of that rather strange burglary at Gaby's flat?'

As soon as the words were out, Carole realized she shouldn't have said them. The incomprehension in Robert Coleman's face showed that he had never heard anything about the break-in, and too late she remembered how unwilling Gaby had been for the police to be notified.

She tried to backtrack. 'Oh, I'm sorry. If you don't know about it, perhaps I shouldn't have mentioned anything. Now presumably you know everyone who's here tonight? I've just—'

But she wasn't allowed to escape that easily.

'Carole, you can't stop there. You mentioned a burglary at Gaby's flat.' His voice was firm and authoritative. 'Maybe you shouldn't have done, but you did, and neither of us can pretend it hasn't been mentioned.'

'No.' She felt like a reprimanded schoolgirl.

'Tell me exactly what happened.'

'Well, I don't know very much. Just what Stephen told me.' Quickly, she ran through the few details she had.

'So nothing at all taken?'

'Nothing obvious, apparently. But, as I say, I've had all this at second hand.'

The twinkle had gone from Robert Coleman's eyes. He was taking the news very seriously indeed. 'And Gaby's personal papers were disturbed?'

'That's right.'

'Hm. I'm going to have to talk to her about it.'

'Well, do apologize to her for my telling you about it. I wasn't thinking.'

'No,' he said thoughtfully. 'I'm very glad you did tell me. Maybe I should have a word with her . . .' He made as if to move away.

'But not tonight. This is her engagement party, after all.'

He thought about this for a moment, then nodded. 'You're right. Not the moment. They're not going back to London tonight, are they?'

'No, they're staying in a hotel. And then Gaby said something about going to her parents for coffee tomorrow morning.'

'Right. I'll talk to her then.'

'Ah. You having a good time, Carole?' asked a painfully familiar voice behind her. 'Good evening, I'm . . . erm . . . the groom's father. David Seddon.'

'Robert Coleman.' The men shook hands formally. 'Well, you two must be very proud of your young man.'

'Oh yes. We . . . erm . . . certainly are.'

'Yes. Though I should point out that we're actually divorced,' said Carole clumsily.

'Right.' There was a silence. The intimacy between Carole and Robert, weakened by her mention of the burglary, had dissipated completely with David's arrival. 'If you'll excuse me – I have to say a few words about the happy couple – must just check through my notes.'

After he had gone, ex-husband and ex-wife looked at each other. 'That was . . . erm . . . Gaby's uncle, was it?'

'That's right.'

'I'm sure we'll get to know them all very well, as the . . . erm . . . years go on.'

'Yes,' said Carole. She felt suddenly very low and miserable. All she wanted to do was to rush out to the sanctuary of her Renault, and find the anonymous haven of her hotel. Or, even better, drive straight back to Fethering.

'. . . and, though Gabs may have come a bit earlier than expected when she was born, she certainly hasn't rushed into marriage. Indeed, I don't think I'm the only one who was beginning to think it'd never happen. For my generation, you see, a girl who's reached thirty is automatically on the shelf. Still, all good things come to those who wait – and, of course, the best wine takes a long time to mature, so I like to think that Stephen has certainly got the pick of the cellar. He's got my favourite niece, and in my book, that makes him a very lucky man. And Gabs is a lucky girl too. From what I've seen of Stephen, he seems a very mature and sensible young man, who I'm sure will curb Gaby's worst excesses—'

'You've got a bloody cheek, Uncle,' Gaby said through the ripple of raucous laughter.

'So all I want to do is to ask you all to raise your glasses, to say to Gaby and Stephen – many congratulations on your engagement, and we wish you many years of happiness together! Gaby and Stephen!'

Marie Martin had been right. Her brother was a good public speaker. And yet, as he went through the motions of his oratory, Carole thought he seemed distracted. The minute the toast had been taken, the bonhomie dropped away from his face, to be replaced by a dour sternness. She wondered if it was the news of Gaby's burglary that was preoccupying him.

Stephen, who – like his mother – was not a natural public speaker, made a perfectly adequate, if over-formal, thank you, particularly expressing his gratitude to 'Marie and Howard for laying on this splendid party.' He wasn't so hypocritical as to praise the venue.

Carole watched Robert Coleman. He clearly wanted to get to Gaby, but the knot of congratulatory guests around her made that impossible, so he moved across to her brother. Phil had to bend down to listen to his uncle's earnest whispering.

Throughout the party, Marie and Howard had hardly moved from their greeting position by the entrance to the suite. They stood nervously, as if, rather than being the hosts of the occasion, they were guests who didn't know anyone. Howard sipped away at a glass of beer, but Carole hadn't seen his wife take a drink all evening. Howard's face was blank; probably the hubbub in the room made it impossible for him to hear anything.

Stephen came to join her, and she could see the strain of the occasion in his pale blue eyes. 'All seems very jolly,' she said, in the teeth of the evidence.

'Yes. Not exactly how Gaby and I would have done it if it'd been our choice, but . . . very generous of Howard and Marie.'

'Oh yes. Very generous.'

'And, if it's done nothing else, I must say I'm really pleased that it's brought you and Dad together.'

The words were out before she could stop them – a waspish 'Only geographically.'

'Yes, but . . . it will be all right for the wedding?' he asked anxiously.

'Of course it will, Stephen. We're both adults, and we're well enough brought up to know how to behave.'

'I'm aware of that. I just hoped that, maybe, by see-ing more of each other, you might—'

'Stephen, if you're hoping there's going to be some rapprochement between your father and me, forget it.' Carole found she was speaking more angrily than she intended. 'We'll not disgrace ourselves at your wedding, but after that we will go back to the only relationship between us that has ever worked – in other words, not seeing each other.'

'I'm . . . erm . . . rather sorry to hear you say that, Carole.'

Damn. She hadn't heard David creeping up to join their conversation. Quite what she should say next was something of a challenge. There was no danger of their having a stand-up row – neither of them had ever been any good at stand-up rows – but Carole couldn't think of anything she might say that wouldn't sour the minimal atmosphere of the engagement party. She certainly wasn't going to take back what she'd just said.

Her dilemma was solved by a sudden commotion over by the door. She looked across to see Howard, Robert, Phil and Gaby looking down in horror at the fallen figure of Marie Martin. They were frozen in surprise for a second, then Gaby knelt down to help her mother up.

As Carole moved towards them, she heard Marie murmur, 'It's all right. I don't want to make a fuss. It's just the heat.'

Gaby held her arm firmly around her mother's waist and looked at her anxiously. Carole felt she was probably intruding into something private, but she couldn't walk away now. Looking up at her, Gaby said, 'Mum does get these fainting spells sometimes.'

'I'm fine. Don't worry about me. Just enjoy the party.'

'This was bound to happen some time.' It was

Howard Martin who spoke, and he didn't sound as though he was referring to his wife's collapse. He looked firmly at his brother-in-law, as he went on, 'I knew he was going to come back. I've talked to him.'

'What?' Robert Coleman sounded in deep shock.

'On the phone. I'm going to meet him tomorrow.'

'Here in Harlow?'

'Yes. He's in the area. He deserves to have his say.'

'Doesn't deserve anything,' Phil said viciously. 'He has no rights.'

This intriguing conversation was stopped when Marie's knees once again gave way. Phil rushed forward to help his sister support their mother's slack body.

'We must get her home,' said Gaby. 'I'll take her.'

'No, you can't,' her mother moaned. 'This party's for you. You can't leave the guests.'

'Well, Steve could—'

'No, it's his party too. Oh, I'm sorry to spoil everything.'

'You're not spoiling everything, Mum. Dad, shall I call for a cab?'

'You'll be lucky. When I tried to book one for later, they said they hadn't got anything all evening. Some big conference, I don't know . . .'

'We'll find someone to drive you back.'

'Well, I'm only on the bike,' said Phil.

'And I walked here,' said Robert.

'I'll do it,' Carole announced. 'I'll drive you home, Marie.'

Chapter Ten

Marie Martin didn't want to say anything beyond giving directions to her flat. It was less than two miles away. She was very grateful for the lift, and she didn't want to be a nuisance, and Carole would have plenty of time to get back and enjoy the rest of the party. Carole didn't say that she regarded the early departure as providential, and, after delivering her passenger, firmly intended to go straight back to her hotel. She didn't care that by doing so, she'd leave David without transport. Seeing her ex-husband in a social context had been a surprisingly disagreeable experience. She hadn't realized how much resentment towards him she had been bottling up over the years.

But hostility towards David was not the only thought in her mind. There was also a huge curiosity about what had happened at the engagement party. She felt sure there was some connection between Robert Coleman's violent reaction to the news of Gaby's burglary and Marie's fainting fit. Even more than that, she wanted to know who Howard had been referring to in his strange utterance about someone 'coming back'. Carole was at least going to try to get something out of her passenger on those two matters.

Still, she'd have to edge her way carefully into the subject. 'It never occurred to me that Robert wouldn't have known about the break-in to Gaby's flat.'

'What?' asked Marie, shocked. 'What break-in?'

'She didn't tell you either?'

'I don't know what you're talking about, Carole. When did this happen?'

'Last weekend.'

'Pascale – Gaby – often doesn't tell me things that she thinks might upset me.' This was said with a degree of satisfaction, as though Marie's hypersensitivity gave her an immunity from some of life's unpleasantnesses.

There was a silence. Carole thought she was going to have to probe again, but Marie Martin's curiosity got the better of her. Turning towards Carole, and peering through her thick glasses, she asked, 'What was taken in the burglary? Did they get away with a lot of stuff?'

'Hardly anything. But Gaby thought someone had been through her personal papers.'

'How do you mean – personal papers?'

'Tax records, passport, address book, birth certificate, that kind of thing.'

'Oh God.' The words came out as an involuntary gasp.

'Are you all right, Marie? Do you want me to stop the car?'

'No, no. I'm fine.' But she didn't sound fine, as she

went on, bleakly, 'You can never get away with any-thing in life. There are always ghosts going to come back to haunt you.'

'What do you mean?'

But Marie Martin realized she'd already said too much, and clammed up.

Carole wasn't going to leave it there, though. 'Who was Howard talking about?'

'What?'

'Just after you fainted, he said to Robert that some-one had come back, that he had talked to him on the phone and that he was going to see him tomorrow.'

'I didn't hear that. I must have been out cold.'

But she wasn't convincing even herself.

'I don't think that's true, Marie. You heard him. Who is this man who's come back?'

'I don't know. Maybe someone Howard used to work with.'

'I think you do know. I think it was hearing he was coming back that brought on your fainting fit.'

There was a silence, which was then broken by the little whimpering sounds of Marie Martin crying.

What an incongruous conversation this is, Carole couldn't help thinking. Here I am, on only the second occasion that I've met my son's prospective mother-in-law, and I'm giving her the third degree in my car, and I've actually made her cry. I'm sure that's not what's recommended for this kind of encounter in all those books of wedding etiquette.

'It's just here on the left. Behind that red car.'

Carole slowed the Renault down and it came to rest

outside an anonymous grey block of flats, whose exterior suggested offices. Beneath the windows, panels of faded green plastic, no doubt at the cutting edge of architecture when the flats had been built, now seemed only to draw attention to the drab greyness of the prevailing concrete.

Carole was determined to get more information out of her passenger, but as soon as the car had stopped, the door was opened and, with a muttered 'Thank you for the lift', Marie Martin had scuttled off and into the darkness of the interior. With a sigh of exasperation, Carole Seddon slammed the Renault back into gear and drove off.

She lay on one of the twin beds in the anonymous room identical to every other anonymous room in that hotel – and in anonymous lonely hotels all over the world. She hadn't undressed yet, but lay on top of the covers, sipping the minibar's white wine directly from the bottle and watching the kind of television she'd never have bothered to watch at home. She felt tired, but still too unsettled for sleep.

At first she couldn't believe it when she heard the tap on the door. Must be a loose window fitting somewhere, or someone along the corridor in another room had a visitor.

But no. The tapping started again. And definitely on her door.

She moved forward with fascinated horror. She wasn't afraid; she just couldn't believe what was happening because there was only one person who could possibly be tapping on her door at that time of night in that hotel.

'Hello? Who is that?'

'It's . . . erm . . . me. David.'

Telling him to get lost – which was what she should have done – suddenly seemed an insuperable effort. She was too tired for any more conflict. Wearily, she opened the door. 'What do you want?'

'Just wanted to have a word.'

He sounded maudlin drunk. Now she came to think of it, he had been putting quite a lot away at the engagement party. Oh God, any sort of David was bad enough, but a self-pitying drunken David – she didn't feel she could cope.

'Aren't you going to invite me in?'

Why the hell should I? We have absolutely nothing in common except for shared memories of unhappiness. What makes you think you can just . . .

But she didn't say any of it. Everything felt like too much effort. She backed away from the door. 'Come in.' She returned to where her wine was. She wished she'd decanted it into a glass, but she took hold of the bottle and sat demurely on the edge of the bed.

'Well, if you're . . . erm . . . having a drink . . .'

'You know where the minibar is: presumably in exactly the same place as it is in your room.'

David opened the little fridge, and produced two miniature Scotches, which he poured into a plastic glass. Dear oh dear, he really was overdoing it. He looked shabbily pathetic, but if he was hoping for sympathy from Carole he surely knew her well enough to realize how slim his chances were.

'Shall I come and . . . erm . . . sit beside you?'

'There's a perfectly good chair over there.'

'Yes, but . . .' Something in her eye stopped him. He subsided into the chair and raised his plastic glass with mock bravado. 'Here's to you, Carole.'

Thank God at least that he hadn't tried, 'Here's to us.'

He drank down about half of his drink, and then said, 'I ended up walking from the other hotel. There weren't any cabs to be had for love nor money.'

'I forgot I said I'd give you a lift. I'm sorry.' Which she wasn't.

David swallowed down most of the rest of his drink, and was silent.

'What do you want, David?' Carole asked in exasperation. 'You said you "just wanted to have a word". About what?'

'Well, there are . . . erm . . . two things.'

Oh God, here we go. David had always itemized, always categorized, always spoken under headings. He had all the props of efficiency, without actually being efficient.

'First, I thought this evening went all right.'

'Presumably it went as Howard and Marie wanted it to go, yes.'

'He seemed very happy, certainly. I was talking to him just as he was leaving. But that wasn't what I meant.'

'Sorry?'

'About this evening. What I meant was that I thought we coped with this evening very well.'

'We?'

'Yes. I'm sure we were both nervous – you know, not having seen each other for quite a while and . . . erm . . . you know, considering what happened between us.'

'"What happened between us", David, was that we got divorced. We decided we no longer wanted to be married to each other. That we no longer wanted to spend time together.'

'Ah, now those are two separate things. I'd like to think that now we've . . . erm . . . come to terms with what happened . . . erm . . . got a bit of distance from it, that we could see each other from time to time.'

Please, no, thought Carole. I've got my life in Fethering. I've got Gulliver. I've got Jude. I just don't need this.

But what she found herself saying was, 'Well, we'll have to see. I'm sure when Stephen and Gaby are married . . . you know, there'll be family occasions when we meet up.'

'Like christenings, eh?' said David, with what she reckoned must have been intended to be a roguish wink.

'Maybe.'

She looked at her watch, which served to give David impetus for the other thing he had to say, 'It's about the marriage I wanted to talk to you.'

'We'll have plenty of time to talk about it before

September. All the arrangements seem to be going fine.'

'No.' He held up a rather unsteady hand. 'What I wanted to ask you about the marriage was . . . erm . . . do you think it's a good thing?'

This was so completely not the question she was expecting that Carole found herself mouthing vacuously. 'Well, yes. I mean, Stephen and Gaby seem to adore each other, which is, after all, what's most important.'

'Yes, but' – he was now wagging a finger at her – 'what about the family?'

'Well, they're very quiet, they're not demonstrative, but it's Gaby Stephen's marrying, not her family.'

'But do you think our son should be allying himself to . . . erm . . . a bunch of Essex gangsters?'

'*What* did you say, David?'

'That boy . . . erm . . . Phil, her brother, he's got a criminal record.'

'I know that, but it doesn't make the family "a bunch of Essex gangsters".'

'And . .' David went on portentously, 'he's not the only one of them who's been in prison.'

'What?'

'I was talking at the party to some man, and he said that someone the Martins know has just been released from prison.'

'All right. Someone they *know*. Not someone in the family.'

'I'm not so sure about that.' He hiccoughed. He really was drunk.

'Anyway, lots of people end up in prison, for motoring offences or—'

David shook his head. 'This wasn't a motoring offence. This man's just been released after serving thirty years for murder.'

Chapter Eleven

It was late by the time Carole managed to get rid of David. He had become increasingly maudlin, and even tried to be affectionate, which was absolutely the last thing she wanted. She was appalled when he tried to kiss her, and even more appalled by the fact that she felt an unwelcome flickering of responsive lust. He was so firmly out of her life that she didn't want him encroaching even on its furthest margins.

Once she had finally ejected him, her mind was too full for sleep to come easily. Seeing David reanimated a whole complex of emotions that she hoped had been safely consigned to inert half-life. The fourteenth of September – the date when she had promised Stephen his parents would demonstrate what a mature, friendly relationship they had – loomed ever more threateningly ahead of her. And the worries David had voiced about Gaby's family were also troubling, particularly as they echoed anxieties that she had not dared spell out to herself.

All she wanted to do was to snatch what sleep she could, get up at half past six, forgo breakfast, leave the hated hotel and set the Renault firmly on course for Fethering.

She was therefore annoyed, when the phone woke her at twenty to eight, to realize that she had overslept.

It was Stephen. And he sounded very tense.

'What's the matter?'

'It's Howard. Gaby's dad.'

'What? Has he been taken ill?'

'No. He's disappeared.'

'What do you mean, Stephen?'

'A car was ordered to take him back after the party last night. He got into it, and that's the last anyone saw of him. He never made it home.'

Chapter Twelve

'Have you rung them?' asked Jude, as soon as she walked in from shopping.

'No.'

Gita spoke with defiant truculence. She was stretched over one of the draped sofas in the Woodside Cottage sitting room, but not in an attitude of relaxation. Her body was taut. She couldn't get comfortable. The television was on, some lunchtime soap, but she didn't seem able to concentrate on the screen.

'It's a good idea.'

'I don't know . . .'

'Yes, you do. You're a professional journalist. You told me at breakfast that it was a good idea.'

'I know, but . . .'

'You woke up with the idea, you were full of it, you said it was the kind of feature you could write standing on your head, and there were at least half a dozen magazine editors who would snap it up.'

'Mm.'

'So why haven't you rung any of them?'

'Because . . .' Gita leant forward and clasped her arms round her shins, making herself into a bundle of misery. 'Because . . . I know I could have done it. I know the old me could have done it. I just don't think – now all my confidence has gone – I don't think I can do anything.'

She sounded so low, too abject even for tears. Instinctively Jude sat down on the sofa and enveloped her friend in a large hug. Gita's body stayed tense. She sighed hopelessly. 'I don't think I am getting any better, you know, Jude.'

'You are, love. You are. You had the idea for the feature. That's the first one you've had since you were ill.'

'Yes, but I still can't follow it through.'

'You will. In time. Come on, you've just got to make one phone call.'

'I can't. Oh, I'm sorry, Jude.'

'There's nothing to be sorry for.'

'There is. I know how sickeningly spineless I'm being. I know how infuriating I am. God, I bore *myself* the way I keep moaning on about the same things, round and round.'

'Don't worry about it.'

'And you have to keep saying the same things back at me. "Don't worry about it." "There's nothing to be sorry for." You must be sick to death of me.'

'I'm not, Gita. Because, you see, I have the advantage of you.'

'In what way?'

'I know you're going to get better.'

Gita broke out into a little, despairing laugh. And then the tears came. Jude continued to hold her, as the body in her arms shook with the regular unloading of grief. It was all she could do, but probably also the most valuable thing she could do.

Calmly, over Gita's heaving shoulders, Jude watched the lunchtime television news.

A man's body had been found in a burnt-out car on the outskirts of Harlow in Essex.

Harlow, thought Jude. That's where Carole's just been. But it can't have anything to do with her.

In her neat white Renault, driving down the M23 towards the South Coast, Carole heard the same news on the radio. And she had an awful feeling it might have something to do with her.

As soon as she got back to High Tor, she found a television news bulletin. Little was added to the information she already had. The body of a man had been found in a burnt-out car driven some way into Epping Forest off the B1393 road near Harlow. That was it.

To Carole, in spite of the horror, it seemed appropriate, confirming her image of Epping Forest as a depository for the bodies of murder victims.

She rang Stephen on his mobile. He was still in Harlow. 'I'm at the hotel. Gaby's with her mother, but they didn't want me there. Marie's in a very nervous state.'

Even in the circumstances, Carole couldn't help thinking, Marie's always in a very nervous state.

'Has there been any sign of Howard?'

'Well . . .' At the other end of the phone, Carole could hear her son swallow. 'Mum, I think it's going to be bad news.'

In her fever of anticipation she didn't notice his use of 'Mum'. 'I heard something on the radio about a body in a burnt-out car in Epping Forest. Surely that wasn't . . .?'

'It looks horribly as if it was. The police have been round to the flat. They haven't got a positive identification yet, but they've said we should prepare ourselves for the worst.'

'Oh, God . . .'

'The body's burnt beyond recognition, but apparently it's the right sort of age. They're going to have to check dental records, or perhaps even DNA – though that may not be easy, because, just to add to the confusion, Phil seems to have disappeared.'

'What?'

'Apparently he didn't turn up for work this morning.'

'Stephen, what on earth's going on?'

'If I knew that, I'd tell you. It just all seems extremely nasty.'

'But what were the circumstances? When was Howard last seen alive – I mean, assuming he's not alive now?'

'Gaby and I didn't actually see him leave, because we were saying goodbye to some other people, but, according to Robert, a car had been ordered for Howard; it arrived at the hotel, and he went off in it. That's the last time he was seen. Then early this morning somebody reported this burnt-out car off the B1393.'

'Was it the same car Howard left the hotel in?'

'Can't be certain, because nobody can remember exactly what kind of car came to collect him, but the police think it's possible.'

'So . . . what? Did the car crash into a tree and burst into flames?'

'No. According to the police, except for the fire, the car appeared to be undamaged.'

'And' – Carole pieced the known facts together – 'there was only one body in the car?'

'Yes.'

'So what happened to the driver?'

'That, I would imagine, is the number-one question the police are currently asking. Who was driving the car?

'And where is he now?'

The next day the police confirmed that the body found in the Essex lay-by was that of seventy-nine-year-old Howard Martin from Harlow. And he hadn't been killed by the fire; he had been strangled before the car was set alight.

Chapter Thirteen

When Carole received that news from Stephen, she knew she had to talk to Jude. On her own. But with Gita in residence at Woodside Cottage, dropping round unannounced was not as simple as usual. So she telephoned.

The timing was good. Gita had an appointment that day with her doctor in London. Jude had initially been reluctant to let her go on her own, but Gita had insisted. Jude, welcoming this new resolution in her friend, had not argued further. Though determined to be supportive, she could not deny that the task of continuously bolstering Gita's seesawing confidence was an exhausting one.

Carole and Jude met at High Tor, and Carole was so full of her story that she forgot her normal rules for the protocol of hospitality and served coffee at the kitchen table. The salient facts didn't take long to spell out.

'Poor kid.' Jude sighed at the end of the narration. 'Gaby. She's a very emotional girl. This is going to hit her hard.'

'It is. I mean, having an older father, she must

always have been preparing herself for his death, but for that death to come so suddenly and like this – as you say, poor kid.'

'So it's definitely a case of murder?'

'Yes. And not much attempt to make it look like anything else. Howard's body was found in the back seat of the car. Maybe the murderer hoped the fire would be so fierce as to hide the fact that he was strangled, but I wouldn't have thought so.'

'Hm. From what you've said, Howard Martin sounded an amiable – even harmless – old guy.'

'He was. Mind you, I don't really know anything about him, his personal history, even what job he did before he retired.'

Jude ran her fingers through her tousled blonde hair. 'So why on earth would anyone have wanted to murder him?'

'I don't know. Maybe a gangland killing?' Carole hazarded.

'Oh, come on. You're only saying that because it happened in Essex, and your image of Essex is as a seething hotbed of East End gangsters.'

'No, I wouldn't say that – exactly. But I just can't think of any other reason.'

'That's because we have insufficient information.'

'*No* information might be more accurate. And a crime scene that's rather a long way away from Fethering. I think we're going to have our work cut out trying to solve this murder mystery.'

'You sound almost disappointed, Carole.'

'No, I don't. I just . . . well, I feel so bad for Gaby's sake. You know, she is almost family now.'

'Yes. She's a sweet girl.'

'She didn't say anything, you know, while you were being an osteopath for her?'

'I'm not an osteopath, Carole.'

'Well, whatever.'

'And there is a code of confidentiality between patient and therapist.'

'Yes, but—'

'No "but", Carole.' Jude sounded quite stern, then relented. 'If there was anything she said that I thought might be relevant to her father's death, then I'd tell you. But there isn't.'

'Oh.'

'What we really need to find out is the identity of the driver who picked up Howard Martin from the hotel after the party.'

'I'd got that far,' said Carole tartly.

'Surely somebody must have seen him go? One of the other guests?'

'Yes, you'd have thought – oh dear.' Carole brought herself up short. 'There was someone who saw Howard leave.'

And it was the last person in the world who she wanted to get back in touch with.

'Erm . . . hello?'

'David, it's Carole,' she said brusquely.

'Oh, how nice to . . . erm . . . hear from you again.'

'You've heard about Howard?'

'Stephen rang me, yes.'

Carole had a momentary pang of jealousy. Had Stephen phoned his father before he'd phoned her? What was the pecking order between them? Resolutely she dismissed the unworthy thought.

'It's terrible, isn't it?'

'Yes, it is. Absolutely . . . erm . . . terrible.' Then, with one of his characteristic lunging changes of subject, he said, 'Incidentally, I was discussing with Stephen the . . . erm . . . possibility of us having dinner.'

'What?'

'You, me, him and Gaby.'

'What are you talking about, David?'

'I suggested to Stephen that we should all meet up for dinner one evening. My treat. In a restaurant. I mean, my cooking's all right for just me, but . . . erm . . .'

'David, we have far more important things to think about. Gaby's father's just been murdered.'

'Yes, but this dinner—'

'I can't think about dinners now,' Carole snapped. 'You have no idea of a reason why Howard should have been killed, have you?'

'No. Well, I suppose . . . I don't know. Maybe a . . . erm . . . mugging that went wrong?'

'Have the police spoken to you, David?'

'Why on earth should they speak to me?' He sounded shocked at the very idea.

'Well, you were at the party, and you said you saw Howard leave.'

'Yes.'

'So you must be one of the few people who actually saw the person who drove him away.'

'Ah.'

'Did you?'

'Well, I . . . erm . . . I saw the car.'

'What was it – an ordinary taxi?'

'I don't think there was anything on it to show that it was a taxi. No illuminated sign, no writing on the side.'

'What make of car was it?'

'One of those smallish ones – you know – a Ford Escort or a Renault or a Peugeot. All cars look alike these days.'

'Colour?' asked Carole patiently.

'Reddish. Dull red. Quite battered. That's the thing that struck me, really. I thought, what an incredibly beaten-up old car that is to be acting as a taxi.'

'Maybe, with hindsight, we could conclude that it wasn't a taxi?'

'Maybe not.'

'You haven't heard the make of the car that was burnt out, have you?'

'No. That hasn't been . . . erm . . . specified in any of the news reports I've seen.'

'Hm. Now, David, the more important question – what about the driver?'

'What about him?'

'Did you get a good view of him?'

'No. I was in the hotel foyer. Howard had just gone outside, so I was looking through the glass doors, and it wasn't very well lit out there.'

'So you got no impression of who was driving the car?'

'Not really. I think he had a baseball cap pulled down over his eyes.'

'A man then. Was he young, or old?'

'Well, I sort of got the impression he was young. But maybe that was just because of the baseball cap.'

'Everyone in Essex wears baseball caps,' said Carole loftily.

'There do seem to be a lot of them, certainly.'

'So, from what you saw of this driver, you would say positively that he was young?'

'Ooh, no.' David had never been much good at saying anything positively.

'Then what did he look like?'

'Erm . . . No, I couldn't tell you. Really couldn't.'

'You're going to be a fat lot of use to the police, aren't you?'

'Carole, do you think they really will want to . . . erm . . . talk to me?'

'Almost definitely. I wouldn't be surprised if they get on to me too. I should think they'd want to check with everyone who was at the engagement party.'

'Yes.'

'They are conducting a murder enquiry, after all.'

'Right.'

'In fact, David, I think you should get in touch with them voluntarily.'

'Why?'

'Public-spirited thing to do. You have information that may be vital to their enquiry. You're a witness.'

'Yes, but I didn't witness much, did I?'

'No, not the way you told it to me, I admit you didn't. But the police have ways of getting things out of witnesses.'

'Really?'

He sounded so anxious Carole couldn't resist teasing him. 'Hypnotism, truth drugs – other methods,' she concluded darkly.

'Oh dear,' said her ex-husband. 'That doesn't sound very . . . erm . . . pleasant.'

Chapter Fourteen

'I think they need to get away, Mother.' Stephen was tense, so he'd returned to his formal mode of address, which was slightly disappointing.

'It must be dreadful for them,' said Carole.

'It is. The phone ringing continuously, reporters actually camping on their doorstep. Constant questioning from the police. Marie's never been very strong emotionally. This is really tearing her apart.'

'I'm sure it is,' said Carole, trying to suppress her knee-jerk reaction to people who weren't 'strong emotionally'. In her view, emotional strength was purely a matter of willpower.

'And it's putting a tremendous strain on Gaby, because she has to field all the phone calls, virtually be her mother's minder twenty-four hours a day. So she's got that on top of the grief and shock she's feeling at her father's death.'

'It must be tough for her, poor kid.' She wasn't conscious that she was echoing Jude's words. 'Can't her brother take part of the strain? Or has he still not turned up?'

'He's around. Apparently the night after the party

he continued drinking with some mates and crashed out on someone's floor. There was nothing more sinister to his disappearance than a massive hangover.'

'But is he being supportive?'

'I gather Phil's always been pretty useless when it comes to anything involving responsibility. Also I don't think he and Marie ever really got on that well. He was closer to his father. No, he's gone back to work.'

'In the warehouse in Hoddesdon.'

'Yes. Which is probably just as well. I don't think Phil's presence would do anything to decrease the tension in the flat.'

'No.'

'Robert's been round a few times. He's been a great source of strength for Marie, but he can't spare much time. He seems to have a pretty busy life, with his duties as a magistrate and what have you. He's also been very helpful dealing with the police.'

'In what way?'

'Well, being an ex-copper, he knows how they work. Sometimes he can give them information and save Marie the stress of another interview.'

'Hm. And you're back at work, are you, Stephen?'

'Yes. I'm really frenetic at the moment.'

Doing what? Carole was tempted yet again to ask the question, but she realized she had left it far too late in their relationship.

'And Gaby?'

'She's off for the foreseeable future. I think she'd give anything to get back to the agency, just to be able to get her mind round something else, but she's afraid to leave Marie on her own. Which is why I was suggesting they should have a break somewhere. Just to get away from the flat, get away from Harlow.'

'Would the police be happy for them to do that?'

'I think it'd be all right. I'd have to clear it with the inspector in charge of the case – Inspector Pollard he's called – but he seems to be a fairly reasonable guy. So long as he knew where they were, I don't think he'd raise any objections.'

'So where are they thinking of going?'

'I thought down your way would be good.'

His words prompted instant panic in Carole. The thought of having people staying in High Tor, people she didn't really know that well, people who were in a highly emotional state – it would be more than she could cope with. The carefully guarded borders of her life were under threat of invasion.

'Well, yes,' she flustered. 'I've only got the one spare room, but if they didn't mind sharing, I—'

'No, I wasn't suggesting they actually stay with you, just somewhere down in your direction.'

'Oh.' Carole hoped the monosyllable didn't reveal too much of her relief.

'I mean, the only hotels I know are like Hopwicke Country House Hotel, which I think might be a bit dauntingly grand for Marie.'

'Well, there are lots of less flashy ones around. I'm sure I could sort something out for you.'

'If you could. As I say, I'm absolutely frenetic here.'

'Leave it with me. Somewhere quiet and comfortable.'

'Yes. With the emphasis on the "quiet". Somewhere where no reporters would think of looking for them.'

'Right. And what – book them in for a week?'

'Something like that. Leave it open-ended.'

'All right, Stephen. It shall be done.'

'Bless you.'

'And from when?'

'Well, if I talk to Inspector Pollard today, and everything's all right, then from tomorrow, I would think. Gaby's got the BMW up in Harlow. She could drive her mum down.'

'I'll arrange it. Can I ring you back at work?' It was something she had very rarely done.

'Trouble is, I've got end-to-end meetings all day. If you don't mind just sorting it out with Gaby. I'll give you her mobile number.' He reeled it off.

'Very impressive memory, Stephen.'

'I get that from you.' Carole was cheered by the thought. 'Anyway, God knows I've keyed Gaby's number in a few times. I wouldn't be so fluent with my own.'

'No, I suppose you don't often dial that.' Carole was as yet unfamiliar with the world of mobile phones. She kept thinking she should get one. But then again, she was so rarely away from High Tor, the landline there was probably adequate for her minimal needs for communication.

'Gaby can't remember her own number for love nor money. It's the first entry in her address book. Mind you, most numbers you put in the phone's memory these days, so it doesn't much matter whether you remember them or not.'

'It matters to me. I try to remember every phone number I've ever been told. It's a point of honour not to have to consult my address book.' It was also, for Carole, rather like doing *The Times* crossword every day, a way of holding at bay the insidious advances of Alzheimer's.

'That, if I may say so, Mother, is entirely characteristic of you.' But, though unarguably a criticism, he said it with affection. 'Anyway, I'll get on to Inspector Pollard, and if there's any problem about them leaving Harlow, I'll let you know within the next hour.'

'All right.'

'Thank you, Mum.' He didn't know how much he had warmed her by saying that. Nor how much more he warmed her by what he said next. 'I'll feel a lot happier knowing they're near you.'

'Is that Gaby?'

'Yes.'

'It's Carole.'

'Just a sec. I'll move next door.' The girl called, away from the phone, 'It's work, Mum.'

Carole heard a door close and then Gaby's voice, closer and more intense. 'Sorry. Mum's getting so paranoid every time the phone rings.'

'I don't blame her. How're you bearing up, Gaby?'

'As well as can be expected, I suppose.'

'Is the back troubling you?'

'No.' Gaby almost laughed at the incongruity. 'Not a twinge. Maybe I'm better at dealing with real disasters than imagined ones.'

'A lot of us are. Look, I was ringing, because you know Stephen called me about finding a hotel down here.'

'Yes.'

'Well, I've got the perfect place. It's in Fethering, but the other side of the river from the main town. Very few people go over there even in the height of summer. Little place called the Dauncey Hotel. Very friendly, very quiet. Nice sea views, and some good walks if that's what you feel like. Alternatively, they serve three very good meals a day, if you just want to dig in.'

'I should think the first couple of days we'd just dig in, then maybe consider venturing out. Oh, Carole, thank you so much for sorting that. If we spend another day in this place, we're both going to go out of our minds – or even more out of our minds than we are already.'

'Well, they're expecting you some time tomorrow afternoon. And I gather from Stephen that the police are happy about you moving away for a while?'

'So long as we don't leave the country. They've got phone numbers for us, and it won't take long to get us back to Harlow if there's any development on the case.'

'And has there been much development on the case?'

Gaby let out a weary sigh.

'I mean, have the police given any indication of the direction in which their enquiries are going?'

'Oh, it's so hard to tell with them. They just seem to ask the same questions over and over again. And then suddenly they get some new idea, go off at a tangent, and find some new set of questions to ask over and over again.'

'So any pointers towards—' Carole recovered herself. 'I'm sorry, perhaps I shouldn't be asking you?'

'Don't worry. It makes a change to have someone who is prepared to talk about it. Mum just clams up. Remembering that Dad's dead is enough to send her off into floods of tears, before you even start on the circumstances of his death.'

'It must be terrible.' There was a silence. 'On the other hand, Gaby, if there is anything you do want to tell me about what the police are saying?'

'Well . . . reading between the lines of their questioning, they seem to think that the person who drove Dad away from the hotel may not necessarily be the one who actually killed him.'

'Oh?'

'Apparently the car was stolen locally, just that evening. The police reckon – don't know how they've got to this point, but they seem to think – that the driver was probably acting under orders, that he just had to drive Dad to some place – possibly the bit of Epping Forest where he was found – to meet someone. And the driver left the two of them there. That's what they seem to be thinking.'

'Hm.'

'They've been asking Phil a lot of questions.'

'Oh?'

'At one time he used to hang around with a pretty unsavoury crowd. I'm not certain that he still doesn't but basically, if you want to find out about a car thief in the Harlow area, you could do worse than ask Phil Martin.'

'You haven't had a chance to talk to him?'

'Not on his own, no. I doubt if he'd confide in me even if he did know something. We've never been that close.'

'How's he reacting to his father's death?'

'Never easy to know with Phil. He was drunk the night it happened, and he seems to have been avoiding confronting it since then by keeping his alcohol level topped up. What he's feeling inside – well, I've never really known what Phil's feeling inside.'

'Right. Oh, incidentally, Gaby, when you're down in Fethering – you know, if you want company – do join me at the Crown and Anchor for a drink or . . .' It went against Carole's nature to make such an unspecific invitation. Normally, she liked to have her social calendar planned out to the minutest detail, but these were exceptional circumstances.

'That's very kind.'

'If you feel like it, the offer's there. If you just want to hide away, that's fine. I won't feel offended. I'm not the sort of person to be easily offended.' Even Carole herself could recognize that that wasn't true.

'Well, can we play it by ear? See how Mum feels?'

'Of course. And if there's anything practical I can do – shopping or whatever – just let me know.'

'Yes, of course we will. Thank you, Carole.'

'Well, I'd better let you get back to your mother. One thing, Gaby . . .'

'Mm?'

'You know how unhappy you were – and your mother was, come to that – about the idea of an engagement announcement in the paper?'

'Yes?'

'Was it because you were afraid something like this might happen – that it might draw attention to you – stir up old issues for your family?'

'Yes, Carole, that's exactly what I was afraid of. And,' she added bitterly, 'as it turns out, with good reason.'

'Don't worry, Gaby, I'm sure the police'll soon find out what happened to Howard.'

'Hm. Maybe they will.'

Carole could not fail to respond to the optimism in Gaby's voice. 'You mean they're close to a breakthrough? Have they actually got a suspect?'

'Well, there's someone they keep talking about. A man who's just finished a long prison sentence and now apparently vanished off the face of the earth.'

'And he had some connection with your father?'

'I assume so. I assume that's why the police keep asking about him.'

'What's he called?'

'Michael Brewer.'

'Have you ever heard of him?'

'No.'

'And have you asked your mother?'

'I've tried, but, as I said, Mum is not being very forthcoming at the moment.'

'But how did she react when the police asked her about this man?'

'She fainted.'

'Oh.'

Chapter Fifteen

'The good thing about it is,' said Jude, 'that our geographical problem is partly eased.'

'What do you mean? The location of the crime scene hasn't changed. Howard Martin was still murdered in Essex.'

'Yes, but now we've got his widow and daughter coming down to Fethering, so at least we have a couple of significant figures in the case close by.'

'Maybe close by, but I don't know that we're going to get much information out of Marie. Whenever the questions get nasty, she just seems to faint.'

'Convenient.'

'Do you mean psychosomatic?'

'I didn't say that. On the other hand, Carole – I know you don't really like the idea – but a lot of illness is psychosomatic. And these things can be hereditary. Gaby reacts to stress by getting a bad back, her mother faints – it could be a similar reaction.'

'Huh,' said Carole, exactly as Jude had known she would.

They were walking along Fethering Beach. The tide was a long way out, and the sand firm beneath their feet. In the warm June sunshine, even the sludge-coloured sea was enriched by the reflected blue of the sky. Down by the water's edge, Gulliver was doing elaborate commando manoeuvres, stalking the bits of seaweed that shuffled on the scummy edges of the waves. For him, Fethering Beach was a canine heaven, full of ambrosial and intriguing smells. Half a day spent on the beach, the other half snuffling sleepily in front of the Aga at High Tor – for Gulliver life could offer nothing more perfect.

'There was something else about heredity I was thinking of,' Jude mused. 'Didn't you say that Howard Martin had had bowel cancer?'

'Yes, but made a complete recovery, I gather. Apparently the scars from the operation were one of the reasons his body was identified so quickly. So they didn't have to take a DNA sample from Phil.'

'Hm . . . I was just thinking . . . I'm not betraying any important confidentiality here, but Gaby did tell me that she had been worried that she might have bowel cancer at one point.'

'But she didn't have, did she?' asked Carole, alarmed at the threat to her future daughter-in-law's health.

'No, no, it turned out she just had a mild form of IBS.'

'IBS?'

'Irritable Bowel Syndrome.'

That got another of Carole's 'Huhs'. She didn't believe in illnesses that were called 'syndromes'. Irritable Bowel Syndrome. False Memory Syndrome.

Chronic Fatigue Syndrome. Restless Legs Syndrome. She thought they were all just excuses for neurotics to hide behind.

'Anyway, there was no problem with Gaby, but presumably she worried about bowel cancer because her father had had it. There's quite a strong hereditary connection.'

'Yes. Oh well, I'm glad to hear that she hasn't got anything serious.'

'No . . .' Jude was still distracted, as though a sequence of thought was escaping her.

They both stopped for a moment. The skin around Carole's pale blue eyes puckered as she gazed through her rimless glasses towards the horizon. 'I just get the feeling that the reasons for Howard Martin's death go back a long way. I may be wrong, but my instinct is that they have some connection with what my son charmingly referred to as "a history of murder in my fiancée's family".'

'But I thought Gaby said it wasn't actually in her family.'

'No. A school friend of her mother's got murdered. This is years ago. Before Gaby was born, I think. And then the police investigating Howard's death seem very interested in someone who's recently been released from prison, where he was serving a sentence for murder.'

'Oh?'

'Someone called Michael Brewer.'

'Do you know anything about him?'

'Absolutely nothing. But I was just wondering,

Jude, whether he was the culprit in this murder of Marie's friend. Because, I mean, Gaby's thirty, so if he'd served a full thirty-year life sentence.'

'Not many prisoners do serve the full term these days, do they? I mean, apart from a few famous cases.'

'Some do. Early release is usually related to good behaviour. So if they don't behave well – if they're violent, or if they don't show any remorse for their crime. Come to that, if the sentencing judge recommended a full thirty-year tariff.'

'Mm. Well, it would be interesting if we could find a connection. Where did this murder take place?'

'Worthing.'

A huge beam spread across Jude's plump face. 'I told you our geographical problem was easing.'

'Yes. But how're we going to find out the details? It could be quite a heavy research job, couldn't it?'

'Yes,' Jude agreed thoughtfully.

'Well, do you have any bright ideas of how we'd set about it?'

An even broader beam took over. 'I do, actually. It will involve someone else—'

'What?' Carole demanded suspiciously.

'But it'll still be secret. We'll still be the only ones who know we're investigating another murder.'

'Really?'

'Yes. I promise. Come on, you'll trust me on this, won't you?'

'Ye-es,' Carole replied distrustfully.

*

'The Dauncey Hotel's perfect. I just wanted to ring and thank you for fixing it.'

'A pleasure. How's your mother?'

'More relaxed already, just because the phone's not ringing all the time. She's crying a lot about Dad, but it's kind of more relaxed, more genuine grief – therapeutic crying.'

'Good. Have you heard from Stephen?'

'Only briefly. Still up to his ears at work. But hopes to get down for a bit of time this weekend.'

'I hope he can manage it. And you haven't had any calls from the police?'

'Nothing, I'm glad to say. Look, Carole, I'd better go. I don't like to leave Mum on her own for too long.'

'No, of course not. And do remember my offer if you fancy getting out for a meal or anything.'

'Sure. Thanks. I'll be in touch. Bye.'

'Have you rung anyone?'

Jude knew the answer before she asked the question. Gita Millington lay listlessly draped over the sofa, the television flickering an unseen cookery programme at her.

'Do you think a glass of wine might help?'

Gita shrugged. 'About all I'm fit for, probably. Drinking up your booze. Leeching on your goodwill.'

Such remarks didn't deserve any response. Jude went through to the kitchen and returned with a bottle and two glasses. When they were charged, she switched off the television and sat down facing her friend. 'Listen, Gita, I have a proposition to put to you.'

'Goodness. I can't remember how long it is since I was last propositioned.'

'Look, at the moment you think you're never going to pick up your career as a journalist again.'

'I don't think it. I know it. Whatever skill I used to have – well, it's just gone. I used to be able to cold-call twenty editors in a morning till one would accept the idea I was flogging. Now I'm afraid even to ring one who's a close friend and to whose daughter I'm god-mother. It's just gone.'

'The confidence has gone. But I'm sure the ability hasn't.'

Gita puffed out a despairing breath. 'I've no idea. At the moment I think the ability's gone too, but it doesn't make a lot of difference either way. Oh, and this was going to be a breakthrough time in my life. I was going to move gradually away from journalism and start writing books. Non-fiction, maybe true crime, but until I can start selling myself again, it doesn't matter whether I have any ability or not.'

'Listen. When you were writing articles, you used to do a lot of research, didn't you?'

'Yes. You had to do research.'

'Right. So if you had a job to do, you'd know where to go to get the right research information?'

'Of course I would. But since I'm currently incapable of picking up the phone to get myself a job . . .'

'Suppose I gave you a job.'

'Jude, you're a very dear friend, and I love you very much, but one thing I can't help noticing about you is you're not a magazine editor.'

'I know that. But there's still something that I want researched.'

'What?' For the first time, there was a little glimmer of interest in Gita's eye.

'I can't tell you why I want it researched, and, I'm sorry to say, I can't pay you for researching it.'

'Jude, after what I owe you in hospitality and kindness and listening to me maundering on, I wouldn't take your money whatever you wanted me to do.'

'All right. Well, what I was thinking was, that if you do this research job for me and you do it well – which I know you will – it might make you realize that you haven't lost all your old skills, that there are still things you can do.'

'So it'd be like a dry run?'

'Exactly. And once you've proved you can still do it, I think the confidence might return for you to do the real thing.'

Gita's lips twisted wryly. 'Nice thought, but I doubt it.' She was hooked, though. 'Come on, Jude, what is it that you want me to research?'

Chapter Sixteen

If it had done nothing else, the prospect of having a research project had sharpened up Gita Millington's personal grooming. When she set off next morning to start her investigations, she was dressed in a smart black trouser suit over a turquoise blouse and black shoes with long screwdriver toes. She'd also done some personal colouring in the shower (she didn't feel she could face a public hairdresser yet), and her hair was back to its uniform dark brown glossiness. And, even more encouragingly for Jude, she'd put on her full war paint. Very skilfully. She had taken ten years off her face. Gita looked what she was – what she feared she would never be again – a successful journalist setting out on an assignment.

Her manner of speaking had also undergone a total make-over. 'I'm going to start in the archives of the *Fethering Observer*. That is your only local paper, isn't it?'

'Only really local one. There's also the *West Sussex Gazette*, which as the name implies, covers the whole county.'

'I'll probably try that too. Then move on to the

nationals. If it was a big murder trial, then there would have been a lot of coverage. I did a bit of preliminary stuff last night on the internet.'

'That's working all right, is it?' Jude had inherited a laptop from her late lover Laurence Hawker. She very rarely used it herself, but had offered Gita the facility.

'Absolutely fine. It's a nice machine.'

'Well, it's already done some useful research into another murder, so let's hope that's a good omen.' Jude felt a slight melancholy pang for the loss of Laurence.

'Yes. Don't worry, Jude, I'll get the information you need.'

And Gita left, as bouncy as the intrepid boy reporter Tintin embarking on a new assignment.

Which made Jude feel very good.

What made her feel slightly less good was the prospect of telling Carole that it was Gita who was becoming a part – albeit an as yet unwitting part – of their murder investigation.

'Carole . . .'

'Gaby, what is it? You sound upset. Is your mother all right?'

'She's fine. Mind you, she wouldn't be if she'd heard the news that I've just heard.'

'What's that?'

'The police have taken Phil in for questioning.'

*

Carole picked Gaby up at the Dauncey Hotel. Marie Martin was having an afternoon sleep, and her daughter felt safe to leave her for half an hour. She didn't want to talk in the hotel, so Carole drove to a car park on a nearby beach. On the far side of the River Fether from Fethering itself were rambling dunes topped with coxcombs of rough, springy grass. At weekends, the car parks and the beach filled up, but that June afternoon there were only a few dog walkers and a couple of young parents with tiny offspring on the sand.

'Do you want to walk or just sit?'

Gaby opted for just sitting. They wound down the car's windows. A slight breeze aerated the car with the smell of the sea, as Carole waited patiently for the girl to get her thoughts together and start talking.

'OK. I had a call from Inspector Pollard this morning. He just told me that "he thought we would like to know" that my brother Philip Martin is currently "helping them with their enquiries".'

'But he hasn't been charged with anything?'

'No.'

'So did Inspector Pollard say what they were questioning him about?'

'"In connection with your father's death".'

'That doesn't necessarily mean he's a suspect.'

'I know it doesn't.'

'You said yourself that Phil's always going to be under suspicion if there's a car theft in Harlow involved.'

'I know. But it's unsettling.'

'Of course it is.'

'The fact that I can't just ring Phil to find out what the hell's going on. The fact that there's yet another thing I have to keep secret from Mum.'

'But there was never any conflict between Phil and your father, was there? You always seemed to imply that they got on well.'

'Yes, they did – in a fairly silent sort of masculine way. You know, they'd go off and have a few beers together. There was maybe a bit of a rift when Phil got sent to prison, but I think Dad was more upset than angry.'

'What did Phil actually go to prison for? I never heard the details.'

'Nicking stuff. Cars, mostly. He was funding a drug habit.'

'And does he still use drugs?'

'Supposedly not. He's meant to have turned over a new leaf since he started this new job in Hoddesdon.'

'You don't sound very certain.'

'No, I'm not. He might have given up, he might still be a user – I don't know. As you may have gathered, Phil and I don't have an enormous amount in common.'

'No. Were you close when you were growing up?'

'Not really. I suppose I liked girlie things. He liked cars and guns and football, you know, boys' toys. And, well . . .' Gaby hesitated for a moment before saying, 'It wasn't really a very relaxed atmosphere to grow up in.'

Carole wasn't sure whether or not she should ask

the question, but she did anyway. 'You mean there were tensions between your parents?'

'Yes, I suppose I do.'

'But when I've met them, they've seemed devoted to each other.'

'Yes, they are devoted to each other, but . . .' Gaby seemed to backtrack, feeling she'd probably said too much already. 'Anyway, Phil and I have never been exactly soulmates. Very different personalities, and, increasingly, very different interests and lifestyles.'

'Yes.' Carole thought of Gaby's life as a theatrical agent, spending most of her evenings watching clients or potential clients strutting their stuff on various stages round the countryside. She somehow couldn't imagine that Phil had ever been to a theatre.

'But, thinking back to your childhood, which is often when patterns of behaviour are established, can you think of any incident where Phil and your father fell out? Anything he might have had against your father?'

'For heaven's sake! You're not suggesting Phil killed him, are you?'

'No,' said Carole, with more conviction than she felt. 'I'm just trying to cover all the possibilities.'

'Well, that's not one of them.'

'Right.' She felt she should be apologizing, but couldn't think of the right words, and so moved on. 'You don't suppose the police might be thinking that it was Phil in the car that drove your father away from the hotel?'

'If they are thinking that, they're wrong. Phil was

still at the party when Dad left. He went off later on his precious motorbike. I remember, because I asked whether he was in a fit state to drive back to Hoddesdon. As usual, Phil didn't listen to me.'

'Though in fact he didn't go back to Hoddesdon, did he? I heard he'd spent that night in Harlow.'

'That's right. Drank a lot more and crashed out on a friend's floor. So hungover the next morning he didn't go into work.'

'Any idea who that friend might have been?'

Gaby shrugged. 'Could have been any one of a number. There's a crowd Phil goes around with. They've all got bikes, and are all probably a bit on the shady side of the law. The one he's most likely to have crashed out on is a guy called Bazza. Small-time crook, nicknamed "Teflon Bazza".' Carole looked quizzical, so Gaby explained, 'So called because he seems to lead a charmed life. Nothing sticks. Keeps getting nicked for stuff, but so far has managed to stay out of prison. Had a really rotten childhood and people feel sorry for him. Magistrates keep letting him off lightly, in the hope that he'll reform and become a useful member of society.'

Gaby's tone showed how unlikely she thought that ever was to happen. Carole, whose experiences in the Home Office had brought home to her both the necessity of prison as a punishment and its useless-ness in changing criminal patterns of behaviour, was also sceptical.

'But you don't know for certain that Phil was with Bazza that night?'

'I'm guessing, but I think it seems likely.'

'Hm.' Carole digested the new information. It wasn't a lot. 'Oh, have you heard from Stephen again. Is he going to come down this weekend?'

'He's hoping to. Thinks Sunday looks pretty good, and with a bit of luck he'll be here for both days. But Uncle Robert's definitely coming. He's booked in for Saturday night at the Dauncey.'

'That's good. It'll take the pressure off you a bit with your mother.'

'Sure. And Mum really responds to Robert. She always perks up when he's around. I've been trying to ring him today, to see if he can get any information on what's happening to Phil – you know, through the police old boy network – but he hasn't rung me back yet.'

'I really wouldn't worry about Phil, Gaby. He can't have had anything to do with your father's death.'

'No.' But her voice didn't ring with conviction.

'I'm afraid he's just suffering from ingrained prejudice.'

'How do you mean?'

'There's a knee-jerk reaction, I'm afraid, in certain areas of the police force. If a crime's committed, they go straight to the nearest person with a criminal record.'

'Yes. I suppose you're right.'

Suddenly, to her surprise, Carole found that Gaby was sobbing. Instinctively – though uncharacteristically – she put her arm around the girl's shoulders. 'It's all right. You've been under a lot of stress.'

'I know. I was just thinking about the wedding – and Dad's death – and the fact that he won't be there.'

'It's dreadful, but' – Carole searched her mind for something comforting to say – 'you'll just have to imagine that the day is dedicated to his memory.'

'Mm. He would have been so proud. Dad wasn't ever very demonstrative, or very articulate, come to that, but he did love me in his way.'

'I'm sure he did.'

'He was very proud of me. Of my career – of every-thing. He would have been very proud to see me married.'

'I know.'

Gaby wiped her nose forcibly with the back of her hand, as though to put an end to her weakness. 'Still – Mum'll get one of the things she wanted.'

'What do you mean?'

'She'll see Uncle Robert leading me up the aisle. Mum always had more time for Uncle Robert than she did for Dad. In fact –' tears threatened again – 'I think Dad had a rather miserable life being married to Mum.'

Carole waited to see if more information might be forthcoming. Rather to her surprise, there was. 'I don't know the details, but they never seemed to be very close physically. Wouldn't surprise me if they stopped having any kind of sex-life after Phil was born. I cer-tainly didn't get the impression there was much going on while I was growing up. Maybe it was something to do with the age gap. And then, of course, Dad was always being compared – unfavourably – to Uncle Robert.'

She turned her blue eyes on Carole, and her tears gave way to a little dry chuckle. 'One thing Steve will never have to worry about in our marriage – being compared unfavourably to my brother.'

Chapter Seventeen

There was a message from Jude on the High Tor answering machine when Carole got back from her talk with Gaby. Gulliver left her in no doubt that he really fancied – and was owed – a walk, but the summons to Woodside Cottage was more intriguing. His brown eyes followed her reproachfully out of the front door. Call yourself a dog owner? they seemed to say.

Carole's excitement was considerably dampened when she found that Jude was not alone. Gita Millington was also there, almost unrecognizable in a smart black trouser suit and full make-up.

Jude dealt with the sticky point of diplomacy by a characteristically frontal approach. 'I asked Gita to do some research for us.'

'What?' Carole was appalled, but, as Jude had anticipated, was too well brought-up to make a big issue of the betrayal while Gita was actually present. When they were alone, recrimination would inevitably follow.

'I haven't heard any of it yet – you know, the stuff

Gita's found out,' said Jude. 'I wanted to wait till you were here.'

The expression on Carole's face did not suggest that this was sufficient compensation for the sin of involving Gita Millington in their own private murder mystery, but Jude felt confident her friend would soon get caught up in the drama of the situation.

On Gita's black-trousered knees was a folder, which she opened with some deliberation. Inside were sheets of handwritten notes and photocopies of newspaper cuttings. 'These are my preliminary findings,' she said, with a new authority in her voice. 'I've got this stuff from local newspaper sources, mostly the archives of the *Fethering Observer*, and what you'll hear is the main outline of the case. But, if you want more detail, I'm very happy to extend my researches.'

Neither of the other women spoke. The transformed Gita Millington held the floor and their complete attention.

'Jude, you asked me to find out what I could about a man called Michael Brewer, who was involved in a murder case in the Worthing area about thirty years ago. I can confirm that on the seventeenth of October 1974 Michael Graham Brewer was found guilty in a trial at the Old Bailey of the murder of Janine Buckley, who had died on the twenty-first of November the previous year. Brewer was sentenced to life imprisonment, and the judge recommended that he should not be released until he had served at least thirty years.'

Gita was confident enough to take a long pause,

knowing that neither Carole nor Jude would want to break her spell.

'The circumstances of the murder were particularly callous. Janine Buckley was a seventeen-year-old girl studying for her A-levels at a convent school in Worthing. Brewer, who was twenty-three at the time, worked as a gamekeeper on a large estate near Fedborough. Janine Buckley had apparently met him at a discotheque in Worthing, and a relationship developed between them. The girl became pregnant and, having been brought up a Catholic, refused to have the abortion that Brewer wanted her to have. Unwilling to take the responsibility for a child, he decided the simplest way out of his predicament was to murder the girl. He strangled her, and then tried to hide the evidence of his crime by putting her body into a stolen car, to which he subsequently set fire.'

That prompted a simultaneous intake of breath from the two listeners. Jude looked across at Carole, glad to see her friend was now so caught up in Gita's narrative that all resentment was forgotten.

'The burnt-out car was found deep into a wood on the estate where Michael Brewer worked. Though he continued to protest his innocence throughout his trial, there was compelling evidence against him. The alibi he put forward for the time of the murder proved to be a lie and, though the victim's body was too badly burnt to show any traces of her murderer, Brewer's fingerprints were found inside the boot of the stolen car and on an abandoned petrol can which had been used as an accelerant to set the vehicle alight. The jury took less than two hours to reach a unanimous verdict of guilty. The trial judge described the murder as "a crime of exceptional wickedness, in the perpetration of which Brewer had showed a cynical disregard for all humane instincts, and had destroyed the life of a young girl and her unborn child from motives of pure selfishness." When Michael Brewer was driven away from the Old Bailey after sentencing, a large crowd of angry protesters shouted messages of hatred and threw various projectiles at the van which was carrying him.'

Gita Millington stopped and looked at Jude for approval. She got it. 'Very good. Exceptionally good.'

'Yes, thank you,' said Carole, in a way that she knew sounded rather graceless. 'So, if he started his sentence in October 1974, and served the full thirty years, he would have been released in October of last year.'

'Yes.'

Carole looked directly at Gita for the first time since she had arrived at Woodside Cottage. 'Were there any other names mentioned in the case? Friends of Brewer's? Accomplices? People who gave him the false alibi?'

'I'm sure I could track down that information. All I have given you today is an overview. I can check the national press and the records of the court proceedings, if you want more detail.'

'I think we do, don't we?'

Jude nodded decisively. 'Yes, it'd definitely help. That is, if you don't mind, Gita?'

'Mind?' The journalist smiled wryly. 'Today is the first time I've felt like a human being in the last three months, the first time I've felt like *myself*. I'll research whatever you ask me to. I can't think of anything I'd like to do more.'

'Good.'

'So, more detail of the trial – fine. I'll write it up like an article. That'll get me back into the right way of thinking.'

'And who knows?' Jude suggested gently. 'One day you might be able to sell it somewhere.'

'I might at that,' said Gita with a determined grin. She picked up a notepad. 'Right. Any other specifics you want to know about?'

'Names would help,' replied Carole. 'Any details of Michael Brewer's life before he committed the murder: who his friends were; who his enemies were, come to that; whether he mixed with Janine Buckley's friends from school.'

Gita Millington scribbled a note. 'OK, I can do that for you. Anything else?'

'Yes,' said Jude. 'Can you confirm that Michael Brewer actually was released last year? And if possible, what he's been doing since?'

'And,' added Carole, with an involuntary shudder, 'his current whereabouts.'

Chapter Eighteen

Robert Coleman phoned Carole at nine o'clock on the Saturday morning. 'Sorry if it's a bit early.'

'Good heavens, no,' she said self-righteously. 'I'm always up by seven. I have a dog that needs walking.'

'Well, listen, I was wondering – I'm coming down to Fethering today, to see Marie and Gaby, and, if it's convenient, I'd like to have a chat with you at some point.'

'Of course.'

'Just to check how they're doing, before I meet them at the hotel.'

'Fine. I haven't actually seen Marie, but I've talked to Gaby.'

'OK. Well, what's best for you? Meet somewhere for a coffee?'

'Be simpler if you come round here.'

'Very well.'

'Now, do you know Fethering?'

'I've been there when we lived in Worthing, but you're talking thirty years ago, so my geography's a bit rusty. I remember the bit where the river goes into the sea, and the Yacht Club.'

'I'm not far from there.' Carole gave him instructions to find High Tor. He arranged to be with her at half past eleven.

He arrived on the dot, casually dressed in off-white chinos and a biscuit-coloured suede jacket. Carole was once again struck by his family likeness to Marie, and once again wondered what had prevented his vivacity from being shared by his sister. Was it just a difference in personality, or had Marie experienced some event in her life which had left her permanently traumatized? The more Carole thought about Gaby's mother, the greater the impression she got of a woman in shock. And that had been the case before the recent blow of her husband's murder.

Carole had coffee ready on a tray in the sitting room, and quickly supplied Robert with a cup. 'Just black – no sugar for me – got to watch my figure – nobody else does.'

She had forgotten how much his brown eyes twinkled, and how they expressed the full focus of his attention on her. Though not conventionally good-looking, Robert Coleman was an attractive man.

'I just wanted to say first of all, Carole, many thanks for organizing the hotel for Marie and Gabs. They're both in such a shattered state that they need someone to make the decisions for them.'

'It was no problem.'

'But getting them away from Harlow was very necessary. Inspector Pollard's a good copper, but not necessarily the most sensitive' – he chuckled – 'of a breed that isn't noted for its sensitivity at the best of times.'

'I was glad to help.'

'And you say you've seen Gabs? How did she seem?'

'All right in herself. But she was very worried about Phil. She'd been trying to contact you that day about him. I assume you know that he had been taken in for questioning?'

'Yes. I heard. It was nothing to worry about.'

'That's not the way Gaby saw it.'

'No. People are very paranoid about the police. Someone gets "taken in for questioning", the general public immediately assume he's about to be charged with murder. Phil was only being questioned because some of his friends have been involved in car theft in the past. Well, so's he, come to that. Pollard was trying to get a line on the car in which Howard's body was found.'

'Would this be through Phil's friend Bazza?'

Robert Coleman's white eyebrows raised. 'How do you know about him? You *have* been doing your research, Carole.'

'Gaby mentioned him when I saw her.'

'Ah.' He seemed relieved by the explanation. 'Yes, Bazza's a bit of a naughty boy. Been up before me as a magistrate more than once. If there's a car theft in Harlow, Bazza's the first person you think of.'

'I thought that was Phil.'

'Oy, oy.' Robert Coleman wagged a finger of reproof. 'No slandering my nephew, thank you very much.' But he wasn't serious. 'Phil may have mis-behaved in the past, but he's a good boy now.'

'Is he?'

'Oh yes.' But his tone suggested Robert was not totally convinced. 'Anyway, Phil's fine. Pollard only had him in for an afternoon.'

'Does Gaby know that?'

'Yes, I told her.'

'Good. Apart from the fact that it was a car theft, were there any other reasons why Inspector Pollard suspected Bazza?'

Robert Coleman grimaced wryly. 'Main one is that he's done a runner. Phil crashed out at Bazza's place the night after the party and saw him the next morn-ing, but nobody's seen him since. Bazza's made him-self scarce. Which, if he did steal the car that got burnt out, might be seen as the action of a guilty man.'

Carole took this in, and was silent for a moment. Then she asked, 'The night of the party, at the hotel – who actually organized the car for Howard? I wasn't there at the time, you remember. I'd taken Marie home.'

'That's right. Well, there was some problem with just ordering a cab the normal way.'

'A big conference or something.'

'Yes. So there were various discussions about how Howard should be got home and . . .' He seemed unwilling to continue, but eventually he said, 'It was Phil who said he could organize a car for his dad.'

'Through his mate Bazza?'

'I've got no proof of that, but it might be a logical inference.'

'So it's no surprise Inspector Pollard wanted to talk to him.'

'No.'

It was a difficult question, but Carole felt she had to ask it. 'You don't think Phil had anything to do with his father's death, do you?'

'God, no.' Robert sounded appalled by the idea. 'Phil had no reason to get rid of his dad. He liked the old boy. And all right, there's some petty crime in his background, but nothing like that. Strangling's a pretty nasty way of killing someone.'

'Yes. Sorry.'

'No, reasonable enough question.' He grunted a little laugh. 'It must be odd for you, Carole, coming into this situation. Your son announces his engagement. Suddenly you're deeply involved with another family.'

'Not to mention an ex-husband,' she said glumly.

'Yes. And then, through the new family, you're involved in a murder scenario. I'm not sure that those natty little books of wedding etiquette cover the proper behaviour for those circumstances.'

Carole grinned. She remembered having a similar thought when she was grilling Marie in the Renault after the party.

'It is a bit odd, yes. And, at the same time, heartbreaking. I'm afraid my main concern in all the business is for Gaby. I mean, I feel sorry for the rest of your family, but Gaby's the one I know.'

'That's as it should be. Gabs is going to be your daughter-in-law.' Robert Coleman looked at his watch. 'Which reminds me, I'd better be off. Said I'd be there for lunch. What's the food like at the Dauncey Hotel?'

'I haven't actually eaten there myself, but its local reputation's very good.'

'Excellent. I'm quite peckish.' He rose from his chair. 'Thank you so much for the coffee, Carole. It's been really good to have a chat.'

'Yes.' Carole hesitated. She didn't want to let him go quite yet. Robert Coleman seemed the most accessible of Gaby's family, and there were questions she could ask him that might be difficult to put to anyone else. On the other hand, she didn't want to make her curiosity about the case too blatant.

She decided to take the risk. 'Robert, there is one thing I'd like to ask you about.'

He smiled easily. 'Ask away.'

'It goes back to things that were said at the engagement party . . . you remember, when Marie fainted.'

'Uh-uh.' He was still relaxed, but a little more guarded.

'Howard talked about someone "coming back".'

'I remember.'

'And he said he had arranged to talk to that person.'

'Yes.' Now Robert was very alert, hanging on what she was going to say next.

'I was just wondering . . .'

'Hm?'

'. . . whether seeing that person, or a connection

172

with that person might have had anything to do with Howard's murder?'

'Well, this is all a bit vague, isn't it? "That person" – Do you know who you're talking about?'

'No, I don't,' Carole admitted. 'But I just wondered if it might be Michael Brewer?'

As at the engagement party when she had mentioned Gaby's burglary, the casualness instantly left Robert Coleman's face. He sank back heavily into his armchair and asked, 'What do you know about Michael Brewer?'

'Gaby mentioned his name to me. I think Inspector Pollard had asked her if she knew anything about him.'

'And did she?'

'No.' He seemed relieved by this news. Then Carole said, 'On the other hand, I know quite a lot about him.'

'What? How?'

She didn't want to mention Gita's work as a research assistant; that might sound too calculating. 'His name came up in conversation. Someone was talking about the Janine Buckley murder case because it was local.'

Robert Coleman didn't appear to be worried about the coincidence. 'Did you know that Janine Buckley was at school with Marie?'

'Yes, Gaby mentioned it,' she replied, truthfully this time. 'So presumably you knew her?' He nodded. 'And Michael Brewer too?'

'I knew him. We used to see quite a lot of each other in those days. Mick and I were in our early twenties. We'd been at school together too. And having a younger sister could be quite useful for young men in search of female company.'

'Were you already in the police force?'

'No, I was working locally round Worthing – crap jobs, driving delivery vans, that kind of thing. I was thinking I needed something more like a proper career, and my ambitions were moving towards the police, but I hadn't started then.' His lower lip hardened into a straight line. 'What happened with Mick was one of the factors that made my mind up for me. Perhaps I felt guilty for not having been able to protect Janine, and wanted to save other people from . . .' He looked troubled. 'Locking the stable door after the horse had gone.'

'It must have been a terrible shock to you, when the murder happened,' Carole prompted.

'That's an understatement. Mick was one of a bunch of us that went round together. Met up in pubs, went to discos – you know. All that music of the time: T-Rex, Slade, Donny Osmond, Gary Glitter. Some of it still stands up even now. But then we were – well, you know how carefree you feel when you're in your early twenties?'

Carole nodded. She didn't think it was the moment to say that she'd never felt carefree in her life.

'And OK, there was a bit of sex going on, you're going to be experimenting at that age, aren't you? No drugs, though. Certainly I didn't do any, and I don't think any of the rest of the crowd did. There was a kind of innocence about the whole thing. Looking back, that's the way it seems to me. And then – this shock. Suddenly we're in the real world. Sex can lead to pregnancy. Pregnancy can lead to murder. And it's been committed by someone you thought of as a mate, someone you thought you knew.' He shuddered. 'Still gets to me. Still, after thirty-odd years.'

'Did it get to Marie too?'

'And how. Sounds a bit dramatic, but I don't think she ever really recovered from what happened. Certainly her personality changed. Seeing her now, it'd be impossible for you to imagine what Marie was like at seventeen. Really bubbly . . . you know, like Gabs, but even more so. And very beautiful. And unafraid of everything. You wouldn't believe that, the way she is now, would you?'

'She must've married Howard fairly soon afterwards, mustn't she?'

'Not long after. Before Michael Brewer came up for trial certainly.'

'But surely Howard wasn't part of your disco crowd, was he?'

'No, he was a lot older. Worked in the business with our dad – fishmonger's.' So Carole had finally found out the dead man's profession. 'But you may have heard Dad died soon after Janine Buckley's murder.'

'I did hear that, yes.'

'Heart attack. Whether it had anything to do with the stress, you know, the state *Maman* was in – I just don't know. Anyway, that meant poor Marie was even more stressed. Howard had always had a thing for my sister, really fancied her, but none of us thought he was in with a prayer. Then suddenly Marie announces she's going to marry him. I couldn't believe it. It was like – don't take this wrong, because I don't want to speak ill of the dead. I liked Howard. He was a good man, an honest man. But it was as though, when Marie married him, she had given up all ambition. I mean, she left school, didn't finish her A-level course, suddenly no more talk of university. It was as if, for her, Howard represented safety. He would protect her from the wicked world that had just betrayed her. They married quietly in the Register Office, and moved away. Dad's business was sold off, and Howard didn't want to stay with the new owner. So he got a job with a fishmonger in Worcester first off; it seemed he and Marie wanted to put as much distance between themselves and Worthing as possible. And then the kids came along, and they moved from place to place, and I suppose they found a kind of happiness – the only kind of happiness they could find – but my sister's life had been totally destroyed by what Mick Brewer did.'

The sadness of this statement seemed almost to wind Robert Coleman. He sat back breathing deeply, like a man recovering from a punch.

'And has he come back?'

He looked at Carole, as though he did not understand her question. The brown eyes had lost their sparkle, and were dull with memories.

'Is it Michael Brewer who has come back? Was it him Howard was talking about at the engagement party?'

There was a new caution in his voice as he answered, 'I don't know. Certainly Inspector Pollard was interested in the history of Marie's connection with the case. That's often how you start an investigation, when you've got nothing to go on. You've got to start from somewhere, so you ask: have any of the principal characters got any connection with another crime, even one that happened thirty years before? And, of course, in this case, maybe they found other parallels.'

'The modus operandi,' Carole suggested. 'A strangling in a car that was then burnt out?'

Robert Coleman gave her a dry look. 'You *have* been doing your research, haven't you? What is your interest in all this, Carole?'

'Simply that I care about Gaby. I don't want her to be hurt.'

He assessed this answer for a moment, then nodded. 'Fair enough. As good a reason as any other.'

Carole felt emboldened to ask a more specific question. 'And have the police found anything that links Michael Brewer to the death of Howard?'

Robert opened his hands wide in self-defence. 'Look, I'm not part of the investigation. I'm not a serving police officer, and when I was I didn't do murder cases. Because we were once in the same profession, Inspector Pollard occasionally shares a little titbit of information with me, but I don't get hourly bulletins of how the investigation's going. All I know is what I told you – that Pollard is seeing if he can find a connection between the murders of Howard and Janine Buckley. I think they're still running forensic tests on the car and the crime scene. Maybe those will reveal something. But if they do, I think the likelihood is against Inspector Pollard immediately notifying *me* of their findings.'

Carole felt duly chastened. 'Sorry. I thought it was worth asking.' There was a moment of silence between them. 'Of course, the next obvious question is: where is Michael Brewer?'

Robert Coleman shrugged wearily. 'That is what no one seems to know.'

'But he is out of prison? He did finish his sentence?'

'Oh yes.'

She digested this unappealing thought. 'What would he have had against Howard?'

'God knows how a mind like his works.'

'And if Michael Brewer did have something to do with Howard's death, who else might be at risk from him?'

'Anyone in the family,' Robert Coleman replied bleakly.

Which, of course, would include Gaby.

Chapter Nineteen

Carole had been surprised when Stephen and Gaby accepted her invitation to join her and Jude for supper at the Crown and Anchor on the Saturday night. She had thought they might want to spend the little precious time they had that weekend alone together. But no, Marie was safe in the Dauncey Hotel, having dinner with her worshipped brother Robert, so Gaby felt safe to leave her. And the engaged couple seemed very happy to join Carole.

Carole deliberately arrived at the Crown and Anchor early, so that she would have time to bring Jude up to date on what she had heard from Robert Coleman. Gita was in London that evening, seeing a friend, a lawyer she had met while researching a crime story. She was also determined to go to her flat for the first time since her suicide attempt. If she felt up to it, she'd spend the night there. If not, she would stay with her friend. All of which Jude thought were very encouraging developments.

Although she'd told Jude, Carole had decided to keep quiet to Stephen and Gaby about her recent conversation with Robert Coleman. Though what he had said was of momentous importance to the investigation of Howard Martin's death, Carole didn't want to frighten Gaby with the image of an avenging murderer on the loose. If the girl initiated the subject of Michael Brewer, then fine. Carole would find out how much Gaby knew and contribute to the conversation accordingly, but she wasn't going to be the first to mention the name.

Both Stephen and Gaby looked tired, he from his work crises, she from the stresses of looking after her mother, but there was still a touching lack of tension between them as a couple. As she looked at them, Carole felt an unfamiliar welling of something she supposed must be maternal warmth. She was determined to do everything she could to remove the cloud that hung lowering over her future daughter-in-law.

The first thing Gaby said, once they were supplied with drinks, did not concern Michael Brewer, but was still something of a bombshell, 'Phil's coming down this weekend.'

'Coming down where?'

'To Fethering.'

In her bewilderment, Carole couldn't stop herself from saying, 'Why on earth would he want to do that?'

'He said he thought he should check that Mum's all right.' Gaby sounded sceptical.

'I gather Robert told you that the police only had him in for an afternoon.'

'Yes. I heard that.'

'So when's your brother arriving?'

Gaby looked at her watch. 'Any time. He's coming

down from Hoddesdon on the bike. He's going to meet us here. I thought that'd be better, so we can have a word before he sees Mum and Robert.'

That's good, thought Carole. Though Phil was very much part of the mystery jigsaw, contacting him in Hoddesdon was almost out of the question. But now he, like Robert Coleman before him, was going to appear conveniently on her doorstep.

There was a break in the conversation as their food order arrived, brought over – they were honoured – by Ted Crisp himself. Before returning behind his bar, the landlord made a bad joke of the 'Waiter, waiter' variety ('Waiter, waiter, do you have frog's legs?' 'Yes.' 'Then jump over the counter and get me a sandwich.').

Then the engaged couple started to talk about their wedding plans, and the sparkle came back into Gaby's eye. For a brief moment, just by keeping off the subject, they could forget the recent tragedy and find a kind of limited normality in a world where people got married and looked forward to sharing happy futures.

The arrival of Phil put an end to this interval of calm. Even without recent events, the appearance of Phil Martin in the Crown and Anchor at Fethering would have been unsettling. The black leathers and black helmet he wore accentuated his height, and he loomed over the bar-room like some legendary avenging warrior. When he removed the helmet to reveal his scowling face, the image became less mythological, but no less deterrent.

He quickly identified who he was looking for, and moved across towards the alcove in which they were finishing their meal. Only then did Carole and Jude notice that he had not entered the bar alone.

Behind Phil, literally in his shadow and looking half his size, followed a man of about the same age. He too carried a crash helmet, and the denim jacket buttoned tightly over a sweatshirt suggested that he had just been riding pillion on Phil's motorbike. Even in June, he'd have needed to wrap up against the wind on the motorway.

Carole had a pretty good idea of who the newcomer might be, and her guess was instantly confirmed when Gaby said, without enthusiasm, 'Bazza. What the hell are you doing here?'

'Come down with me, didn't he?' said her brother ungraciously.

'But I thought the police were looking for him.'

Phil shook his head. 'Don't know anything about that, Pascale.'

'It's Gaby.'

Her knee-jerk reaction showed that his use of her given name was part of an ongoing conflict between the siblings. Whenever Phil wanted to rile his sister he used her original name.

'Hello, Phil. Nice to see you again.' Carole felt that social decorum should be observed. 'Now, you haven't met my friend Jude, have you?'

Phil agreed that he hadn't, but didn't seem that interested in remedying the deficiency. 'Where's the place Mum's staying then?'

'Just the other side of the estuary. Ten minutes in the car.'

'Right. And Robert's with her there and all?'

'Yes, he is.'

'Are we off then?'

'Phil, we haven't finished eating.'

Stephen recognized his cue to ask Phil and Bazza if they'd like a drink while they waited. Both opted for pints of Stella. At the bar, Ted Crisp gave Stephen a rather old-fashioned look. 'Those bikers friends of yours, are they?'

'Yes. The tall one's my fiancée's brother.'

Ted Crisp didn't say anything, but he didn't need to. His face expressed his disapproval of the connection. He didn't want the Crown and Anchor to get the reputation of being a haven for bikers.

Phil and Bazza said very little while they downed their lagers. Both looked ill at ease, keen to be on the move. Bazza looked up in panic each time someone new came into the bar, fearful presumably that the police had tracked him down.

But when the party for the Dauncey Hotel was ready to leave, Phil made it clear that his friend wasn't coming with him. 'No, you stay here. I'll sort it out with Robert. There won't be a problem. I'll give you a bell on the mobile when it's sorted.'

'Leave it out, Phil,' Bazza complained. 'I should come with you, otherwise I'm stuck here without any wheels.'

'I'll call you,' said Phil, with a menacing firmness that stopped further argument.

The threesome left sitting at the Crown and Anchor was an unusual one. Though so different in personalities and attitudes, Carole and Jude weren't an incongruous couple. But the addition of a small-time car thief from Harlow did make for an unusual mix.

Carole was sorely tempted to go home, but she could recognize the sense of Jude's offering to buy another round of drinks. Circumstances had brought them together with someone the police wanted to interview in connection with Howard Martin's death. Sleuthing opportunities rarely came better gift-wrapped.

Bazza consented to another Stella, so Jude bought that and a couple of Chilean Chardonnays from a surly Ted Crisp. Even though the one who actually wore leathers had gone, he remained suspicious of the other 'biker'.

While the drinks were being organized, Carole racked her brains for something she could say to Bazza, but not an idea came. She had to fall back on a polite smile, which was rather wasted because the boy refused to look up at her.

Needless to say, as Jude sat down, she pitched in with a perfect conversation-opener. It was characteristically direct.

'Dreadful for Phil and Gaby, isn't it, their dad having died in that ghastly way?'

Bazza conceded that it was 'a bit of a choker.'

'You weren't at the engagement party, were you?'

'No. I'm more Phil's mucker than Pascale's. You know, I've met her the odd time, but we're not, like mates.'

'And did you know Phil's parents?'

'Met them, like, the odd time.'

'But you can't think why anyone might have wanted to kill Howard Martin?'

Carole would never have dared be as direct as that. Bazza looked more uncomfortable than ever. His eyes flickered towards the door, contemplating flight. But some logic within him seemed to argue that he was off his home turf, he had nowhere else to go, and he could be in a worse situation than talking to two old biddies with a nearly full pint of Stella in front of him.

'No idea,' he replied stolidly.

'I couldn't believe it,' Jude went on ingenuously, 'Gaby was saying that the police wanted to talk to you about the murder.'

'Don't know what the police want, do I? All I know is, if you ever once got the wrong side of them, you never hear the end of it.'

'And you had got on the wrong side of them?'

'Look, everyone's done some iffy stuff when they're young, haven't they?' He looked at the two middle-aged ladies he was with, and realized he was asking the wrong audience. 'OK, yeah, I've knocked off the odd car in my life. I was skint and I only took them from people who could well afford them. I mean, rich people don't really suffer anything much more than inconvenience when their car's nicked, because they've all got insurance, haven't they? If you nick a car from some bloke who can't afford the insurance, then all right, he's going to suffer.'

To Carole this was a very bizarre justification for stealing cars, but Bazza seemed to believe what he was saying. He had managed to convince himself that he was committing victimless crimes.

She took up the conversational baton from Jude, remembering what she'd been told in the car park on the beach. 'Gaby said that you'd been very lucky, that you'd got off quite lightly when you'd been caught by the authorities.'

'Well,' said Bazza, aggrieved, 'like I say, I never done that much wrong. And, OK, I been lucky enough to come up before magistrates what've given me the benefit of the doubt. I wish more was like that. Most kids when they commit their first crime and get caught. Well, they get sent down the nick, or the Young Offenders Centre, you know, depending on their age – and that's it. All they learn in places like that is how to commit more crimes, so when they come out, they're lifetime villains. Much more sensible to give those kids a ticking-off and another chance. That's what happened to me – and it ain't done me no harm.'

Exhausted by this long disquisition on the criminal justice system, Bazza sat back and took a long swill from his pint of Stella.

Carole had a sudden thought, a synaptic linking of two pieces of information in her brain. 'Tell me, Bazza, did you ever come up before Robert Coleman? In the magistrates' court?'

'What if I did?'

'He's a kind man. Is it possible that you owe your light treatment by the magistrates to him?'

For a moment, the boy seemed as if he was about to reply more fully, but then he sat back and took another swig of lager. 'Don't know what you're on about.'

'Are you sure?' asked Jude, who was catching up with the direction of Carole's thinking. 'When Phil was here, he assured you that Robert Coleman was in the Dauncey Hotel with his sister. Is that why you've both come all this way – to see whether Robert Coleman can help you out of another hole?'

'I'm not in a hole. Phil's come down to see his mum. I'm his mate. He asked me if I fancied a trip down the South Coast. I said yes. That's all there is to it.'

'You say you're not in a hole,' said Carole sternly, 'but apparently Inspector Pollard wants to talk to you, and he hasn't been able to find you.'

'Don't know who you're talking about.'

'Inspector Pollard is the officer investigating the death of Howard Martin.'

'I didn't have anything to do with killing him.'

'I'm sure you didn't. But did you have anything to do with procuring the car in which he was killed?'

'Procuring? What's this? What do you mean by procuring?'

'Stealing, Bazza.'

'I never stolen anything in my life.'

'Really? But you've just told us you've nicked the odd car.'

'Yeah, but when I nick something, it isn't stealing.' Bizarrely, a high moral tone had crept into his voice. 'Look, all right, I have occasionally *borrowed* a car. Mate needs one for a little while, I'll sort it out for him.

Car almost always goes back undamaged – just a bit less fuel in the tank. Sometimes not even that. Often the owner doesn't even know it's been borrowed. So who's suffering here?' Bazza, it was becoming clear, was something of an expert on the concept of the victimless crime. 'OK, maybe it's not strictly legal, but I don't see it's doing much harm to anyone.'

'Surely,' suggested Jude quietly, 'that rather depends on what your mate does while he's in possession of the car?'

Bazza had his moral defence ready for that one. 'I never ask. That's not my business, is it?'

Carole snorted her disapproval. 'But presumably your *mates* pay you for your car supply service?'

'Well, of course.' He was self-righteously offended by her tone. 'I can't do stuff for nothing, can I? I got to make a living.'

Suddenly, quite unexpectedly, there was the sound of a dog barking. Carole and Jude – and other pub customers – looked around for the animal in question. With a complacent grin, Bazza drew a mobile phone out of his pocket. 'Not a bad ring-tone, that?'

He pressed a button and the dog ceased to bark. He checked the number on the display, and pressed another button. 'Case in point. This mobile's my office. Another little business call. I'll get back to them.' He returned the phone to his pocket.

'Get back to who?' asked Jude hopefully.

He laughed indulgently at the idea she might even think he'd answer that.

There was a silence; then, very deliberately, Carole

filled it. 'Bazza, did you "supply" the car that took Howard Martin from the hotel the night he died?'

'Course I didn't. I had nothing to do with it.'

'No?' Carole took a risk. 'Someone actually saw you driving up the hotel entrance to pick him up.'

'Nobody could have seen me – because I wasn't there.' The break between the two parts of his sentence was tantalizing. He could have made a slip and be covering up for himself. Equally – and frustratingly – his words could be perfectly innocent.

Carole continued with her risk strategy. She didn't see that it could lose her anything. 'You didn't think anyone could see you, because you had your baseball cap pulled down over your eyes.'

This did seem to catch him on the hop. There was a definite pause before he said, 'Nah, you're making it up. Nobody could have seen me at the hotel, because I wasn't there.'

'My ex-husband was there. He saw you.' Time for the big lie. 'You exactly match the description he gave me.'

The boy looked really worried now. 'Has he – your ex-husband – has he talked to the cops?'

Carole didn't know that for a fact, but it didn't stop her saying, 'Oh yes.'

Bazza's eyes darted to the Crown and Anchor's main entrance, then back to the remaining third of his drink. He wanted to get out, but not before he'd finished his Stella.

Jude took over the interrogation. 'Do you know someone called Michael Brewer?'

The instinctive flick of the head appeared genuine enough. 'Never heard of him. Why should I?'

'It's possible that he was the one who organized that car from the hotel.'

'Well, it wasn't. Like I said, I only do that kind of job for mates.'

It took a second for Bazza to realize the implications of what he'd said. When he did, he rose to his feet, downing the last of his drink.

'And Phil's your mate,' Jude persisted. 'Are you saying that Phil asked you to organize that car to drive his father?'

'Mind your own bloody business, you nosy cows!' he snapped, as he stumped out of the pub. It wasn't much of a parting shot, but it caused a little ripple of reaction among the other Saturday night customers. Behind his bar, Ted Crisp smiled with grim satisfaction. He didn't want any bikers in the Crown and Anchor.

Chapter Twenty

When she got back from taking Gulliver for his walk on Fethering Beach the next morning, Carole was surprised to see her son's BMW parked outside High Tor. Stephen had his own key, and was sitting in the kitchen waiting for her. He came into the hall when she opened the front door.

'What's up, Stephen?' she asked, as she used a towel to brush the sand off Gulliver's paws. 'Is Gaby all right?'

'She's fine. Well, she's OK, anyway. No, it's her brother I'm worried about.'

Carole closed the door and followed Gulliver through into the kitchen. 'Why? Where is he?' Without asking, she started preparing coffee.

'That's what we don't know. After we'd left you in the pub, we went over to the Dauncey Hotel and booked a room for him. He was a bit iffy about that, until I said I'd pay. Then Gaby and Robert and I had a drink in the bar, while Phil went up to talk to his mother. Marie had been feeling tired, so she'd gone up to bed early.

'Gaby and I were tired too, so we were off to bed

after one drink with Robert. Gaby just dropped into her mother's room to say goodnight, and found Marie in a terrible state. Apparently, she and Phil had had some kind of row, and he'd stormed out. He wasn't in his room or anywhere else in the hotel. Robert reckoned he'd have just gone off to the nearest pub, and went out to look for him. But I saw Robert at breakfast, and he hadn't found him. Nobody's seen Phil since he left his mother's room.'

'He might just have leapt on his beloved bike and driven back home to Hoddesdon.'

'He might. But there's no reply from there. Or from his mobile.'

'Oh, come on, it's still pretty early on a Sunday morning, Stephen. We know Phil has a habit of going on overnight benders. He's probably passed out in some pub car park somewhere.'

'Yes, maybe.' Her son sighed. 'Sorry to bother you with this. It's just that Gaby's worried. She's in such a highly strung state at the moment.'

'Who can blame her?'

'Anyway, Gaby was thinking that, wherever Phil is, he's probably with his chum Bazza, so she was wondering when you last saw him?'

Briefly Carole detailed the timing of Bazza's departure from the Crown and Anchor the previous night. 'And he did have a call on his mobile while he was there. Said he was going to call back. Maybe that was Phil fixing up to meet?'

'Maybe.' Stephen took an almost despairing sip from his coffee.

'You are all right, are you?' Carole dared to ask. 'I mean, you and Gaby?'

'Yeah, yeah, we're fine. It's just . . . well, I don't need to tell you, Mum, this is all very stressful, particularly for Gaby. All she wants to do is to get back to the work she loves and to plan her wedding, and yet the chances of her doing that just seem to get more and more remote. Every time she thinks she can relax, something else happens to tighten up the screw of tension. I mean, Marie seems to be in a worse state than ever after her row with Phil.'

'Did you discover what that was about?'

Stephen shook his head. 'Impossible to get that kind of stuff out of Marie, even when she's in her normal state. Now she's totally illogical.'

'Hm. Robert seems to be the only vaguely normal member of that family.' As soon as she'd spoken she realized her tactlessness. 'Except for Gaby, of course, when she's not so stressed.'

Her son smiled bleakly.

'By the way, Jude and I talked to Bazza last night.'

'That must have been an interesting conversation. I'm sure Oscar Wilde wished he could have been there, taking notes.'

'Don't you believe it, Stephen. Bazza's not as inarticulate as he might appear. Has some very interesting views on the definition of criminal activity.'

'Oh?'

'The main one being that if *he* does something, then by definition it's not a crime.'

'Ah.'

'But, more importantly, I got the pretty firm impression that Bazza was involved in arranging the car for Howard Martin that night.'

'Really?' Stephen was shocked.

'Yes. Can't prove it, but he virtually admitted as much.'

'No wonder Inspector Pollard's keen to talk to him.'

'I wonder where he's been lying low the last few days? Phil clearly had no difficulty contacting him.'

'No. I'll give Pollard a call. He should be informed that Bazza's down here.'

'I agree.'

'Mum, you said you thought Bazza *arranged* the car for Howard, but you don't think he's the murderer?'

'No. Murder's way out of his league. Someone else asked him to arrange the car.'

'Who?'

'Bazza said he only did that kind of work for his mates.'

Stephen sighed wearily. 'Things aren't looking too good for Phil's innocence, are they?'

Jude sounded excited when she summoned Carole round to Woodside Cottage later that morning, but Gita Millington looked even more excited. She was bouncing and bubbling with energy. Her clothes were not as formal as the black trouser suit, but still very smart casual. The make-up was perfectly in place, and again she looked the epitome of the successful career woman.

As soon as Carole was sat down with a pre-lunch Chardonnay, Gita launched into her routine. 'Jude's probably told you that I went to London last night. In fact, I stayed the night in my flat.' Carole was not aware of what an achievement that represented. 'And Jude probably told you that I had dinner with a friend. What she didn't tell you – because she didn't know – was that in fact the friend I had dinner with was a solicitor called Jerome Clancy.'

'Oh! I know him,' said Carole, with some surprise.

'Really?'

'I used to have quite a lot of dealings with him when I worked at the Home Office. Big on human rights issues, prison reform, that kind of stuff.'

'Exactly. Anyway, I've consulted him before when I've been doing articles on legal issues or the prison service. Well, I'd talked to Jerome on the phone about the questions you'd put to me . . . you know, Michael Brewer's release from prison and his subsequent movements, and last night, over dinner, he told me what he'd found out.'

So animated was Gita as she spelled this out that Carole began to wonder whether there was a romantic element in her friendship with Jerome Clancy. Or maybe it was just the excitement of achieving something concrete after her months of evident depression.

'Michael Brewer was released from Parkhurst Prison in October 2004, having served the full term of his thirty-year sentence for the murder of Janine Buckley. To the end, incidentally, protesting his innocence of the crime.'

Gita Millington left another dramatic pause, and Carole took advantage of it to ask, 'But there was never any question of his guilt, was there?'

The journalist shook her head. 'No. Brewer's lawyers made two appeals against the conviction, but both claims were rejected. The amount of evidence against Michael Brewer was overwhelming.'

'All right,' said Jude excitedly. 'So where is he now?'

'This is the bizarre bit.' Gita Millington frowned at the incongruity of what she was about to say. 'Since his release, Michael Brewer has vanished off the face of the earth.'

'I heard that,' said Carole, 'but do you have any detail on what happened to him?'

'From the moment he left Parkhurst, there's been no sighting of Michael Brewer anywhere.'

'Well,' said Jude reasonably, 'after what he'd been through, you could hardly blame him if he just wanted to slip off the radar, settle down somewhere quiet with a new identity or . . . surely it's up to him.'

'Yes, it's up to him, but there are still obligations he has, as an ex-prisoner. He has to keep in touch with the authorities, turn up for appointments with his probation officer. Weekly at first, then at greater intervals.'

'And has he not turned up for any of them?'

'Not a single one, Jude.'

'But surely he can't just get away with that? Aren't the police looking for him?'

'Oh yes. There's been a warrant out for him for some time. But I'm not sure that finding him was that high up the police's priorities – until recently.'

'So, as you say, he's vanished off the face of the earth.'

'Yes, he has.'

There was a silence while the two women took in the implications of this news. Then Carole said, 'Which could mean one of two things. Either he's lying low, for reasons of his own – possibly plotting revenge on the people who he believes to have done him wrong . . .'

'Or?' asked Jude.

'Or he's lying even lower.'

'How do you mean?'

'In a shallow grave, perhaps? Maybe somebody wanted revenge on Michael Brewer?'

Carole heard it on the early evening news. A man's body had been found in a burnt-out car on a lonely part of the South Downs near Fedborough.

Chapter Twenty-One

'That's all they said, Jude. I've been listening to other bulletins and watching the local news, but there's been no more detail. Certainly no indication of who the victim might be.'

It was Monday morning, and the two women were sitting over coffee in the kitchen of High Tor.

'Of course, it's entirely possible,' said Jude thoughtfully, 'that this death has absolutely nothing to do with Howard Martin's.'

'But the modus operandi—'

'Oh, come on. Villains who want to get rid of other villains have been using that method for years. The same modus operandi doesn't necessarily mean the same perpetrator. You can't patent a murder method.' Carole looked so cast down that Jude grinned and said, 'But we mustn't allow boring old logic to get in the way of our conjectures. Let us assume that there is a link between the two deaths.'

'And if that is the case, the victim's identity does become rather pivotal. But,' Carole continued glumly, 'we have no means of finding that out until there's an announcement from the police.'

'Perhaps we should put Gita on the case? No doubt she's got a convenient friend in the police force, just as she had a convenient friend who knows about prisons.'

This was said with a little mischief, because, although Gita's researches had already proved so useful, Jude knew Carole was still unhappy about having got her involved.

'I don't think that'll help.' Carole was predictably huffy. 'We'll have to wait till it's on the news.'

'Well, just running with the logic of our conjecture for a moment – If this latest body is connected with the Martins, who might it be? Who's missing?'

'Phil . . . Bazza, I suppose.'

'Or what about the mysterious Michael Brewer?'

'As victim, are you suggesting?'

'Why, Carole? Were you thinking of him more as perpetrator?'

'That had been the way my mind was moving, yes. If he was behind Howard's murder, then he must have had contact with Phil and Bazza.'

'Assuming that Phil gave Bazza the order to steal the car in which Howard was driven off?'

'Yes. So either Phil or Bazza might know too much about Michael Brewer's activities – or indeed whereabouts – and might need silencing.'

'Mm. So if one of them does turn out to be the victim, you'd reckon Michael Brewer was responsible for both murders?'

Carole nodded, then gave a little shudder. 'I get this feeling that Michael Brewer is not far away. Worthing was his old haunt thirty years ago. I think he could be hiding out round here again. And I feel he represents a real threat.'

'To whom?'

'To Gaby.'

But Gaby didn't look threatened when she met Carole at the Crown and Anchor later that morning. In fact, she looked better than she had at any time since her father's death. Because it was a nice morning, she had walked from the Dauncey Hotel, over the road bridge which crossed the Fether. The mile's stroll in the fresh air had brought colour to her cheeks and restored the sparkle to her eye. Though her protectors had gone – Robert Coleman back to Essex, and Stephen Seddon to his work crisis – she looked relaxed.

She didn't mention the latest body in a burnt-out car, and Carole reckoned, after some casual probing, that the girl hadn't yet heard the news. Carole wasn't about to tell her, either. The longer Gaby remained in ignorance, the longer her sunny mood might be preserved.

Because the day was sunny too, they sat at one of the pub's outside tables, looking over a stretch of rough grass to Fethering Beach. Early holiday-makers – mostly couples with pre-school children – added splashes of colour to the sandy expanse.

Having unwittingly established that she didn't know about the new murder, Gaby proceeded to eliminate one of its potential victims. 'We've heard from Phil.'

'Oh, what'd he been up to?'

'God knows. Out drinking somewhere, I imagine. Anyway, he was back in his flat yesterday evening, and said he was going in to work today.'

'Did he say anything about Bazza?'

'No.'

'And you haven't seen or heard anything of him?'

Gaby shook her head, puzzled by the question. 'Why should I?'

'No reason. I must say, you're looking so much better.'

'Thanks.' Gaby ran her hands through her bubbly curls, and grinned. 'It was good to see Steve at the weekend, got things in proportion. I feel a lot more relaxed about everything, as though it's possible that normal life can, one day, continue.'

'And how's Marie?'

'She's much better too.'

'Did you find out what her row with Phil was about?'

'No. I should think probably just him saying something insensitive. He does rather lumber into things with big hobnail boots on. And Mum's still so upset about Dad. Probably Phil just said something thoughtless about him.'

'Mm.'

'No, Mum is a lot better. Much more relaxed. That's actually why I wanted to see you, Carole.'

'Oh?'

'I was thinking of trying an experiment tomorrow.'

'That sounds intriguing.'

'Actually going back to work.'

'Really?'

'Yes, I've got to do it soon. Work'll get me back to sanity. So I was thinking of trying a few days commuting.'

'From here?'

'Mm. I don't think Mum's up to being back in Harlow quite yet.' (Carole didn't think she herself would ever be up to being back in Harlow.) 'But if I'm away during the days, and she has the security of knowing that I'll be back in the evenings – well, it could be a good start, weaning her back on to the idea of life getting back to normal.'

'I think it's a brilliant idea.'

'And what I wanted to ask you, Carole, is would you mind vaguely keeping an eye on Mum? I don't necessarily mean going to see her, but, you know, being at the end of a phone if she gets a panic attack or anything like that.'

'I'd be delighted to do that for her. And, if it turns out she does want company, then I'd be happy to oblige.' This was not total altruism. Carole had been thinking that there were further questions she'd like to put to Marie Martin.

'Thanks so much. Then maybe soon we'll be able to get on with some of our other plans.'

'For the wedding?'

'Yes. And just getting back some kind of social life.' Gaby hesitated for a moment, before she said, 'You know David wants us all to have dinner together one evening?'

'What?'

'He said he'd mentioned it to you.'

'As a vague idea. He mentioned it just after we'd heard about your father's death. Sensitive timing was never one of David's skills.'

'No. Well, he's mentioned the idea again to Steve.'

'Has he?'

Gaby looked awkward. She was moving on to territory where her professional poise deserted her. 'Carole, it would mean a lot to Steve just to feel that you and David could have some kind of workable relationship.'

'The fact that we got divorced, I would have thought, showed just how impossible it is for us to have any kind of workable relationship,' Carole said tartly.

'Yes, I know you find it difficult, but – well, Steve would really appreciate it if you two could get more used to being together again. I mean, not on a permanent basis . . .'

'There's not a chance of it being on a permanent basis!' But then Carole moderated her tone. Gaby was after all only trying to please Stephen, to show her love for him. In working to that end, the two women should be on the same side. 'Look, Gaby, I'm sure David and I will get much more used to seeing each other again. There won't be any problems, I promise.'

'And you would maybe accept his invitation to dinner with us?'

Carole could not think of a prospect that she found less appealing. But then again, it wasn't her comfort she should be thinking about. Her priority should be the happiness of her son and his bride-to-be. 'I'm sure that'd be possible at some point.'

'David was going to ring Steve with some possible dates,' said Gaby eagerly.

'Yes, well, there's time enough for that. The most important thing is getting your life back to normal.'

'You're right, Carole. Oh, I feel so much better already, just at the thought of getting back to work – of life settling down a bit – with no more traumas.'

Carole hoped it would be as long as possible before Gaby finally heard about the body in the burnt-out car on the Downs. Or, maybe, by the time she did hear, the police would have identified the victim as someone with no connection to the Martin family. To ensure Gaby's peace of mind, shattering Carole and Jude's conspiracy theory would be a small price to pay.

At that moment a mobile phone trilled. 'Excuse me while I get this,' said Gaby, reaching into her pocket. 'It's probably from work.'

She grinned at the prospect and pressed a button to put the call through. She listened. Whatever she heard had a devastating effect. The colour drained from her face and she snatched the phone away from her ear, as if it was scalding hot. She put it on the table and shuddered, her eyes staring.

'What on earth's the matter?'

Instinctively, Carole picked up the phone and held it gingerly to her ear.

'Are you still there?' she heard. The voice was rough and male. 'I thought you'd hung up on me. Listen, Gaby, my name's Mick Brewer.'

Chapter Twenty-Two

Carole's first thought was that another potential identity for the body in the car on the Downs had been eliminated. Her second thought, after a look at Gaby, was to rush to the bar and buy a large brandy from a slightly bewildered Ted Crisp. He wasn't used to her ordering brandy, least of all before lunch.

But she'd done the right thing. The alcohol did at least stop Gaby's trembling, and soon she was able to talk again.

'What did he say to you?'

'Just that his name was Mick Brewer.'

'Did he say how he'd got your number?'

'Yes.' An involuntary shudder ran through Gaby's body. 'He said he'd got it from my address book.'

'How could he have got your address book?'

'There's only one way.' Gaby looked terrified as she pieced the thought together. 'It must have been him, Mick Brewer, who burgled my flat. My address book was there, among the things that had been moved, so he must have looked at it. That means he knows where I live. He must have been following me for months.' She let out a little gasp of pure fear. 'He must know where I am now.'

'No, he doesn't,' said Carole, more reassuring than she felt. 'You're safe here.'

'But for how long? Anyway, who is he? Who is Mick Brewer?'

'You know who he is. Inspector Pollard asked you about him.'

'Yes. But he didn't give me any detail. Except that he'd just come out of prison after serving a very long sentence – which I would assume means he committed some violent crime. Do you know anything more than that about him, Carole?'

Her future daughter-in-law was in no state to hear all the details that Gita Millington had unearthed about the murder of Janine Buckley. So Carole ignored the question, as if she'd just had a new and urgent thought. 'You must ring Inspector Pollard.'

'What?'

'He was asking you about Michael Brewer, wasn't he? You must tell him about the call. I'm sure the police can trace where he was ringing from. They might be able to find him. Then you won't have to worry any more.'

Gaby saw the logic. She quickly rang a number she'd scribbled on the back of a till receipt, and was put straight through to Inspector Pollard. It was clear from her reactions that he took what she was saying very seriously indeed.

When the call was over, Gaby looked ruefully at

Carole. 'So much for my idea of normality returning, of going back to work. The Inspector wants me in Harlow.'

'And your mother too?'

Gaby nodded. 'He says he reckons we'll be safer there. Though Harlow didn't turn out to be very safe for Dad, did it?' A sob caught her unawares. 'God, this whole thing's a nightmare, isn't it?'

'Yes, but it's a nightmare that's about to end. By phoning you, Michael Brewer's broken cover. It won't take the police long to find him now.'

'I hope to God you're right, Carole. I don't know how much more of this I can take!'

Carole found herself instinctively reaching across to take the girl's hands in hers. This surprised her, because she didn't think she ever did anything instinctively. Maybe Gaby's troubles were helping to find a new softness beneath the carapace of Carole Seddon's personality.

'It'll be all right,' she found herself saying. 'Come on, I'll drive you back to the Dauncey Hotel. It'll be quicker that way. Soon you won't have anything else to worry about.'

How untrue that remark turned out to be. As soon as Carole switched on the ignition of the Renault, Radio Four came on, right in the middle of the *World At One* opening news bulletin '. . . and the man whose body was found in a burnt-out car on the South Downs near

Fethering in Sussex has been identified as Barry Painter of Harlow, in Essex . . .'

'Oh, my God,' Gaby breathed. 'Bazza!'

Chapter Twenty-Three

Marie Martin was not at the Dauncey Hotel when they arrived. Gaby's instinctive panic was allayed by the girl on reception who said her mother had just gone along the beach for a walk. In other circumstances, this would have been good news – the fact that Marie was feeling sufficiently together to do something on her own – but Gaby couldn't see that. She was too stressed by the need to get back to Essex as soon as possible.

'Don't worry,' said Carole. 'You go up to your room and get packed. I'll go and meet Marie.'

There was only one direction in which her quarry was likely to have walked: east on the path through the dunes. The other way led back into Fethering, and Carole felt sure Marie Martin would have chosen privacy over people.

The woman was not in sight, but there was no danger that Carole would miss her. Only a thin strip of the dunes was available to walkers, separated by a high fence of wire netting from the inland golf course. On the other side the dunes gave way to the beach, which could be seen clearly from the pathway. Carole was bound either to catch up with Marie while she was still on her outward course, or meet her coming back.

The second proved to be the case. Carole saw a small figure in a beige raincoat – hardly necessary on such a warm day – coming towards her. At first glimpse she suspected it to be Marie, and a closer view left her in no doubt.

When the woman saw who it was coming towards her, she looked panicked, but there was no escape. The encounter could not be avoided. She had managed to manufacture a smile by the time Carole was within speaking distance.

There was no point in trying to sugar the pill. Marie Martin had to hear the truth. She couldn't be protected from everything all through her life. The kid gloves with which she was habitually treated had to come off. And it gave Carole an unworthy feeling of satisfaction that she was the one taking the kid gloves off.

'Marie, I'm afraid you're going to have to go back to Harlow. Gaby's had a call from Michael Brewer.'

The woman's first reaction was to totter, as if she was about to faint, but she recovered herself. Cynically, Carole reckoned that Marie had weighed up the options and realized that her customary exit route from a sticky situation wasn't going to work. Fainting out there on the sparsely peopled dunes would have little effect. It wouldn't cause a disruption, and when she came round, her nemesis, Carole Seddon, would still be there confronting her.

'I don't know who you mean,' Marie faltered. And

she started to walk briskly back through the dunes towards the Dauncey Hotel.

'You know perfectly well. Robert told me the whole history.' That was only partially true – she'd got other bits from other sources – but it would do at that moment. 'Michael Brewer was someone you and Robert knew when you were at school. He murdered your friend Janine Buckley.'

Marie Martin couldn't argue against that level of research. 'And you say he called Pascale?'

'On her mobile.'

'How on earth did he get the number?'

'It seems pretty certain that he was the one who burgled her flat. Her mobile number's right in the front of her address book.'

Gaby's mother looked pale and shocked, but not as though she were about to faint. She'd temporarily given up on that form of escape.

'Marie, you could make things a lot simpler if you told me more of what you know about Michael Brewer.'

'Why should I tell you? What business is it of yours?'

Which was actually a perfectly reasonable question. And one which amateur sleuths have always found difficult to answer. Still, Carole came up with a reasonable justification. 'It's my business because Gaby is about to become my daughter-in-law. I care about her welfare. She's under a tremendous amount of stress at the moment, and a lot of that stress has something to do with Michael Brewer. If you shared a bit more of what you know about him, we might see ways of making things easier for her.'

'Of course Pascale's under stress. My husband was murdered last week.'

'And do you think the person who committed that murder was Michael Brewer?'

Marie's eyes avoided Carole's. 'There are obviously similarities with the way Janine was killed.'

'So, thirty years on, as soon as he's served his sentence, Michael Brewer kills again. But why did he pick on Howard? Was it revenge? What might he have against your husband?'

'I don't know.'

Carole felt certain that wasn't true, but it was said with a determination that offered no prospect of a climb-down. Still she persisted. 'Howard was going to meet Michael Brewer the day after he died. He said so at the engagement party. Just before you fainted.'

'I don't remember,' said Marie unhelpfully.

'And you yourself have had no personal contact from Michael Brewer?'

'I haven't seen or heard from him since he was arrested for Janine's murder.'

A new thought came to Carole. 'And did you think you'd escaped him? Did you think he'd never track you down?' Now she'd made the connection, the ideas were tumbling out. 'Is that why you always wanted to keep a low profile? And why you didn't want any announcement of Stephen and Gaby's engagement in the national press? You thought that might give Mick Brewer a clue to find you?'

Carole was convinced that she was right, but got no admissions from Marie Martin. Instead, as if she'd heard none of the questions, the woman asked, 'Why do Pascale and I have to go back to Essex?'

'She spoke to Inspector Pollard, told him about the telephone call. He wants to talk to her. Maybe he wants to protect her.'

Marie thought about this idea. 'Being in Essex didn't protect Howard,' she said finally.

'Are you suggesting that Gaby's in real danger?'

A bleakness came into the woman's faded eyes. 'After what happened to Howard, everyone's in real danger.'

They were nearly back at the hotel. Carole was about to lose her unwilling interviewee. 'Marie,' she pleaded, 'have you any idea where Michael Brewer might be at the moment?'

'Well, he won't be in Essex. This is Mick's area. He knew this bit of the country like the back of his hand. This is always where he would come back to.'

'But where specifically? If the police are looking for him . . .'

Marie Martin smiled a pale smile. 'The police caught Mick Brewer once. No way he'd let that happen a second time. He's a devious character. And you forget, he used to work as a gamekeeper. He always had his own secret places. If Mick Brewer doesn't want to be found, he won't be found.'

And with that frustrating incomplete parting shot, Marie Martin scuttled off into the Dauncey Hotel.

*

'You're low.'

Gita Millington agreed listlessly that she was low.

'It's after all that excitement of researching Michael Brewer.'

'Yes. That put me on a high, made me think I could do things again, even made me think I could start my career again. Now I don't think I could start a rumour.'

'It'll come back, the confidence.'

'Will it, Jude? I wonder. I just see myself getting older and older, and less and less attractive, and more and more out of touch with the world of work . . .' Her voice spiralled down into despair.

Gita was again flat out on the sitting-room sofa. She was back to T-shirt, jogging bottoms and not a dab of make-up. Jude felt the weariness of responsibility. Inviting Gita into her home had been a voluntary act, and not one she regretted, but she wished she could do more to make her friend feel better. She had contemplated suggesting alternative treatments for depression, but felt that might be taking advantage of her privileged position as the patient's hostess. Jude knew of cases where acupuncture had worked, reflexology, even some of her own healing techniques. But she felt that, while Gita was under the hospital's regime of medication, she shouldn't interfere. Though Jude's own belief was that traditional and alternative medicines could work in a complementary way, she didn't want to impose her views. Gita was sufficiently traumatized already by the suddenness of her depression; she didn't need further confusion.

Still, there was one therapy which had been proved

to work, if only for a short time. More of the same was at least worth trying. 'You know, I have a theory about murder cases . . .' Jude announced.

'Oh? Really?' Gita was bewildered by the abrupt change of subject. 'What are you talking about? Michael Brewer?'

'I'm talking in general terms, but it applies to him too.'

'All right. What is your theory?'

'It's not a very revolutionary one. Just that what happens before the murder is at least as relevant as what happens after it.'

'How do you mean?' Already Gita's back was straighter. She was more alert. Jude had hooked her attention.

'Well, a murder is a shock to a community . . .'

'I'll say.'

'Probably the ultimate shock, really. And in a lot of cases, the murder is the culmination of a lot of things that have been going wrong, tensions that have been building up. So to understand the crime, you have to understand the circumstances which led to that crime. In other words, a good murder investigation not only fingers the perpetrator, it also gives an understanding of the society in which it took place.'

'I'd go along with that, Jude. So, if you apply this to the Michael Brewer case?'

'I'm saying that to understand his crime, we need to know the world in which it happened.'

'Find out what his life was like before the murder?'

'Exactly.' It was disingenuous, but in the cause of

Gita's recovery, Jude asked, 'Any thoughts how we might set about doing that?'

A large smile crept across Gita Millington's unpainted lips. 'Do you know – I think I might have.'

Chapter Twenty-Four

Jude had her own research methods too. As part of her varied work portfolio, she still did occasional discussion sessions at Austen Open Prison, which was a little way along the coast from Fethering. They were called 'New Approaches', discussion groups involving a shifting repertoire of prisoners, with subjects ranging from alternative therapy through guilt and morality to life skills and philosophy. Many of the attendants were lifers – which meant murderers – spending the last few years of their long sentences in an environment which was supposed to be more like the outside world than a high-security prison. These sessions had been organized by Austen's Education Officer, Sandy Fairbarns, someone who, though they'd never met outside work, Jude regarded as a friend.

Her next 'New Approaches' session was scheduled for the Tuesday after Gaby had received the call from Michael Brewer, and Jude had set her plan in motion with a call to Sandy Fairbarns that morning.

'I have found someone,' Sandy announced immediately Jude arrived at the Austen main entrance prior to her session. 'Name's Jimmy Troop. He came across

Michael Brewer in Parkhurst, and he's prepared to talk to you.'

'Does that mean I'll need one of those – what are they called? V something?'

'VO. Visiting Order. Yes, you'd have to get that if you did it in normal visiting times. But there's another way.'

'Really?' They were walking towards the education building, between the pale yellow one-storey blocks that housed Austen's inmates. The borders that fringed the path were beautifully kept, a regimented profusion of marigolds, alyssum, blue and red salvias and lobelias, which bore testimony to the painstaking horticultural skills of the prisoners.

Sandy grinned. 'I've checked it out with the guard who's on the education block this afternoon. You can have a quarter of an hour with Jimmy after your session.'

'Brilliant. And he's agreeable?'

'Jimmy is extremely agreeable. Very cultured and amiable man, Jimmy. One of nature's gentlemen.'

'Ye-es. Except presumably at some point in his life, he did murder someone.'

Sandy Fairbarns gave her a look of mock-reproach. 'Really, Jude. You mustn't let yourself be prejudiced by things like that.'

The session Jude conducted that afternoon followed the pattern of her previous ones. About a dozen prisoners attended. Some were there for the first time, some were regulars. And some regulars whom she'd been expecting weren't there. They might have been released, they might have got bored, they might have found a game of football a more attractive option; inside a prison you could never know. Jude no longer went into the education block with any expectations of who might be there; she worked with the attendance she had.

Perhaps influenced by her recent conversations with Gita Millington, Jude started that afternoon with the issue of self-esteem, the roots of confidence and the threats to it. As ever, the topic mutated into something else, this time the issue of aggression, in both its internal and external manifestations. And as ever, after a jerky start, the dialogue developed, the inarticulate became more fluent, and the shy encountered subjects on which they could not keep silent.

Even before he gave his name, Jude would have recognized Jimmy Troop from Sandy's description. He was in his early sixties, a tall thin man whose thick brown hair was white at the temples. Even though dressed in prison denims and trainers, he carried the air of a man in tailor-made suit, highly polished brogues and Garrick Club tie. What crime had brought him to his current circumstances, and how someone of his background had survived the considerably tougher circumstances of other prisons, though intriguing questions, were ones to which Jude never expected to find the answers.

In that afternoon's debate Jimmy Troop was extremely articulate, but did not allow his superior education to upstage the contributions of his rougher colleagues. Jude was interested to observe the respect and positive affection with which he was treated by his fellow inmates.

The two hours of 'New Approaches' flashed by, and, on a nod from the guard who sat in the corridor outside their classroom, Jimmy Troop lingered as the other prisoners filed out. This was always a moment of transition. The articulacy – and even intimacy – of the recent discussion suddenly dissipated as the reality of prison life reasserted itself. The men became awkward, their farewells to Jude clumsy or often non-existent.

'Well, I'm very honoured,' said Jimmy Troop, when they were alone in the room. Whatever else prison might have done to him, it hadn't diminished his patrician charm. He still remembered how to treat a lady.

Jude went to close the door.

'No, I wouldn't do that.' She stopped at Jimmy's words. The guard sitting on the landing didn't look as if he cared much whether the door was open or closed. 'Kind of thing that gets misinterpreted in a place like this,' the prisoner explained. Jude moved away from the open door and sat down, facing him. 'Not of course that you wouldn't be safe with me – I know what befits a gentleman – but there's always the risk of making the other fellows jealous.'

Once she was safely seated, he sat down and smiled a rather wistful smile. 'Mind you, I'm not sure that I would be much threat to a lady these days, anyway. The years pass, you know, and it's rather a while since I had the opportunity to put it to the test.'

'Still, you'll be out soon, won't you?'

'Yes. Yes . . .' he agreed, but not as though he regarded freedom as an unmixed blessing. Quickly shutting off introspection, he went on, 'Still, we mustn't waste our time. I have been granted a bonus quarter of an hour of your delectable company –' The compliment was played with light irony – 'while you have a quarter of an hour of detailed brain-picking.'

'Sandy did tell you what it was about?'

'And who it was about, yes. Michael Brewer. I read everything in the press about the Janine Buckley murder – in happier times – little thinking that I would one day find myself in the same situation as its perpetrator. I joined him later. I wasn't given such an extensive sentence for my own . . . peccadillo.' He pronounced the word lightly, but without real humour. 'Very well. What can I tell you about my fellow-participant in Her Majesty's pleasure?'

'Michael Brewer was released last year, having served his full thirty-year sentence.'

'I suppose he would have been. I haven't done the arithmetic, but, yes, that would be about right.'

'Since his release, though, no one's seen him. He hasn't turned up for any of the scheduled meetings with his probation officer.'

'Ah.' Jimmy Troop nodded.

'You don't look surprised.'

'No, dear lady. I got the impression that Michael Brewer – a few people in Parkhurst called him Mick, but I never attained that level of intimacy. Anyway, I got the impression that he was of a reclusive nature, so after thirty years of enforced human society, I think he might well have got away from people as soon as he had the opportunity.'

'How well did you know him, Jimmy?'

The man shrugged his thin shoulders. 'Relationships in prison are mostly tangential. Oh, you hear stories of love affairs and things. In my experience, not a lot of that went on. Generally, there are some people you never speak to – and never want to speak to. The occasional – very occasional – real soul mate, and the vast majority with whom one might exchange a word at a meal time, or during exercise.'

'And for you, Michael Brewer fitted into that "vast majority" category?'

He nodded, then smiled wryly. 'I hope you don't mind my saying, Jude – It is Jude, isn't it?'

She confirmed that it was.

'Then I hope you don't mind my saying what a rare pleasure it is for me to sit and talk to an attractive woman?'

She giggled, playing along with his gallantry. 'It's a fairly rare pleasure for me to sit and talk to an attractive man.'

She had got the tone just right. With another wry smile, he thanked her. 'But enough of this flirtatious badinage. The sands of our quarter of an hour are trickling away. What can I tell you about Michael Brewer?'

'Would you describe him as a violent man?'

'Given the nature of his crime, he was always going to have that reputation.'

'But any signs of violence inside the prison?'

'No. He kept his nose clean. A model prisoner.'

'Any vices, habits, hobbies?'

'He played cards. Well, no, that's probably the wrong thing to say – playing cards implies that you play them with other people. Michael Brewer just played patience. Endlessly, round and round. Always had a pack of cards with him. I think he must have known a variety of versions of the game. You'd go mad just doing the same thing time and again.'

'Or maybe the appeal of the game was doing the same thing time and again?'

Jimmy Troop thought about this for a moment, then nodded. 'You could be right. A good name for a prisoner's game, isn't it? Patience?'

For the first time in their encounter, a shadow of pain crossed his face. But his customary urbanity was quickly reasserted.

'Anything else I can tell you about my fellow inmate?'

'I heard that he always protested his innocence of Janine Buckley's murder.'

Jimmy Troop spread his hands wide. 'Show me the prisoner who doesn't protest his innocence. Oh, there are the hard ones who boast all the time about the crimes they've committed, and a good few crimes they've only committed in their imaginations, but for most of us the image of innocence is very potent. You'd wake up in the morning from a dream that you hadn't committed your crime, a seductive dream, a very real dream, and then you'd look around your cell, and the unarguable reality would hit you . . .' He

224

paused, again straying dangerously close to personal territory, then, with a patrician smile, moved on. 'Sorry, you were asking me about the violence in Michael Brewer.'

'Yes. You think it was still there?'

'Very definitely. He wasn't demonstrative, but there was a lot of anger bottled up inside him. He had scores to settle.'

'To settle when he was finally released?'

'I would assume so, yes.'

'He never told you what those scores were?'

An apologetic shake of the head. 'As I say, I wasn't one of his close associates. And I'd have been surprised if he had confided that kind of information even to a close associate, assuming that he ever had any.'

'Did he mention where he might go when he was released?'

'He always spoke fondly of Sussex. Brighton area, Worthing, round there.' Jimmy Troop looked out through the metal-framed windows to the grey-blue humps of the South Downs. 'Pity he wasn't sent here to Austen. He'd have liked it.' A second thought came to him. 'Though maybe he would have found it even more frustrating, being so close to where he wanted to be. Maybe he'd have done a runner. Not difficult to get out of a place like this.'

'Jimmy, from what you know of Michael Brewer, which I know isn't a lot, but going on your instinct, do you think he'd be capable of committing another murder?'

The gentleman in denim laughed, then fixed

Jude's brown eyes with his and said, with total seriousness, 'Oh yes. But then we'd all be capable of that, wouldn't we? It's committing the first one that takes us by surprise.'

As he spoke the words, he seemed to open a window on to a vista of infinite pain. But only for a second. The mask of languid charm was quickly put back in place, as he looked up to see the guard on the landing tapping his watch.

'Dear lady, I fear our most enjoyable quarter of an hour is at an end.' Jimmy Troop rose from his seat, the complete gentleman. 'I'd offer to see you to the gate, Jude –' he gave a self-depreciating shrug – 'but, sadly, circumstances do not allow me to do that.'

Chapter Twenty-Five

The afternoon that Jude was talking to Jimmy Troop, Carole had a phone call.

'Erm . . . it's . . . erm . . .'

'Hello, David.'

'I gather . . . erm . . . that Gaby and her mother are no longer down in Fethering.'

'No. I think they're both in Harlow.'

'Marie is certainly, but I believe Gaby's back in her own flat now. She's returned to work.'

'Has she?' Carole couldn't repress a feeling of pique that he had this information and she didn't.

'Yes, I was talking to Stephen last night and he told me,' said David, rubbing it in. 'Which, anyway, I thought was a good . . . erm . . . opportunity for us to go back to my plan.'

'Your plan? What on earth are you talking about, David?'

'My plan for the four of us to . . . erm . . . as it were, have dinner together.'

'Oh. Well, yes, I'm sure . . . at some point.'

'Stephen said he and Gaby could do Thursday evening.'

'Could they? Well . . . um . . .'

'Have you got anything on on Thursday night, Carole?'

'I might have – I'm not entirely sure.'

'It would be good for us to . . . erm . . . get together as a foursome.'

'Maybe. But I'm sure Gaby's not ready for something like that yet. She's in a very bad state about her father's death, and she's worried about her mother, so I'm sure she'd rather put off that kind of social encounter for—'

'Yes, I suppose she might. But if she did feel up to it, then you would join us, wouldn't you? It would mean so much to Stephen.'

First Gaby, now David, thought Carole. Why's everyone trying to blackmail me about my duty to my son? Trouble was, the blackmail was working, making her say things against her better judgement.

'Well, look, David, if it happens, I suppose I could be free.'

From David's enthusiastic reaction no one would have guessed how gracelessly she had said the words. 'That's terrific, Carole. I knew you'd be up for it. Look, I'll . . . erm . . . ring you before Thursday with the fine-tuning – details of times and . . . erm . . . where we're going and . . . erm . . .'

Oh God, thought Carole savagely as she put the phone down, why do I get myself into situations like this? But she hadn't time to brood, because at that moment there was a ring at her doorbell. She opened it in expectation of a misdirected delivery or a young man of dubious provenance selling tea towels and oven gloves of equally dubious provenance. The only person in Fethering who would ring the bell of High Tor without pre-arrangement was Jude. And Carole knew Jude was away somewhere that afternoon.

She was therefore surprised to see Gita Millington standing on her doorstep. This was the new, fully made-up, efficient Gita Millington. Carole was for a moment nonplussed, before ingrained manners asserted themselves and she said, 'Oh, how nice to see you, Gita. Won't you come in?'

But she didn't feel comfortable. Gita was Jude's friend, and Carole had never been in her company without Jude present. Gita on her own in High Tor felt like an obscure invasion of privacy.

But the atavistic rituals of politeness had to be followed. Coffee was offered and accepted, and nothing more than small talk exchanged until the two of them were sitting over a tray in the sitting room. Carole assumed Gita must have some reason for her call, but behaved as though someone dropping in for coffee unannounced was the most natural thing in the world.

The coffee-pouring ceremony performed, Gita revealed why she had come round. 'Jude's out this afternoon, but I thought you'd like to know, Carole, that I've got some more information on Michael Brewer.'

Carole certainly did like to know that, but couldn't totally repress the resentment she still felt at the inclusion of a third person in their investigating team.

Gita qualified what she'd said. 'Well, it's not information as such that I've got, more a source of information. I've found someone you could contact to find out more details.'

Carole liked that a lot better, Gita in her proper position as junior researcher, not as a main investigator.

'I should have thought of it before, but I got on to Friends Reunited.'

'Oh?' said Carole blankly.

'A website service whereby old school friends can track each other down.'

Carole's face revealed her distaste for the concept. Her own schooldays had been a time of complex emotions and continuous embarrassment, certainly not a time of her life she wished to revisit. Nor indeed were there any people from school with whom she wished to renew contact.

'Anyway, Carole, I suddenly realized that Friends Reunited might be the simplest way to make contact with people who were at school with Janine Buckley.'

And, of course, with Marie Martin – or Marie Coleman, as she would have been then. Carole almost said the name out loud, but then remembered Gita knew nothing of the connection between the Martin family and Michael Brewer.

'That's an excellent idea, Gita,' she was forced to concede.

'I found quite a few contact names, a lot of them still local. Surprising how many of the girls stayed in the Worthing area.'

'But how did you get into the website? Surely it's meant only for people who actually were at the school?'

Gita blushed. 'There are ways round that kind of thing. You don't have to use your own name to log in.'

Carole didn't probe further.

'Look.' A printout of names was proffered. 'Here's a list of girls who were in the same year as Janine Buckley. All local. A lot are married and have changed their names, but I've managed to get phone numbers for all of them.'

'Well, that's wonderful,' said Carole, with something approaching enthusiasm.

'And look –' Gita's finger found a name. 'There's one who lives right here in Fethering. Libby Pearson.'

'Oh. Goodness . . .' Carole was instantly besieged by social doubt. What, she wondered, was the correct protocol for ringing someone out of the blue to question them about the murder of a school friend more than thirty years ago? She supposed she could wait till Jude was back. That felt rather wimpish, though. She should seize the opportunity she had been given. But what pretence could be fabricated to justify the initial contact?

Gita must have identified her dilemma, because she said, 'Are you wondering how to break the ice?'

'Well, it might be rather awkward, you know, just ringing someone up. One ought to have some kind of reason.'

'Like writing a book about the Janine Buckley case?'

'That would do it, certainly.' But Carole had never had the ease with tactical lying that Jude had. 'The trouble is, I'm *not* writing a book about the Janine Buckley case.'

'No.' There was a silence, then Gita Millington said firmly, 'But I am.'

The two women's eyes met. Carole recognized that Gita was offering her a deal. I'll make the next stage easier for you – if you include me in your investigation.

The phone in High Tor rang while Gita was back in Woodside Cottage, touching up her make-up. It was logical, really, that there should be a call from the police. Carole hadn't followed through the implications, but of course she and Jude had been among the last people to see Barry Painter – known to his friends as Bazza – before his death.

'I'm Inspector Pollard from Essex Police,' the humourless voice on the phone identified itself. 'I'm collaborating on this case with West Sussex, so it is permissible for me to talk to you. Have you had any contact yet from West Sussex Police?'

Carole said that she hadn't.

'Right. I'm sure you will soon. They're always a bit slow off the mark.' There was a satisfaction in this, some point-scoring in an inter-constabulary rivalry. 'I've obviously been talking to Marie Martin and her daughter Gaby. I believe you know them?'

'Gaby is the fiancée of my son Stephen.'

'Fine. Given what happened to Mr Painter, we are needless to say trying to reconstruct his movements during the last hours of his life. And I believe' – a note of disbelief came into his voice – 'that he had a drink in the Crown and Anchor pub in Fethering with you and your friend, Jude something-or-other – I don't have a record of her surname.'

'She's just called Jude,' said Carole loyally.

For a moment Inspector Pollard seemed about to press for a surname, but decided he had more important questions. 'May I ask, Mrs Seddon, how Mr Painter came to be having a drink with you? Was he a friend of yours?'

'Good heavens, no.' Carole couldn't keep the instinctive distaste out of her reply.

'Or of your friend Jude?'

'No.'

She wondered why he was asking. He surely must already have got this information from Gaby or Marie or Phil. Was he asking in the hope that she would point up some inconsistencies in their stories? Or that she would show herself to be a liar? She felt on her guard, as though already under suspicion. It was not a pleasant feeling.

Quickly she ran through the circumstances of how she and Jude had ended up with Bazza in the Crown and Anchor. She had the impression of Inspector Pollard at the other end of the line with a notebook, ticking off points of corroboration. He then asked her to go through the conversation they had shared with the late Mr Painter. She provided as much detail as her memory could offer.

'This call he had on his mobile phone – you say it was from a friend?'

'That was the implication. He said it was a business call, and he only did business with his mates.'

'But he didn't identify who made the call?'

'No. I assumed it was Phil Martin. Maybe asking Bazza to organize another car theft just as he had on the night of his father's death? Maybe organizing the car in which Bazza met his own death?'

Her conjectures were greeted by a silence. Then Inspector Pollard said magisterially, 'Our job is already a difficult one, Mrs Seddon. It is not made easier by members of the public fancying themselves as amateur sleuths.'

'No, I can see that. But it does seem likely, doesn't it,' she persisted, 'that Phil got Bazza to organize that car for Howard Martin on the night of the engagement party?'

'I hope you're not expecting me to make any comment on that suggestion, Mrs Seddon.'

'Well, it would be nice if you did.'

She thought that was a reply worthy of Jude, but it didn't produce any thaw in Inspector Pollard. 'Even if I wished to, I would not be at liberty to discuss any details of the case.'

'No, of course not. Interesting, though, isn't it' – time for a big stab in the dark – 'that Bazza claimed never to have heard of Michael Brewer?'

'What?' His voice was tight with surprise. 'Where have you heard that name, Mrs Seddon?'

'Oh, come on. Gaby's my son's fiancée. She's told me some of the things you've asked her. Also, I was actually with her when she took the call on her mobile from Michael Brewer.'

'Oh. Right.' He couldn't argue with that.

'So it's no surprise that I've heard of Michael Brewer. And living down here, it's no surprise that I've heard about the fact that he murdered Janine Buckley.'

'I suppose not.'

'And I gather no one's seen him since he was released from Parkhurst?' Inspector Pollard made no reply. 'So is he one of your suspects?'

'Michael Brewer is one of a large number of people we wish to talk to,' the Inspector conceded.

'But he's disappeared off the face of the earth?' Again no response. 'Though we know he's alive, because he rang Gaby.'

'Mrs Seddon, if we could move on? That is,' he added sarcastically, 'if you have no further comments to make?'

'Well, all I would say is that it doesn't take a massive intellect to observe that the same murder method was used in the killings of Janine Buckley, Howard Martin and Barry Painter.'

Now she had gone too far. 'Mrs Seddon, I am calling you to ask about the time you spent in the Crown and Anchor with Mr Painter. I would be grateful if we could confine our conversation to that subject. I'm afraid I haven't got time to listen to your ill-informed amateur speculations. I know that members of the general public all believe they have greater skills in the business of crime solving than professional police officers, but I'm afraid statistically that is not the case. It is a pernicious fantasy prompted by ill-researched and inaccurate television programmes.'

This long speech had the intended effect of cowing even Carole Seddon into silence. 'Right, I may need to contact you again. I will definitely be speaking to your friend Jude Nicholls.' So he'd known the name all along. 'In the meantime, are there any further questions you wish to ask me, Mrs Seddon?'

'Yes, there is one.'

'Well?'

'Is Michael Brewer your chief suspect for the murders of Howard Martin and Barry Painter?'

Inspector Pollard put the phone down on her.

Chapter Twenty-Six

Libby Pearson was a large, over-enthusiastic woman in her late forties, and Carole got the feeling she had been a large, over-enthusiastic schoolgirl in her late teens. She entertained them in the large family kitchen of her large family house on the Fedborough side of Fethering. There was a strong smell of meat and herbs in the air, and their conversation was punctuated by clangs, as Libby moved pans from oven to oven of her large double Aga.

'Sorry, cooking. Always cooking. That's the way it's bound to be with a husband and two teenage sons.'

She offered them tea or coffee, but they said they'd just had some. This was true; it was not much more than half an hour since Libby Pearson's name had first been mentioned in the sitting room of High Tor. The alacrity with which she had invited them round had been almost alarming, and in keeping with her all-round heartiness.

She pointed to a metal grille of aromatically steaming biscuits. 'Those have just come out of the Aga, so if you fancy one, help yourself.'

She took a casserole out of the bottom right oven,

took off the lid and sniffed it. 'Bit more rosemary, I think.' Expertly stripping the spines from the stem, she added the herb, replaced the casserole and turned to face them.

'So you're writing a book about poor Janine?'

Carole wondered why she'd made such a fuss about making contact. Libby Pearson seemed so ready to talk, she probably wouldn't have needed any reason. And whether Gita or Carole herself was the potential author didn't seem to worry her either.

Gita fielded the question. 'Yes. It's not just about her, obviously, but about the whole case: the circumstances out of which it arose.'

'The circumstances out of which it arose,' said Libby Pearson ruefully, 'were too much drink and teenage sex.'

'Oh?'

'The school we went to was a convent. We were all taught Catholic values, but with people like Janine, they didn't stick. Which was why she got into trouble.'

'Are you saying,' asked Carole incredulously, 'that if she'd been a good Catholic, she wouldn't have been murdered?'

'Of course I'm saying that. Janine Buckley was murdered because she got pregnant.'

'But you could say she got pregnant because she was a good Catholic. She didn't use any form of birth control.'

'She shouldn't have got herself into a situation where she even needed to think about birth control.

The ruling of the Catholic Church is quite clear on such matters.'

Carole's instinct was to continue the argument. But she reminded herself that they weren't there to discuss Catholicism and morality. They were trying to find out all they could about Michael Brewer.

Smoothly, Gita Millington took up the questioning. 'From what you say, it sounds as though you and Janine Buckley weren't close friends. Are you suggesting that she was part of a kind of – fast set?'

'No, I wouldn't say that. I *was* good friends with her.' But whether Libby Pearson said that to gain a retrospective association with notoriety, Carole couldn't judge. There was something about the woman that seemed to try too hard. Carole could visualize her in the playground, unsubtle and ungainly, desperate to be part of the gang.

'Did you ever meet Michael Brewer?' Carole asked.

'Oh yes. I certainly did.' Libby Pearson didn't want to miss out on that bit of reflected evil either.

'What did he look like?'

'Tall. Very thin. Very good-looking he was, but quite intense. I remember saying to Janine and Marie that I wouldn't have liked a boyfriend who was so intense.'

'But you never went out with him?'

'No. We went around in a crowd.' The eternal answer of the teenager who didn't have a particular partner.

'So how many were you in that crowd?' asked Carole.

'I suppose eight or ten. We used to go to discos.'

'And when you say eight or ten, those were all girls, were they?'

'No, no, there were boys.' Some recollected teenage gaffe embarrassed Libby Pearson, and she turned to check a pan in the bottom left oven of the Aga.

'The boys were regulars?'

'Pretty well. I mean, it varied a bit. People fell in and out of, you know, relationships.'

She turned back to them, seeming to have recovered. The redness of her face could have been caused by the heat of the Aga.

'And Michael Brewer was one of those regulars?' Libby nodded. 'Along with Janine Buckley and Marie Coleman?'

'Yes. How did you know about Marie?'

'We've already done quite a lot of research,' said Gita efficiently.

'Ah. Well, she and Janine were very close. Best friends. And, though usually with female best friends, there's a pretty one and an ugly one,' Libby Pearson spoke as if she had had personal experience of this syndrome and had not been the pretty one, 'they were both absolutely gorgeous. All the boys wanted to be with them,' she concluded wistfully.

'Were they just gorgeous, or were they lively personalities as well?' asked Carole.

'Oh, incredibly bouncy, both of them. So much energy, always giggling. Full of life and—'

She stopped short, perhaps aware of the irony of her words in connection with Janine Buckley. But

Carole was more struck by the contrast between this description of Marie and the pallid, traumatized woman she had been speaking to the day before on Fethering Beach.

'Which other boys,' she asked, 'were regular members of the disco crowd? Apart from Michael Brewer?'

'Ooh, Lord.' Libby Pearson's brows wrinkled with the effort of recollection. 'We are talking a long time ago here. Let me think. I can see some of the faces, but I didn't know any of them that well, because we weren't at the same school.'

And I wasn't very close to any of them. Carole supplied the thought.

But Libby's memory clicked into action. 'Well, there was Marie's brother Robert, of course.'

'Robert Coleman.'

'Yes. He was always around in the crowd. He was a great friend of Michael Brewer's.'

'And did Robert have a particular girlfriend in the group?'

'Not so far as I remember.' Thinking back became hard again. 'I don't know. There was a certain amount of couples forming and breaking up, but . . . Robert . . . I can't really remember. I always got the impression that Robert's main job was to keep an eye on his little sister Marie.'

'Oh?'

'Their parents were very strict Catholics. Her mother was French and wouldn't have allowed Marie to go out at all in the evenings if Robert hadn't been there to see she behaved properly.'

'And did he do that? Did she behave properly?'

Carole realized that she was rather hogging the questioning and looked across to see if Gita minded. A flicker from the journalist's eyes gave her carte blanche to continue.

'I think,' Libby Pearson replied, 'that Marie behaved more or less as she wanted to behave. Oh, nothing very bad. But she could twist Robert round her little finger – like she could twist all men round her little finger. She was a bit of a flirt, really. Like Janine Buckley. They both were. They knew the power they had over men, and were just trying to see how far they could go with it.'

Again this image was totally at odds with the Marie of thirty years later.

'And Janine, of course,' Libby Pearson added self-righteously, 'went too far.'

'What about Howard Martin?' asked Carole. 'Was he a regular in the disco crowd?'

'Howard Martin?' The repetition was one of pure bewilderment.

'The man who Marie married, very soon after Janine Buckley's death.'

The girl shook her head. 'I've never heard of him. All I know is that, only a short while after the murder, Marie's family moved away from Worthing. I never heard what happened to her.'

'So Howard Martin means nothing? Worked as a fishmonger, with Marie's father?'

Another determined shake of the head. 'I certainly never met him.'

There was a silence. Then, smoothly journalistic, Gita Millington came in with a question. 'Just before the murder happened, Libby, were you aware of any trouble? Any row between Janine Buckley and Michael Brewer?'

'No. To be quite honest, I didn't even know they were a couple. I mean, our social lives were very circumscribed. It was just Saturday nights at the disco, really, and for some of us, our parents were waiting outside to pick us up at midnight.' They were left in no doubt that Libby had been among that number. 'So what went on, what various couples got up to privately – well, we didn't really know about that. A lot of gossip, but most of it pure invention.'

'So,' asked Carole, 'you didn't actually see Michael Brewer and Janine Buckley together as a couple?'

'I saw them dancing together, but then everyone danced together. Well, everyone in a certain group danced together.' She had clearly not been part of that group. Libby Pearson had been the eternal wallflower. She turned away awkwardly for some unnecessary banging of Aga doors.

'So there was no one time when you saw them, sort of . . . kissing or cuddling?'

'Well . . .' Libby Pearson turned back towards them and was silent. She had a story to tell, and was going to do it at her own pace. 'There was one occasion. It was a party, at Marie's place. Her parents were away, in France I think, visiting some relatives, and Marie invited us all back after the disco. It was very naughty, felt very daring at the time, and we'd got in some more booze, and drank and smoked, and played music and did a bit more dancing. And then we mostly passed out – you know, slept on the floor and helped clear up the next morning, so that Marie's mum and dad would never know what'd happened. And that's the only time I saw Janine and Mick together.'

Libby Pearson let the silence ride, before picking up her dramatic narrative. 'I was sleeping on a sofa in the sitting room. We were all scattered round the house – well, except for Marie and Robert, who were asleep in their own rooms. Anyway, I woke up in the middle of the night, and was terribly thirsty, and went to the kitchen to get a drink of water, and when I opened the door to the hall . . .' she allowed another pause '. . . I saw Janine and Mick going upstairs together.'

Another silence.

'And I've thought about that a lot since. They must've been going up to Marie's parents' bedroom to – you know – and I think the timing would have been about right; I think that was probably the night that Janine got pregnant. And I've often wondered if I should have done something. I mean, obviously I had no idea what was going to happen, how it would all turn out so badly, but I've wondered if I'd made a noise and they'd seen me, or if I'd said something, come to that, whether they might not have gone on upstairs, and Janine Buckley might still be alive today.'

The way she concluded her speech left no doubt that it was a party piece, with which she had delighted many listeners over the years when they had asked her if she knew anything about the Janine Buckley murder.

'And did you ever tell that to the police?' asked Carole.

'The police never asked me. I was never interviewed by them.'

There was no reason why she should have been. The same information could have been gleaned from Marie or Robert or any number of other witnesses.

'And they were the only ones – Janine and Mick – the only couple who went upstairs that night?'

A sneer formed instantly across Libby Pearson's features. 'There was another girl – year below us at school – who'd come to the party with her boyfriend, and she kept going on about the way they were always having sex all the time. She took him upstairs earlier in the evening.'

'Do you remember their names?'

'I don't remember his. Don't think I ever knew it, actually. But hers . . . she was a right little madam – wouldn't forget her in a hurry.' A wave of recollected playground jealousy swept through her. 'She was called Diana Milton.'

'Any idea what happened to her?'

'I don't know and I don't care,' came the childlike response.

Carole looked across at Gita Millington, and they silently agreed that the interview was probably at an end. 'Thank you so much. You've been an enormous help for the book.'

'It was my pleasure. As you see, all I'm doing is cooking. For a husband and two teenage sons.'

She finished this with a laugh, which seemed to emphasize the hollowness of her life. Cooking was more than a necessity for Libby Pearson. It was a validation of her existence in a house full of three men. She was always going to be the galumphing one, running behind the others in the playground, wanting to join in their games and rituals.

And she would talk to anyone about the murder of Janine Buckley, because it was the only time when Libby Pearson, even for a few minutes, could hold centre stage.

Chapter Twenty-Seven

Carole was glad when Jude suggested a drink in the Crown and Anchor on Wednesday evening. And even gladder when she heard that Gita had gone up to London for the night.

With customary instinct, Jude understood her friend's feelings. 'Nice for us to have a chat together. Sounds like this Libby woman you met was a mine of information.'

'Oh, Gita's told you all about it, has she?' In spite of her best efforts, there was an edge of pique in Carole's voice.

'No, not all the details. I wanted to hear all those from you. Don't forget, Gita's only our research assistant in all this. We two are the investigators.'

Part of Carole knew that this was a kind of soft soap, but there was such honesty and warmth in Jude's brown eyes that she yielded happily to being soft-soaped. 'Gita has been very useful to us,' she conceded magnanimously, 'though probably a lot of the information is stuff we could have got for ourselves.'

'Of course we could,' Jude agreed soothingly. 'You could have done it standing on your head.'

Carole tried not to show how flattered she felt.

'But it has been incredibly important for Gita. It's helped her get her confidence back. And I really appreciate what you've contributed to that process, Carole.'

'Well . . !' Carole had a nasty feeling that all she had really contributed had been jealousy and prejudice. Still, if Jude didn't see it that way . . .

'What I want us to do tonight is to pool the new information we've got. You bring me up to date with what you learned from Libby Pearson, and I'll tell you what I've been up to.'

'Oh? You've been up to things too, have you?'

'Yes. An idea I followed through.'

'With Gita?'

Sometimes Carole's insecurity was so naked as to be almost comical, but Jude just smiled and said, 'No, not with Gita. I've been following up a contact at Austen Prison.'

'Oh, do you still do all your *alternative* stuff down there?' Carole Seddon was incapable of pronouncing that adjective without disapproval.

'Yes, I still do. Anyway, you first. Tell me what you got from Libby Pearson.'

So Carole did. Then Jude brought her up to date with the information she'd been given by Jimmy Troop.

'I'm amazed,' said Jude, when they both knew as much as each other, 'given her family background, how remarkably sane Gaby is.'

'You really think she is?' asked Carole anxiously.

'Yes. Absolutely, yes. I don't know her as well as you do, but I think she's got a remarkably strong personality. She and Stephen will be great together.'

'I hope so.'

'Of course they will, Carole.'

'But, given her family history, particularly on the female side, I do worry. Her grandmother had a breakdown, her mother seems permanently on the edge of a breakdown . . .'

'The great thing about heredity, Carole, is that it's an indicator of possible behaviour, not a form of predestination. Everyone can escape their background.'

'Do you really think so?'

'I'm absolutely certain of it.'

'Hm.' Carole didn't sound convinced. But then she looked across to the bar, where Ted Crisp was sharing his store of elderly jokes with a group of elderly customers, and she felt a little surge of confidence. She thought back to the deep shame and embarrassment she had felt at the end of their brief affair, and compared it to the amiable friendship she and the landlord now enjoyed. Yes, maybe Jude was right. Maybe it was possible to grow away from the past.

'You can't hold a breakdown against someone, Carole. It could happen to any one of us.'

'Nonsense. I can't see it happening to you, for one.'

'Don't you believe it. I've been very close.'

Carole was too taken aback to ask the proper immediate follow-up questions. And another opportunity to find out more about her enigmatic friend was whisked away, as Jude went on, 'Everyone who's human must have been very close.'

'Well, I never have,' Carole pronounced firmly.

'No?'

'No.' Carole confirmed this with even more vehemence.

'What do you think a breakdown is?'

'It's . . . losing control.'

'And you'd hate to do that?'

'Yes.'

'Well, for some people I think it's necessary: part of the way they grow as human beings. The personality they had before wasn't working, that's what led to the breakdown, and after it they have to rebuild a personality that fits them better, a personality they can live with.'

'And is that what Gita's doing?'

'Yes, that's exactly what Gita's doing.'

'And you really don't think Gaby's going to go the same way?'

'Carole, if Gaby was the sort to crack up, she'd have cracked up over the last few weeks. The strain she has been under has been enormous. No, she's a survivor.'

'Mm. That's good, isn't it?'

'It's very good.' Jude leant across and patted her friend's hand. 'Now listen, I'm going to buy you supper.' She held both hands up to stop the inevitable remonstrances. 'No, no argument. Hm, I wonder how special Ted's special is tonight?'

When she got back, slightly unsteadily, to High Tor,

Carole Seddon felt relaxed. For the millionth time, she asked herself: what was it about Jude?

Never mind what it was, it worked. Carole had had a really good evening. Certainly better than the one she expected to have the next day.

Chapter Twenty-Eight

Had she thought about it, Carole could have predicted exactly the sort of restaurant David would have chosen for their dinner *à quatre*. (Her anticipation that her son's fiancée wouldn't feel up to the evening had proved unfounded. Gaby had gone back to work, had returned to her Pimlico flat, and Marie was safe in Harlow, with her beloved brother Robert round for the evening. By the time David's 'fine-tuning' call came through, Carole had left it too late to come up with a decent excuse not to be there. In desperation she contemplated inventing some veterinary emergency for Gulliver, but hadn't had the courage to go through with it.)

David's choice of restaurant was a rather dimly lit Italian, whose dark wood alcoves, red gingham tablecloths and much-dribbled candlesticks seemed to hark back to the bistro boom of the late sixties – and indeed probably hadn't been redecorated since. A lot of objects dangled from the ceilings: smoke-stained pennants from Italian football clubs, raffia-bound long-necked wine bottles, boxes which had once contained – and might indeed still contain – rich fruit cakes, spindly tin knight-in-armour puppets. The atmosphere should have been cosy, but only felt cramped.

The choice of restaurant was also archetypically David because, a glance at the laminated menus had told Carole, it was cheap. Not embarrassingly cheap, but marginally underpriced. David was not exactly mean, but he derived great satisfaction from shaving a small percentage point off the price of anything. He was not capable of making the grand gesture. This particularly annoyed Carole because she knew she shared elements of the same trait. She was capable of generosity, but never of unthinking generosity.

The *padrone* of the restaurant was a short, stout man with an unfeasible wig, whose automatic bon-homie David took to be the recognition of a much-loved regular. The restaurant was in Swiss Cottage, 'just round the corner' from the flat whose address and phone number Carole willed herself not to memorize. David seemed determinedly hearty, ready to be a good host and demonstrate what an habitué he was of such eateries. Having seen his performance in Harlow, Carole wondered whether his heartiness was alcohol-aided, whether he'd had a few bracing Scotches straight from the bottle before he arrived.

In the long catalogue of David's irritating modes, she probably found the bonhomous one the most irritating. (On the other hand, if he had been in his self-pitying mode, or the one where he nitpicked about her character, or the one which made him sullenly resentful of the success of others, that would have been equally annoying. Basically, so far as his ex-wife was concerned, David Seddon couldn't do anything right.)

But Carole knew the evening wasn't set up to rehearse old antagonisms. She and David, she had to keep reminding herself, were not the principal characters of the occasion. The dinner was for Stephen and, particularly, for Gaby, who had just been through a series of terrible traumas. The job of Carole and David was to give her as uncomplicated and enjoyable an evening as possible, to reassure her that normal life could continue, and to remind her that she was a young woman on the exciting verge of marriage. Nothing else – least of all the aggravation that had precipitated the end of another marriage – was important.

But, given the circumstances of their last encounter, Carole could not suppress a curiosity about her future daughter-in-law's encounter with Inspector Pollard back in Harlow, and was therefore relieved when Gaby herself raised the subject.

'Look, I do just want to bring you all up to date. About the investigation into Dad's death. Just so's we can get it out of the way now, and not have it hanging over us all through the evening.' She smiled across at her fiancé. 'Steve knows all this, so you'll just bear with me, won't you, love?'

He nodded willing acquiescence, as Gaby continued. 'Inspector Pollard is not a great one for volunteering information . . .' You can say that again, thought Carole '. . . but in questioning me, he couldn't avoid letting out certain facts. There seems no question that Bazza – Barry Painter – did steal the car that picked Dad up from the hotel in Harlow the night he died. Who arranged for him to do that Inspector Pollard either didn't know or didn't reveal to me, but I wouldn't say that my dear brother Phil has been completely cleared of suspicion. I personally don't think he had anything to do with it – or if he did, he didn't realize the consequences, didn't know where Bazza would take Dad . . .' she could not repress a shudder '. . . you know, into Epping Forest. Phil's done some dodgy things in the past, but he's not really evil. And he got on well with Dad. He wouldn't knowingly have put the old boy in danger.'

For a moment she wobbled, emotion threatening. Having to be strong for her mother had forced Gaby to suppress her own feelings of loss for her father, but they were nonetheless powerful. Sensing her distress, Stephen put a large hand on top of his fiancée's. With a grateful smile, Gaby took a deep breath and continued, 'The police do seem to have a suspect, though. Inspector Pollard didn't spell it out – indeed, he probably tried to keep the information from me – but from what he said, and from things that Uncle Robert told me, I think they're after this man called Michael Brewer.' She looked across at Carole. 'The one from whom I had that call on my mobile. I don't know much about him.'

Jude and I probably know a lot more, thought Carole. But, with David present, she wasn't about to share what she knew. She realized a new level of her resentment towards her former husband. She didn't like the fact that Gaby was including him so automatically in her talk about what Carole thought of as 'the case'. Her work with Jude on murder investigations was part of her painfully created change of identity: the new Carole Seddon who lived at High Tor with her dog Gulliver. She resented someone like Gita Millington being involved in that aspect of her life, but the thought of David as part of it was even more distasteful.

'But the good thing is,' Gaby went on, 'now the police know who they're looking for, they're pretty confident they'll soon have caught him. So we'll all be able to relax.'

'Are you saying that Michael Brewer is definitely the police's suspect for both murders?'

'That's the way it looks.'

'Did Inspector Pollard tell you why they're convinced it was him?'

Gaby shook her head. 'No. The inspector wasn't going to tell me more than he had to. But Uncle Robert was able to fill things out a bit. It's useful having someone in the family with contacts in the Force. Apparently there's strong forensic evidence linking Michael Brewer with both crime scenes.'

'Do you know what that evidence was?'

'No, Carole, I don't. But apparently it's pretty unarguable.'

'And have the police any idea where Michael Brewer might be now?'

'They're concentrating their searches on the South Coast.'

'Oh yes, he was brought up in Worthing.'

Gaby did look slightly surprised at the depth of Carole's knowledge, but she didn't comment. 'And that call to my mobile . . .'

'Yes?'

'It was made from a public phone in Brighton.'

'Ah.' It made Carole feel a little uneasy, the confirmation that a double murderer was at large, not far from Fethering. 'Did Robert say any more about Michael Brewer? Because they used to be friends.'

This detailed knowledge again prompted a rather curious look, but Gaby gave a straight answer. 'No. He said they used to know each other, but that was it.'

'But surely—'

Her son came in to stop further questioning. 'That's all Gaby knows. So we're all up to date. And I think it'll be a relief all round if we now moved on to talk about more pleasant things.'

Though frustrated in her further researches, Carole was impressed by how masterful Stephen could be. Masterful and protective. The look of gratitude that Gaby flashed at him augured well for their life together. He showed a sensitivity to his fiancée's needs that Carole would never have suspected he had in his nature.

The thought inevitably reminded her of David's presence. Here they were, a family group, mother and father, son, son's fiancée – it should all have been so normal. Talk of weddings, talk of the future, and the unspoken thought of the family developing into another generation. Yet to Carole it all felt uncomfortably abnormal.

But the engaged couple, the people who mattered, did not seem aware of any unease. Having got the distasteful topic of the evening out of the way, they did as Stephen had suggested, and talked about more pleasant things. These mostly concerned their wedding plans, their invitation list, the friends Carole and David had yet to meet, the 'characters' from their separate work environments. Gaby's theatrical connections promised a lively group of party-goers, and even Stephen's professional colleagues sounded quite a jolly bunch. (Carole could not repress the mental 'even'. Whatever it was that her son did, she somehow hadn't expected his colleagues to be amongst the sparkiest of individuals. Prejudice again.)

Stephen and Gaby also talked further about their house purchase plans. They still seemed to want to move south. When Carole had first met them together, they had come down to the Hopwicke Country House Hotel to check out the local property scene, and their intentions had not changed. A large house near the South Coast remained their ambition. Feasibility of commuting might put them nearer Brighton than Fethering, but the likelihood remained that Carole would have them as relative neighbours. For her, the attractiveness of this situation was tempered by the knowledge that it would also bring David close to her on a regular basis.

She really did want to make the evening a success, and it was, but she still could not relax in her ex-husband's presence. Maybe constant encounters would dilute her distaste for him, but she didn't feel optimistic. There was too much history, too many spoken – and, even worse, unspoken – resentments between them.

She could not understand why David himself was so relaxed. Surely he was feeling the same tension that she was? But if so, he was disguising the fact well. He seemed very at ease, drinking too much certainly, but exchanging badinage with the *padrone*, even telling bad jokes to Stephen and Gaby, entering into the spirit of the occasion in his habitually inept, hesitant way. Maybe, thought Carole coldly, David really believes that we have achieved that goal so desired by all divorced couples – 'a civilized relationship', in which they can meet up socially without rancour. Well, he might have attained that plateau; Carole couldn't see herself making it until – various formulae of words involving 'hell' and 'freezing over' came to her mind.

At the end of the dinner there was an elaborate routine between David and the *padrone* (whom he insisted on calling *padrone*) about sambucas 'on the house'. The narrow glasses with the colourless liqueur and coffee bean were brought forth and ceremoniously ignited, and there was much comment from David about the blue flame. He even, ill-advisedly, tried to express his gratitude to the *padrone* in Italian.

The winding-down of the evening was far too extended for Carole's taste. Wasn't he ever going to ask for the bill? She kept sneaking glances at her watch, assessing the tube journey between Swiss Cottage and Victoria, along with the limited timetable of trains to Fethering. It was a huge relief when Stephen suggested giving her a lift. He was going to take Gaby to her flat in Pimlico. Victoria was virtually on their way.

Finally, they were standing up. Carole submitted to a slobbery kiss from her ex-husband, and smiled non-committally at his hope 'that this will be the first of many such evenings'.

Once inside Stephen's ultra-comfortable BMW, she had two predominant emotions. First, massive relief that the evening was over. And, second, deep guilt for the ungracious thoughts which had filled her mind throughout it.

Because of the vagaries of the SouthCentral timetable, to avoid Carole having a half-hour wait in the inhospitable wastes of Victoria Station, Stephen decided he would drop Gaby at her flat first, take his mother to catch her train and then return to Pimlico. There had been an unspoken sexual semaphore between the couple all evening, and as soon as they were alone together, Carole felt sure they'd be in bed. She found the thought rather heart-warming. She certainly felt no jealousy. An evening in the company of her ex-husband had proved a powerful anti-aphrodisiac. The thought that Carole Seddon might ever again entertain desire for another human being seemed unlikely. And yet her mind could not erase the unwelcome sexual frisson she had felt for David at the hotel in Harlow.

Never having been there, Carole was curious to see

where her future daughter-in-law lived. She'd just missed a train and at that time of night there was only an hourly train service to Fethering, so there was going to be time for a 'quick cup of coffee'. Carole also wondered whether she was about to meet Gaby's flatmate, the actress Jenny.

It was a road of early nineteenth-century terraced houses, well-proportioned with tall windows. All were iced with white paint, and fronted by shining black railings. The parked cars bespoke affluence. 'This is very nice,' Carole murmured.

'Yes. Lucky to get it. Belongs to one of our clients. He's now making it big in Hollywood, but he's kept this on, and Jenny and I are the lucky tenants.'

Stephen eased the BMW into a space. 'The gods are with us tonight,' he said.

'Certainly are. Sometimes, you know, Carole, Steve has to park about half a mile away. Traffic here's appalling. But tonight, *voilà* – we're right outside.'

'Sure I've got time for that coffee?'

'Yes, course you have, Mum. Quick one. Don't worry, I'll see you're in good time for the train to Fethering.'

The three of them mounted the three steps of the white portico, and it was Stephen who unlocked the tall black door. He moved proprietorially across the dimly lit hall to one of the two apartments and inserted another key into the lock.

He had hardly begun to turn it before the door burst open. A girl's scream sounded from inside the flat, as a tall, thin man pushed forward, sending

Stephen flying backwards across the hall. A tied scarf obscured the man's face. He paused for a moment at the sight of the two women, then, before she had time to recoil, grabbed Gaby's throat with his hand.

For a long, terrifying second, the man stared at Gaby. Then, he seemed to change his mind. As suddenly as he'd grabbed her, he released his hold, and rushed out of the front door, slamming it behind him.

In the doorway of the flat, a distraught girl approached, sobbing. If logic hadn't done so already, her histrionics would immediately have identified her as the actress flatmate Jenny. 'He said he'd come to see you, Gaby. He was expecting you to come back alone. He only decided to leave when he saw through the spy hole that you'd got other people with you.'

'Jenny, did he say who he was?'

'He said his name was Michael Brewer.'

Chapter Twenty-Nine

When he got inside the flat, Stephen became very masterful. He sat the two hysterical girls on the sofa, and dispatched Carole to the kitchen to make strong sweet tea while he called the police. In the emotion of the moment, she hardly noticed the smart minimalist decor of Gaby's flat, which under different circumstances would have fascinated her.

By the time Carole returned with the tea, Gaby had more or less calmed down. Her pale face showed the effort she was putting into battening down her feelings. But her flatmate Jenny was doing enough emoting for both of them. As if auditioning for the role of some tragic diva, she kept telling them how ghastly it had been to come back and find someone in the flat, how he'd told her to be quiet, implying a variety of threats if she disobeyed. And how awful it had been just to sit there waiting till Gaby's return, knowing there was nothing she could do to warn her friend of the danger.

'Yes,' Stephen agreed grimly, 'I think it's lucky I didn't just drop you, love, and go straight on to the station with Mum.'

Gaby nodded bravely. Carole could see on her face the strain of not letting her thoughts wander to what might have been.

'The good thing about it is, though—'

'There's a good thing, Stephen?' she asked incredulously.

'Yes, Mum. At least now we've got an up-to-date physical description of Michael Brewer.'

'Have we, though?' asked Carole. 'Couldn't see much of his face, with that scarf wrapped round it. I could say that he was tall, thin and probably bearded – that's about it. The light in the hall was pretty dim.'

'Yes, I didn't see much more. What about you, Gaby? He looked at you very closely. Would you be able to identify him in a police line-up?'

His fiancée shook her head firmly, as if hoping to shake out unwelcome images. 'I don't know. I just thought he looked . . .' She decided not to pursue the thought, and shook her head again.

'He looked what?' asked Carole. 'Were you about to say he looked familiar?'

'No. Well, he couldn't be, could he? I could never have seen him. Not if he's been in prison for the last thirty years.'

Carole felt sure Gaby was leaving something unsaid, but the girl would not give any more.

Stephen turned his attention to her flatmate. 'You were with him for longest, Jenny. Did you see his face?'

'No.' Onstage the word would have been a thrilling whisper. 'He had the scarf on when I came in. He was sitting here waiting. At first he thought I was Gaby. I had to show him a credit card to prove I wasn't. It was *terrifying!*

'Did he talk much?'

'Hardly at all.'

'Did he threaten you, Jenny? Say he'd hurt you?'

'Not exactly. But I don't think he would have been afraid to hurt me. There was something, I don't know . . . *obsessional* about him.'

'Was he carrying a weapon?'

'I couldn't see anything, but I got the impression that he probably was.'

'Did he say anything that . . .' Stephen tried to find the right words, but ended up with the rather feeble '. . . anything that sort of seemed important?'

'He said –' Jenny dropped her voice to another audition-tingling whisper, '"After the old man died, and the boy, Gaby had to be next."'

At these words, an involuntary shudder ran through their subject. Instinctively Stephen put his arm round his fiancée's shoulder.

At that moment the doorbell rang, and a couple of local detectives arrived, somewhat disgruntled at being summoned to a crime scene where no one had been hurt and nothing stolen. Stephen had to spend some time impressing on them the seriousness of the incident before they agreed to put a call through to Inspector Pollard of the Essex Police.

By the time the two girls had been calmed, and the police arrived, the last train to Fethering was long gone. It was agreed that Stephen would stay in Pimlico to give Gaby moral support – and support through the police interrogations – while Carole took Gaby's set of keys to Stephen's house in Fulham. Carole was slightly miffed at not being on the scene for the next stage of the investigation, but knew the chances of her finding out anything further from the police were pretty minimal. So, obedient to her son's instructions, she took the cab he had ordered for her round to his house.

She had been there before, but only a couple of times. First, on a tour of inspection just after he'd bought the place, perhaps her first realization of quite how successful her son had become in his career (whatever that might be). And then second, a few months after that, for a rather formal and awkward Sunday lunch party to which he'd suddenly invited her (a social experiment that had not been repeated).

But she remembered her way around. Following Stephen's instructions, she found the drinks' cabinet in the sitting room, and surprised herself by pouring a large Scotch. Her rationale was that she wasn't going to sleep, anyway, so she might as well take something to calm her nerves.

She took the drink upstairs with her, located the new toothbrush Stephen had described in the bathroom cupboard, had a perfunctory wash, and slipped under the crisp clean sheets of the spare room bed. She thought to herself how well organized her son was domestically, with his cleaning lady and his—
Instantly, she was asleep.

*

A creak of a floorboard woke her and she looked up to see Stephen just closing the door to her room.

'Sorry, Mum, didn't want to wake you. I had to come back to pick up a clean shirt and some papers I need for a meeting.'

He lingered by the door, as if about to beat a hasty retreat, embarrassed by her presence in his house.

'How's Gaby?' asked Carole.

The question made up his mind for him. He came back into the room. Carole patted the side of her bed, then immediately felt awkward because she only had on bra and pants under the duvet. She shouldn't feel awkward with her own son. Or perhaps it was worse with her own son.

Stephen sat down heavily on the bed beside her. He didn't look as if he'd slept at all. With Gaby and Jenny to keep calm, not to mention questioning from the police, he probably hadn't.

'Oh, Gaby's bearing up,' he said. 'Inspector Pollard arrived in the early hours.'

'All the way from Essex?'

'Yes. They're taking this very seriously indeed. No more pussy-footing around the subject. Pollard is now actually saying that Michael Brewer is their chief suspect for the two murders.'

'God. Which makes it even worse. For Gaby, I mean, to think what might have happened last night if we hadn't—'

'I don't need to be told to think about it, Mum. I haven't thought about anything else all night.'

'Did Inspector Pollard let slip any reason why they're so sure of Michael Brewer's guilt?'

'Yes. There's a DNA match from both sites. They've still got samples on file from the Janine Buckley murder. There's no question it's him.'

'But the cars were burnt out. How can you get DNA samples under those circumstances?'

'Oh, Brewer left them very deliberately. He's not trying to disguise the fact that he's involved.'

'You mean – he left calling cards?'

'Almost literally that, Mum. Playing cards.'

'What?'

'At each crime scene, a playing card was found. They definitely belonged to Brewer. Traces of his DNA all over them.'

The image came to Carole's mind – something Jimmy Troop had described to Jude – of Michael Brewer in Parkhurst, playing endless silent games of patience. And, as he flicked over the cards, who could say what fantasies of vengeance had run through his head?

Well, he'd revenged himself on Howard Martin. Though for what offence it was hard to imagine. Bazza's death, Carole felt pretty sure, had not been for revenge, just a necessity to stop the boy talking about his involvement in Howard Martin's. Leaving a playing card there was just an act of bravado – or maybe the intention had been to frighten someone.

And now, Carole realized with sickening impact, this man was targeting her son's fiancée. 'So where's Gaby now?'

'At the flat. Pollard's still with her and Jenny. Trying to get anything else he can out of them about Brewer. Seems like it's becoming a full-scale manhunt.'

'Well, he can't stay hidden for long, can he? Nobody could. Least of all someone who's spent the last thirty years in prison. The world must seem a pretty alien place to him, and I'd have thought it was hard for anyone to hide in an alien landscape.'

'Hope you're right. Until Brewer's caught I'm just not going to relax about Gaby for a second. I feel I shouldn't be going in to work today, but if I don't – well, that'd be the equivalent to chucking in the job, the way things are going at the moment.'

'Look, the police're bound to catch Michael Brewer soon.'

'Yes,' her son said wearily. 'Yes. I know, I know. And at least Gaby's safe for today.'

'What? Is Pollard taking her into protective custody?'

'No, nothing like that is needed. Her Uncle Robert's coming over to the flat. Pollard's promised he won't leave till Robert's there, so at least I can feel vaguely relaxed for the rest of today.'

He scraped his fingernails up through his greying hair. 'Oh, I wish Gaby were out of this. Somewhere safe.'

'Would she be safe in France?'

He looked up at his mother in puzzlement. 'Why France?'

'Gaby has said on a couple of occasions that she'd like to see her grandmother in France before the

wedding. Hoping to introduce you to the old lady.'
Carole spread wide her hands. 'Maybe this is the perfect opportunity?'

'Wouldn't work. I can't possibly take the time off at the moment.'

'Good idea, though, isn't it?'

'Yes. Or it would be if we could get someone else to go with Gaby, to look after her.'

'Do you know,' said Carole, 'I think that could be arranged.'

'I've done it.'

Whatever Gita had done, Jude knew, as soon as she walked into Woodside Cottage, that it was something good. Her houseguest was wearing a biscuit-coloured trouser suit over a jade-coloured silk shirt, and inordinately pointy shoes. The clothes, Jude recognized, were new. That was a good sign. So was the fact that there was not a chink in Gita's armour of make-up.

'I rang one of the editors.'

'Well done.'

'Don't know why I haven't done it before. She's a close friend, for God's sake.'

'You weren't ready to do it before. You are now.'

'Anyway, I pitched an idea to her, on the back of the research I've been doing for you and Carole.'

'Oh?'

'A major feature about lifers: how they manage when they're finally released; how they come to terms with freedom; how the outside world comes to terms with them. The editor loved it. A definite commission. I'm going up to town to have lunch with her today, to talk it all through.'

For the first time, Jude noticed Gita's luggage on the sitting-room floor. Not just the scruffy nylon knapsack she had arrived with: a smart black wheelie suitcase stood beside it. Also new. However much the fee for the new commission was going to be, Gita had surely already overspent it. But that too was a good sign.

Jude's friend saw where she was looking. 'Got the train into Chichester this morning. A major consumerist splurge.'

'Very necessary. And very therapeutic.'

'You bet.' Gita grinned. Suddenly she was a stunningly attractive woman. 'And yes, the luggage does mean I'm about to get out of your hair.'

'You don't have to.'

'That's very kind, Jude. And I can never thank you enough for what you've done. But it's time. I need to go.'

Ever since Gita arrived at Woodside Cottage, Jude had been longing to hear such a positive statement. But she still couldn't help asking, 'You sure you'll be all right?'

'Yes. I'll go down again, I know. I'm in a manic phase at the moment – I can recognize that. But the medication does control the mood swings a bit. And I've rung other friends in London. I'm rebuilding my network. Yes, I'll go down again, but I've got people I can turn to. I can take the burden off you.'

'Gita, you haven't been a burden.'

'Oh no?' There was a twinkle in the journalist's eye. 'I know you very well, Jude. You volunteered to have me here, and you've supported me all the way. But you'll be glad to have Woodside Cottage to yourself again.'

Jude was not one for polite lies. She nodded a smiling acknowledgement of the truth.

'Well, whenever you need me, I'm just at the end of a phone. You've got my mobile number?'

'Of course I have.' Gita Millington looked at her watch. 'Must go. The next Victoria train leaves from Fethering Station in a quarter of an hour. And, incidentally, I'm very glad to know that you're there for me, but don't forget that I'm also there for you. I'm not expecting you to need me as an emotional support – though if you do, I'm more than ready to take on that role – but if you and Carole need any other research done . . .' she smiled as she echoed Jude's words '. . . I'm just at the end of a phone. Incidentally . . .'

'Yes?'

'I've been very good about not asking why you wanted that research done.'

'You have indeed.'

'But I can't deny that it's made me curious.'

'You wouldn't be human if you weren't curious, Gita.'

'No.' There was a silence. 'I gather, from the fact that you're not volunteering anything that I'm not going to get any more information at the moment.'

'How right you are. I'm sorry, but what it's all

about – well, it concerns Carole more than me. I don't want to betray any confidences.'

'No.' Gita quickly reconciled herself to the frustrations of ignorance. 'But when everything's sorted?'

'When everything's sorted, which I hope will be very soon, you will know the whole story.'

'Thank you, Jude.'

'And maybe you can get another story out of it. That true crime book you were talking about?'

Gita grinned, accepting the thought. Then another quick look at her watch. 'I must – Jude, I can't begin to thank you.'

'Then don't.'

And the two women enveloped each other in a huge hug.

Chapter Thirty

It had been Carole's intention to leave Stephen's house as early as possible, catching the first available train from Victoria to Fethering. After her son had hurried off to work, she was on her way out when she heard the phone ring. The thought of answering did not occur to her, but after Stephen's recorded message, curiosity kept her listening to identify the caller.

It was a male voice. 'This is a message for Carole.'

She was thunderstruck, like some haunted victim in a ghost story.

'I don't know if you are still there, but if you are, please pick up the phone.' With massive relief she had recognized the voice before he identified himself. 'This is Robert Coleman. If you are there, please pick up the phone. Or if, by chance, you pick up this message later, please call me on—'

She picked up the phone. 'Hello, this is Carole.'

'Oh, I'm so glad I caught you. Listen, Stephen probably told you that I'm coming to London to be with Gaby. I was just wondering, if you're still in town, whether you'd care to join us for lunch?'

Carole's immediate reaction was to say no, she had

to get back to Fethering and Gulliver. But she curbed this instinct. Jude had already seen to Gulliver that morning; she wouldn't mind taking him out again, if necessary. And, if Robert was willing to talk about it, he probably knew more about the background to the Janine Buckley murder than anyone, except for Michael Brewer.

Robert Coleman's choice of venue was a club, not one of the patrician Pall Mall ones, but a sensible convenient meeting place for professional men and women, particularly those involved with law and order.

Gaby looked much better than she had when Carole had last seen her. The colour had returned to her cheeks, and some of the verve to her personality. She seemed relaxed with her Uncle Robert. Like her mother, Gaby had always known him as a rock throughout her life, the one stable element in the insecurity of family life. And he responded to his niece's affection. There was a palpable warmth between them.

When they met, in the club's rather severe, no-frills bar, Carole's first question was about Marie. 'Is she all right on her own in Harlow?'

'She's fine,' Robert reassured her. 'Pollard's got a man keeping an eye on her. Anyway, I don't really think *Marie*'s at any risk.'

His emphasis froze the gin and tonic on its way to Gaby's lips. 'Meaning I am?'

'After last night,' he said grimly, 'I think there can no longer be any doubt about that.'

Carole thought it was time for a few straight questions. 'Robert, you knew Michael Brewer well, didn't you, before he was arrested for murder.'

A nod of the head. 'Which made it all the worse. Something like that's ghastly, but when you find out the perpetrator is someone you thought of as a friend, well, that doesn't make it any easier to take.'

'I met someone in Fethering recently who was a school friend of Janine Buckley and Marie.'

He didn't seem surprised by the news. 'It's a small area. A lot of people never move far away from where they were born.'

'Her name was Libby Pearson. Mean anything to you?' He shook his head. 'Maybe Pearson's her married name. Do you remember one of Marie's friends called Libby?'

Another shake of the head. 'We are talking a long time ago, Carole. At the time I saw a lot of Marie's school friends, but it was a very brief period of my life. I doubt if I'd even remember the name of Janine Buckley if circumstances had been different.' He was troubled by the memories the name prompted. 'When I think she could now be a wife and mother, a grandmother even, if Michael Brewer hadn't . . .' His head shook again in pained disbelief.

'Libby Pearson talked about a party at your parents' house.'

'Goodness, she's got a long memory. When was this supposed to have been?'

'1973, I should think. Your parents were apparently away in France.'

'Doesn't ring any bells with me. So, what does this Libby say about that clearly unmemorable social event?'

'She says it's the only time she saw Michael Brewer and Janine Buckley together.'

'Then she definitely wasn't part of our group. Mick and Janine were all over each other all the time.'

That rather confirmed Carole's image of Libby Pearson as a fringe player, someone who desperately wanted to be at the centre of the action, but was doomed always to remain peripheral.

'Libby also reckons that was the night that Michael Brewer got Janine Buckley pregnant.'

Robert Coleman shrugged. 'Could have been. There were plenty of other opportunities, though, the way those two went at it.'

'You still don't recall the party?'

'Some vague recollection's coming back, but not much detail, I'm afraid.'

'Libby said that, when Michael Brewer and Janine went upstairs, you and Marie were already up there.'

'Well, we would have been, in our beds, if it was the middle of the night. And I'd have been fulfilling my duty of preserving my sister's honour. If our parents were away, then I was in charge. And I knew they'd take a pretty dim view of Marie getting up to anything of a sexual nature. Our mother had strong – even old-fashioned – views on moral issues.'

'And she now lives in France, is that right?' asked Carole.

'Yes. In a home down there. She went back to be near her family after our dad died. She was very ill . . . I think I told you that she'd had a major breakdown after his death?'

'You did tell me, yes.'

'Well, she'd never really settled in England, although she'd lived here for nearly thirty years, so when she came out of hospital, it made sense for her to go back to near where she was born. She'd got sisters and cousins over there.'

'Near Villeneuve-sur-Lot?'

Gaby confirmed that, and Robert went on, 'I think it worked out pretty well for her. She was always going to be quite fragile emotionally, but she was happy to be back in France. She had a nice little house there, and we'd all go out and visit, till she was too feeble to look after herself and went into the home. She's pretty gaga now, I'm afraid.'

'I wouldn't say that.' Gaby, who had been silent during their previous conversation, now came to life. 'She's frail, but she's still got all her marbles.'

Robert Coleman shook his head sadly. 'You haven't seen her for nearly a year, Gabs. I'm afraid she's gone downhill quite a bit.'

'Oh dear. I've meant to go and see her. I've just been so busy the last few months, particularly since Steve and I announced our engagement. I must get out there soon.'

Carole was about to announce her brilliant plan,

which would both salve Gaby's conscience and ensure her safety, but Robert Coleman spoke first. 'I wouldn't bother, Gabs love. She won't recognize you.'

So Carole decided the moment wasn't right. She'd make the suggestion when she could get Gaby on her own.

Once they were through in the club dining room, eating solid British fare, she reverted to the subject of the 1973 party at the house of Robert and Marie's parents. 'This Libby Pearson woman also mentioned a girl called Diana Milton. Does that ring any bells?'

A slightly mischievous smile crossed Robert Coleman's face. 'Now I'd be lying if I denied knowing that name. Right little raver she was.'

'That's rather what Libby implied.'

'A year below Marie in school, as I recall. But you'd never have known it. One of those girls who has an instinctive knowledge of her sexuality and what to do with it.' His smile became sheepish. 'I'm afraid, Carole, mention of that name has brought back the party of which you speak in full Technicolor detail. Yes – preserving my sister's honour was not my sole occupation that particular night.'

'Diana Milton?'

He nodded, with that mixture of apology and pride that men usually apply to their sexual conquests. 'Yes.'

'But I understood she was at the party with her boyfriend.'

'They had a row. And I – took advantage of the opportunity.' A nostalgic smile. 'Diana was . . . aah.

Lost touch, I'm afraid, when I moved away from Worthing. I wonder what happened to her.'

'Probably ended up a dumpy housewife and mother, like every other teenage fantasy figure,' suggested Gaby.

'You're probably right.' Her uncle chuckled wistfully. 'Funny, I hadn't thought of her for years until you mentioned the name, Carole.'

'I also asked Libby Pearson about Howard.'

'Hm?'

'Well, we're only talking – what? Less than a year before Marie married Howard? Libby had never heard of him. She certainly had no recollection of him being at that party.'

'Well, no, Howard moved in different circles. He knew us all because he worked with Dad, and we lived above the shop. His thing for Marie was a kind of secret between them, until suddenly it all came out in the open and they got married.' His face scrunched up with the effort of recollection. 'I don't know. Maybe Howard was there.' Another chuckle. 'Quite honestly, now you've introduced the name of Diana Milton into the conversation, I'm having a bit of difficulty remembering anything else.'

But Carole wanted him to remember other things. 'What I find odd about this whole situation . . . you know, Gaby being stalked by Michael Brewer—'

'But is it exactly stalking?'

'I don't know what else you'd call it, Gaby.'

'No,' Robert agreed. 'And most of the other descriptions are even less attractive.'

'But what I don't understand,' Carole went on, 'is, if Inspector Pollard is right and Michael Brewer did kill Howard and Bazza, then *why*?'

'From what I've gathered from Pollard, his feeling is that Bazza's murder was done simply to shut him up. He knew too much about what had happened to Howard.'

Gaby wanted explanations too. 'The bit I still don't get is how Bazza got involved.'

Her uncle grinned ruefully. 'I'm afraid that is down to your brother. Your father was stuck at the hotel without means of transport. Phil immediately thought of the one person he knew who could produce a car at short notice. So he rang Bazza.'

'Are you saying that he was in on the plot to kill Dad?'

'No. Pollard thought he must have been. That's why Phil was pulled in for questioning. The inspector could not imagine that anyone existed in the world whose first thought when a taxi was needed would be to get a friend to steal a car.'

'Ah. Shows he doesn't know our Phil.'

'No. I'm afraid your brother was never quite the sharpest knife in the drawer. But, anyway, Phil's off the hook, at least so far as the murder's concerned. He could still be in trouble over his involvement with Bazza's car-stealing activities, but I doubt if Pollard'll bother to pursue that.'

'All right,' said Carole, as though drawing a meeting to order. 'We've established why Michael Brewer needed to kill Bazza, but I still can't see what he had against Howard. I can believe he spent thirty years in prison, dreaming of revenge. But why should he take his revenge on Howard Martin? What had Howard ever done to him?'

'Ah.' Robert Coleman was silent for a moment, making a decision. He looked tenderly at Gaby before opting to go ahead. 'Gaby, this may not be pleasant to your ears, but I'm afraid it's something you're going to have to know some time, and since the topic has come up, I think I may as well tell you now. What I'm about to say doesn't reflect particularly well on your dad, but that doesn't change the fact that he was a good man and, in his own way, he loved you very much.'

He allowed himself another silence, before continuing. 'As you know, your dad worked for my dad, in a fishmonger's in Worthing. After he married your mum – and after our dad had died and the business had been sold – Howard and Marie went off to Worcester, where he continued working in the same line. But when he was young, he also had a hobby that was . . . well, not strictly within the law. He had a shotgun, and he liked to go off after rabbits and hares, pheasants too. Some of them might appear in our dad's shop, though he never knew where they came from.'

'Uncle Robert, are you saying my dad was a poacher?'

'Yes.'

'Well, that's no reason to murder anyone.'

'Not in itself, no. Trouble was, Howard used to go shooting on the estate where Mick Brewer worked as a gamekeeper.'

'That's still no reason—'

'Wait for it, Gabs. Will you please wait until I've finished? The night Mick killed Janine Buckley, your dad was out shooting on the estate. He saw the car being torched.'

'He saw Michael Brewer actually setting fire to it?'

'Don't know if he was close enough to be sure it was him, Carole. But he saw the fire erupt. And he called the police – anonymously, he didn't want to draw attention to the fact that he'd been trespassing for the purpose of poaching. But, Gabs, if your dad hadn't seen that car go up, it could have been years before the remains were found. Mick had driven it into a very remote part of the estate. He was reckoning it'd be a long time before anyone found the car, and by then getting any forensic detail from the site would have been a lot more difficult.'

Robert Coleman sighed and took a reflective sip from his beer glass. 'So you see, that's why Mick Brewer wanted revenge on poor old Howard. So far as he was concerned, it was your dad who got him convicted.'

'But, Uncle Robert, there's no logic to that. Dad didn't know who he was—'

He silenced her with an upheld hand. 'Gabs, if you spend thirty years in prison plotting revenge, I don't think logic is at the top of your priorities.'

'No. Perhaps not,' she conceded.

'All right,' said Carole. 'Let's accept that as the reason why he targeted Howard, but why's he after

Gaby? She wasn't even born at the time of his first murder.'

In a hopeless gesture, Robert Coleman put thumb and forefinger to the bridge of his nose and screwed up his eyes. 'I don't know. Who knows how a mind like his works? Gaby belonged to Howard, maybe that's all there was to it. Or maybe she represents what he couldn't have – the child Janine Buckley was carrying when . . . I'm sorry, I don't know. All I do know is that Gaby's in danger.'

He sat back in his chair and Carole suddenly noticed how tired he was looking. Recent events had taken their toll on his sister and niece, but Robert's own supportive role had also been exhausting. Being the family rock was not an easy job.

'Still,' he said, 'it'll soon all be over.'

'What do you mean?'

'I mean, Carole, that Mick Brewer can't be at large for much longer. The police are closing in on him, they must be.'

'They've been looking for him since last October.'

'Not very hard. Someone who missed the odd appointment with his probation officer isn't worth a lot of manpower. But now they're really looking for him.'

'In West Sussex?'

'Yes. He's somewhere down there. Got some hideaway, I'll put money on that. Don't worry, they'll find him.'

'And then he'll be charged with both murders?' asked Gaby.

'Bound to be. The police have got DNA evidence. He definitely killed your father and Bazza.'

Gaby sighed wearily. 'Oh, I can't wait till they get him. I don't think I'll ever relax again, until I know that Michael Brewer is safely back behind bars.'

Her uncle reached across and patted her hand. 'Won't be long. And till then, we need to see that you're kept somewhere very secure, somewhere where he'd never think of looking for you.'

'But not Fethering,' said Carole.

Robert Coleman grimaced. 'No. Not down there again. I didn't know about that little excursion until after it had happened. I'm afraid, of all the places in the world to go to be away from the attentions of Michael Brewer, Fethering is the last one I'd have chosen.' He looked fondly across the table at his niece. 'Maybe you'd be best to come back to Essex with me. Stay with Marie. As I say, the police are keeping an eye on her up there.'

But Gaby shook her head. 'No, I'll be fine in London. I've got friends I can stay with.'

Or I've got an even better idea, thought Carole.

Chapter Thirty-One

Like everything else in Robert Coleman's club, the ladies' room was severe with no frills. But it was spotlessly clean. As she washed her hands, Carole thought about their host's abrupt departure. Just as they had reached the foyer from the dining room, he had received a call on his mobile.

Its content was clearly urgent because, with the most perfunctory of farewells, he left the two women alone. Robert Coleman's anxiety about his niece's safety seemed to have suddenly evaporated. Though, of course, that could mean that the news he'd had related to the capture of Michael Brewer, which would in turn mean that the threat to Gaby was at an end. Carole, not for the first time in her investigative career, felt deeply frustrated. Why were the police – and by extension, their intimates like Robert Coleman – always so uncommunicative about how their enquiries were progressing?

Gaby came out of a cubicle to join her at the washbasin, and Carole decided the moment had arrived to put forward her plan. 'A coincidence that your grandmother's name came up at lunch.'

'Why? Oh, I do feel terribly guilty about her, you know.'

'I do know. Which is maybe why the coincidence is one that you could turn to your own good.'

Gaby looked at her curiously.

'I was talking to Stephen this morning, when he came to fetch some stuff from his house . . .'

'Yes?'

'And he's terribly worried about you.'

'I know.'

'He wants you away from here, away from all your familiar haunts, away from anywhere where that man might be able to find you.'

Tears trickled from Gaby's eyes. The relentless stress still had a hold on her.

'I suggested you should go to France.'

'France?'

'To see your grandmother.'

'On my own?'

'No, not on your own. You'd need someone with you for security.' A silence. 'Stephen thought it was a very good idea.' A longer silence. 'Well, do you think it's a good idea, Gaby?'

'Yes. I think it's a brilliant idea.'

When Jude told her that Gita Millington had returned to London, Carole could not suppress a feeling of unworthy glee. Jude had anticipated and noted this, but did not comment.

She was quickly brought up to date with developments on the case: Michael Brewer's appearance in Gaby's flat the previous night, and Carole's brainwave as to where the girl should go.

'I agree. A great idea. Because, apart from anything else, if anyone is going to know the whole history of the case, then it's going to be Gaby's grandmother. She was around when the whole thing happened.'

'Exactly, Jude.'

'So, what are you planning to do? Drive down to the South of France? Or fly?'

'Flying'll be quicker.'

'Have you booked a flight?'

'Stephen's PA has sorted it out. They're holding two seats for a Gatwick flight to Bordeaux at 7.55 tomorrow morning. But I didn't want to confirm until I knew the names of the passengers.'

'What?' Jude looked perplexed. 'Come on, Carole. You know Gaby's name. And I assume you know your own.'

'No. I wanted to check first that you'd be willing to go with Gaby.'

'Me?'

'It's logical. I'm in touch with Stephen and Marie and Robert. You're not, really. So if anything happens here, I'll be able to keep in touch with developments. Besides . . .' said Carole, with one of her hard-nosed moments of self-knowledge, 'I think Gaby might be more relaxed with you than she is with me.'

'All right.' The bird's nest of blonde hair quivered with the vigour of Jude's nod.

'And there's another thing.'

'What?'

'You speak good French.'

Jude acknowledged this was true.

'Because you told me once that you lived in France for a couple of years.'

'Yes, you're right. I did. And I'm sure, once I'm actually there, the language will come back.'

Carole had been hoping for more details of her neighbour's sojourn in France, but as so often happened with Jude, the moment for elaboration was quickly past, and the conversation moved on.

'One small matter, Carole.'

'Yes?'

'Who's actually paying for this little jaunt?'

'Stephen.'

'Well, it's logical that he should pay for his fiancée, but—'

'He's paying for both of you. Anyway, it's not just a jaunt for you. You have a job of work to do.'

'As what?'

'Gaby's minder.'

After their lunch with Robert, Gaby had gone into work for the afternoon, the reasoning being that if Michael Brewer was trying to get at her, he wouldn't choose to do so in a busy office full of theatrical agents. She found being in her work environment a blessed distraction; arguing with tight-fisted theatre managements brought out her competitive instinct and drove all other thoughts from her mind. At the end of the day she stayed late, her colleagues supporting her with a few glasses of wine, until Stephen came to pick her up. He was her minder overnight in the Fulham house, and he drove her down to check in before seven o'clock at Gatwick's North Terminal.

Stephen had explained their plans to Inspector Pollard, who approved them. The police effort was concentrated in West Sussex as the noose tightened on Michael Brewer and, so far as he was concerned, the further away Gaby Martin was, the better. He made sure they all had the relevant contact numbers, and gave the expedition his blessing.

Gaby had also phoned the retirement home near Villeneuve-sur-Lot where her grandmother was in residence, and told them she'd be coming to visit. The receptionist she spoke to was delighted at the news because the old lady was not getting any stronger, and she kept talking about her granddaughter and her impending marriage.

Jude was waiting for them at the North Terminal. Carole had driven her up from Fethering in the Renault, but, with characteristic economy, had avoided the cost of parking and just dropped her at Departures.

Stephen kissed his fiancée an anxious goodbye, and returned to his latest work crisis. Neither of the women needed to check bags in. They only had hand luggage: a neat executive rectangle for Gaby, and a squashy patterned fabric bag for Jude. The plan was only to be away two nights. Gaby had booked them in to the small hotel in Villeneuve-sur-Lot that the Martins always used during their visits to *Grand'mère*.

They sat down for a coffee and waited for their flight to board.

'God,' said Gaby. 'I cannot wait to be on that plane. It'll be the first time I've felt really safe for ages.'

The flight time was only an hour and thirty-five minutes, but quite a lot was achieved in that time. Though, apart from their therapy session, Gaby had only met Jude once – the evening in the Crown and Anchor when they had been joined by Phil and Bazza – there was no reticence between them. As ever, Jude's easy presence elicited confidences. (The knowledge of this was one of the reasons why Carole had decided that her neighbour should take on the role of minder for the trip.) In spite of the age difference, Gaby soon found herself talking as though to a contemporary she had known since childhood.

'The back's been all right, has it, during all the nightmares of the last few weeks?'

'Yes. It's amazing, isn't it, Jude? When I was under minimal stress, my back packed in. Now I'm facing real disasters, real threats, I haven't got a twinge.'

'I don't find that at all amazing. Your body, or your mind, or the two of them working as a conspiracy, have decided that you need all your strength. Your being incapacitated at the moment wouldn't serve any useful purpose. It wouldn't remove the stress.'

'No, that's only going to happen when Michael Brewer's been caught.'

'And when the stress is removed, that's when you're going to have to be careful.'

'About my back?'

'About your back or any number of other physical symptoms which may try and get at you. If you think about it, Gaby, for the last few weeks, you've been putting so much energy into just keeping going, you've shut out all kinds of negative thoughts simply in the cause of survival. When the pressure's off, you'll be very vulnerable.'

'I know what you mean. Sometimes in the past, after a sustained period of pressure, I've gone down with a fluey cold.'

'And you've rather enjoyed that, haven't you?'

Gaby grinned, acknowledging Jude's intuition. 'Yes, it's been very welcome. Snuffling round the flat, watching daytime television and endless mushy DVDs.'

'But you only got ill when you'd completed the project in question, didn't you? Illness has never stopped you from doing some work you had to, has it?'

'No.' Gaby chuckled. 'Why are we such idiots? Why do we let our bodies play these tricks on us? We should be able to recognize their little games. Yes, I've been stressed. When the stress is off, I will be ill. And yet, every time it happens, it's like a big surprise. Same as when there's snow in England. Everyone has always known it's a possibility, but there's still total shock when it happens, and the whole country grinds to a halt.'

'Illness is often a very good medicine, Gaby.'

'Mm.' The girl was thoughtful. 'Maybe Mum needs a nice comfortable little illness, to make her less uptight.'

Jude shook her head. 'From what I hear of your mother, she controls things by being uptight, by being publicly uptight.'

'I know what you mean. Everyone knows she's nervy. You only have to meet her to know that.'

'So instantly you have less expectation of her. I think that's how your mother has insulated herself from the unpleasantnesses of life.'

'You're right. She seems very self-effacing and unassertive.'

'But in fact the entire life of her family revolves around her.'

Gaby nodded, as if at the confirmation of something she had always suspected.

'Power,' Jude continued, 'comes in different packages.'

There was a silence. They both looked out of the plane window. The wide green fields of northern France – so different from the greens of England – rolled away below them. Both felt that little burst of liberation that flying can bring.

'Do you know what changed your mother, Gaby?'

'What do you mean – "changed her"?'

'Carole met someone who'd been at school with

her. Apparently, as a teenager, she was an incredibly lively personality, real life and soul of the party.'

'Mm. I've always suspected there was another side to her, but I've never seen it.'

'So what do you think changed her?'

'I don't know. Getting married? Having kids?'

'A lot of people regard getting married and having kids as very positive experiences.'

'Yes, but I don't think Mum and Dad really got on very well. I mean, as a kid, you're really too close to know what's going on, but it was a very tense atmosphere to grow up in. I don't know what was wrong between them, but there did seem to be something.'

'Did your mother ever talk to you about it?'

A firm shake of the head. 'Emotions were a no-go area. Mum just got on with life, though always with the air that the whole business was a major imposition.'

'Did she ever talk about the time when you were born?'

'No. But I get the impression it was round then that something changed for her. Maybe it was the worry because I was premature. Maybe she got post-natal depression. I should think that's the most likely explanation. But of course, it's something that she would have kept quiet about. And I don't think Dad would have been aware there was a problem – he was a sweet man, but not very sensitive to the feelings of others. I'm sure Mum would never have gone to a doctor or anyone like that for help. I've thought about this quite a lot, Jude, as I'm sure you can imagine, and that's the best explanation I've come up with.'

'Sounds reasonable,' said Jude, although she had thoughts of her own on the subject. 'And your father – was he a dominant presence around the house?'

'No. He was very quiet. I mean, he went out to work and came back in the evenings and watched television. But he was kind of . . . I don't know. I wasn't very aware of him when I was growing up.'

'When you came to see me about your back, you mentioned that your father had had bowel cancer.'

'Yes. What, eight years ago, I suppose? But he made a complete recovery – survived so that he could be murdered,' Gaby added bitterly.

'You also told me that when you'd got stomach trouble, you'd been worried that it might be bowel cancer presumably because of the family history of the disease?'

'Yes, but it was all right. I talked to Mum and— ooh, look at that big lake down there!'

Jude duly looked in the direction of the pointing finger, wondering whether the interest of the lake was sufficient to justify the change of subject. Anyway, she wasn't going to be side-tracked so easily.

'Gaby – sorry to go back over unpleasant memories – but thinking back to when your father's body was found in Epping Forest . . .'

'Yes?'

'Carole told me everything that happened. It must have been terrible for you when the body had been found, but still not identified.'

'It was, awful. Because part of me thought, so a body's been found in Epping Forest. It's not the first and it won't be the last. But, because Dad hadn't gone back home the night before, another part of me was having all these awful fantasies which, sadly, turned out to be true.'

'Yes. Carole said that initially the police weren't sure how they were going to identify the body.'

'True. Talk of DNA matches, which was another complication, because Phil had gone missing that night, but it turned out all right. They identified Dad from his dental records and the scar where he'd had the cancer surgery.' Gaby shuddered. 'Oh God, I never want to live through anything like that time again. The thought of something like that happening to Steve.'

'It's not going to happen to Stephen,' said Jude, automatically reassuring, while her mind raced, building up a new edifice of logic which she longed to share with Carole.

Their conversation broadened and they started to talk about France. Clearly visits to Villeneuve-sur-Lot had featured large in Gaby's childhood, and she spoke of her *Grand'mère* with deep affection.

'How long has she been living there?'

'She moved fairly soon after Grandpa died. I suppose I was about five or six. I don't really remember him very well.'

'But he was English, your grandfather?'

'Oh yes.' Gaby hugged her knees. 'I've always loved France. I always feel a part of me belongs here. I'm longing to show my favourite places to Steve.'

'I'm sure you'll soon be able to when all this is over.'

This reminder of her situation cast a slight shadow over Gaby, so she determinedly moved the conversation on. 'You said you lived in France for a while, Jude. What were you doing?'

And, because Gaby had asked a direct question, Jude told her. She was still telling her when they arrived at Bordeaux Airport. Carole would have killed to have been there.

Chapter Thirty-Two

You're being stupid, Carole Seddon told herself. It was something she had told herself many times over the years. Indeed much of the interior duologue of her entire life had been castigating herself for some real or imagined lapse. Such was the penalty of being a post-war middle-class woman.

But that morning on Fethering Beach, Carole wondered whether she really was being stupid. She had picked up Gulliver as soon as she got back to High Tor from Gatwick, and taken him straight out for his walk. He was, as ever on the beach, in canine nirvana. He scuttled around on missions of desperate urgency, whose purposes he kept forgetting. He faced up to the threats of weed-fringed plastic bottles, and boldly challenged strips of khaki bladderwrack to single combat.

The day was sunny, June getting seriously warm as July approached.

And Carole Seddon could not get out of her head the feeling that she was being watched.

*

Stephen's PA had arranged a hire car for Gaby and Jude to pick up at Bordeaux Airport. Gaby drove. She knew the way to Villeneuve-sur-Lot; it was a route she had followed many times before. And, besides, Jude had not been behind the wheel of a car for a long time.

The first part of the journey was motorway, not that different from a motorway in any other part of the world. The service stations, stacked with knick-knacks and souvenirs, were different from English ones, but not as different as when Jude had last been in France. She regretted the homogenization of Europe. How far would you have to go at the beginning of the twenty-first century to find somewhere that felt foreign?

Things improved when they left the motorway and pottered through small towns, past distant vineyards and dusty fields of tobacco. Painted signs to restaurants offered untold gastronomic delights. But even in the countryside, the multinational logos on petrol pumps and hoardings diluted the sense of being abroad. Jude thought back wistfully to her first visit to France as a teenager, when everything, from the bedclothes to the taps, to the sugar-lumps, to the bitter black chocolate, to the previously unheard-of yoghourt, to the corrugated iron cars, breathed the excitement of foreignness.

Conversation with Gaby continued to flow. They didn't talk of anything momentous, just their shared love of France and the uncompromising arrogance of the French.

They stopped in Villeneuve-sur-Lot to pick up

some fruit as a gift for *Grand'mère*, and found they had arrived on a busy market day. This felt more authentic, the profusion of fruits and vegetables on the stalls, the variegated beans and greens, the strings of plump purple garlic. Huge slabs of unknown cheeses were on offer, giant skin-straining sausages, olive oil in plastic mineral water bottles, infinite arrays of herbs and nuts. Yet even these were not as exotic as they once had been. Most of the goods would be available in any large English Sainsbury's.

There were a few individual touches. Live chickens with trussed legs, and rabbits shut in tiny boxes defied English sensibilities. A few ancient crones sat over trays offering handfuls of meagre root vegetables. But set against these survivals of peasant tradition were the omnipresent stalls selling replica designer T-shirts, CDs, DVDs and the other initialized technology of the twenty-first century. The music that blared from the speakers was American.

Nor could the crowd of sellers and buyers be characterized as uniquely French. The ethnic mix was much more varied since the last time Jude had been at a French country market. Tall deep-black North Africans and women in saris mingled with the locals. In the crowd, bright Romany skirts balanced the severity of Muslim headgear.

Jude knew the development was good, that the only future for the world lay in the celebration of its diversity. But she could not suppress a slight nostalgia for the days when countries felt different, when you could recognize a person's nationality by their footwear, before the ubiquitous trainer achieved world domination.

As she had the thought, she smiled inwardly, thinking of the robustness and lack of political correctness with which Carole would undoubtedly have expressed not dissimilar views.

The retirement home was an old farmhouse, most of whose land had been long sold off, one of those four-square symmetrical buildings with tall windows flanked by neat white shutters. This, at least, thought Jude, as Gaby brought the car to rest in the visitors' car park, is archetypally French.

The smartly suited woman on reception instantly recognized Gaby, and, once her travelling companion had been introduced, a flurry of voluble greetings ensued. Jude was pleasantly surprised by how readily her understanding of French returned, though she feared fluency of speech might take longer. Despite the unhappiness in which her two-year sojourn in France had ended, she still felt a charge to be back among French speakers.

The receptionist said she'd better show them the way to Gaby's *'belle Grand'mère'*, because she had changed rooms since the girl's last visit, 'now she cannot move around so well.' Gaby would probably see a change in the old lady, 'But she still manages, and is grateful for every day she remains with us.'

The room was at the back of the building. The bed was empty, a wheelchair stood by the French windows, and a blanket-wrapped *Grand'mère* was propped up in a lounger on a small balcony that looked over fields to the dark green edge of a forest. The balcony could be completely glassed in, but that warm June day one window was open and the room was full of the smells of outdoors.

'Your visitor has arrived, Madame Coleman,' said the receptionist, as Gaby rushed forward to greet her grandmother, wrapping the frail body in her plump arms. After much excited banter and the ceremonious handover of the fruit from Villeneuve-sur-Lot, Jude was introduced. There seemed no problem in her being there. No explanation of her presence was requested or given.

When she got a chance to look at the old lady, she was struck by the family likeness, emphasized by *Grand'mère*'s fragility. Marie's prematurely pinched face was uncannily reflected in the old lady's age-eroded features. The short-sighted vagueness in the faded eyes was also reminiscent of her daughter. And the tight perm – she was evidently very well *soignée* by the staff at the home – echoed her granddaughter's bubbly curls.

Grand'mère and Gaby spoke instinctively in French, but Jude did not have too much difficulty in keeping up. She was surprised by how on the ball the old lady seemed. From what Carole had passed on of Marie and Robert's opinions, she had been expecting someone totally blind and in the last stages of Alzheimer's. But, though physically very frail and with limited vision, there seemed to be nothing wrong with the old lady's mental processes.

And for her, there was no question of her

granddaughter being called 'Gaby'. Her birth name was Pascale, and that is what she was called. Gaby did not argue; she had learnt over the years not to challenge the old lady's formidable will.

After the initial affectionate greetings, *Grand'mère* said how shocked she had been to hear of Howard Martin's death. 'It is terrible that once again the happiness of our family should be darkened by the shadow of murder.'

'Yes.' As she agreed, Gaby looked straight at Jude. There was a lot of meaning in her look. Although they had never discussed the subject, the girl knew that Carole and Jude had taken more than a casual interest in the two recent murders and were desperate for explanations. Part of Carole's motivation for the trip had been removing the threat to her future daughter-in-law, but the two neighbours were also caught up in the fascination of the puzzle for its own sake. Gaby's look at Jude seemed to say that she knew all that, and that she too wanted to use the visit to find out a few basic truths about her tainted family history.

'You know, *Grand'mère*,' she said firmly, 'that the police believe Michael Brewer killed Dad.'

'That is the way the police think, in every country. Here in France too. The person who has committed one murder is the first suspect when another murder occurs.' She sighed. 'Yes. It is thirty years. He has served his sentence for his wickedness, and now is the time for the next stage of the process. Evil cannot be hidden for ever. He caused so much pain to our family.'

'Did you know Michael Brewer well?' The question was instinctive; only once she'd spoken did Jude realize that her interposition into a family discussion might be out of place. But *Grand'mère* seemed either not to notice or, if she did, not to mind.

'Oh yes. My husband was very keen on shooting. Mick was a gamekeeper. They would shoot together. Often they would make a night of it, drive round, I think, in Land Rovers with big lights, you know, to shoot rabbits. And then they would go off somewhere to drink. Mick had drink stashed away somewhere on the estate. Always, after my husband went off shooting at night with Mick Brewer, he came back drunk. I did not approve of this.' The asperity in the last line reminded Jude of the old lady's reputation for strictness on moral matters.

'And I gather Howard would also sometimes shoot with Michael Brewer too?'

'Yes. He was often one of the party. But then, I don't know, they fell out. Howard I think took advantage, went shooting somewhere without Mick's permission perhaps.'

That tallied with what Carole had reported from her conversation with Robert Coleman. 'And I heard that Howard was shooting the night Janine Buckley was killed. He alerted the police to the burnt-out car.'

The old lady did a small, quintessentially Gallic, shrug. 'That is quite possible. I do not know the details. All of that period is a blur of great unhappiness. With my dear husband dying and – I was very ill,' she admitted. 'For a long time I was very ill. There is much from that time that I have done my best to forget.'

'*Grand'mère*,' asked Gaby, 'if you knew Michael Brewer so well, were you surprised when you discovered that he was a murderer?'

'But of course. You do not expect this from anyone, least of all from a family friend. But I do not claim to understand the workings of evil – what drives someone to do something of that nature. Only the good Lord can give an explanation of such terrible things.'

'But you knew Janine Buckley too, did you?'

'Oh yes. She was a very close friend of Marie. She was often in the house. They were two very lively girls, so high-spirited, so talkative, so naughty.'

'Naughty?' echoed Jude.

'Yes, she was always supposed to be doing her school homework, supposed to be behaving like a good Catholic girl, but her head was only full of thoughts of pop music and of boys.' The disapproval in *Grand'mère*'s voice was strong. 'Fortunately, Marie behaved herself in that respect. She knew what was expected of a good Catholic girl. Sex before marriage is always wrong.'

Gaby's eyes evaded the stern look that accompanied this. *Grand'mère* sighed. 'If only poor Janine had remembered that. I often think, if Janine's parents had brought her up as a better Catholic, she would still be here with us today.'

Jude, with Gaby's tacit approval, continued the questioning. 'Given the fact that Marie was so high-spirited and lively, wasn't it rather a surprise when she suddenly gave up on her A-levels and married Howard?'

'Perhaps, in one way. In another way, it made perfectly good sense. I don't think you can understand, Jude, what it was like for all of us after the murder of Janine Buckley. A terrible shock. We all felt it. Poor Robert had to be so strong. He was the one who held the family together at that time. My husband died very soon after the murder. I was distraught and had to be hospitalized, but Marie also was totally shattered. It changed her personality entirely. At that age, you think only about having fun, you don't have a care in the world, you think perhaps that you can have relationships with boys with freedom, with no strings. Even though this is wrong, that is what a lot of young people think.

'And then this thing happens in your life. Suddenly you're in the real world. It is brought home to you that sex can lead to pregnancy. Even worse, you discover that, in extreme circumstances, pregnancy can lead to murder.'

Had Carole been there, she would have recognized *Grand'mère* almost echoing Robert Coleman's words.

'So for Marie,' the old lady went on, 'it was a terrible time. She had no security. Her father was dead, her mother in hospital. Everything she had believed in had been proved to be false. And there was Howard, a good man who had been holding a candle for her for a couple of years. He loved her and wanted to marry her. For Marie, he represented security, and a chance to get away from Worthing.'

'Did you approve – and would your husband have approved – of Howard as a husband for your daughter?'

Another little Gallic shrug, with an equally characteristic 'Phwoof' noise. 'We had always known he was an honest man, and a good Catholic. He had been in the shop working with us for a long time. It was maybe a surprise when Marie said she wanted to marry him, but she was happy about the idea and it seemed a good solution.'

'And do you think it continued to be a good solution?' It was Gaby who asked this question, and, from her lowered voice, Jude got the feeling it was the first time she had talked to her grandmother about the state of her parents' marriage.

'Howard was a good man and a good Catholic. I think he made your mother as happy as anyone could have done. After Janine died, Marie – well, she shut off so much of her personality. She was never really complete after that.'

Jude heard a discreet cough behind her. A uniformed nurse stood in the doorway. 'I am sorry, but I am afraid I must take Madame Coleman now for her bath.'

Gaby's offer to help her grandmother into the wheelchair was politely rejected. The indignities of age were to be witnessed by professional carers, not by family members.

As they were leaving – with promises that they'd be back the following morning – Gaby noticed a photograph in the array on *Grand'mère*'s dressing table. She and Stephen smiled out, caught in a relaxed moment at some friend's wedding. 'Ah, I'm glad to see we've made it into your gallery.'

'But of course you have. Your fiancé is a fine-looking man. A little serious perhaps, but I think you can be relied on, my dear Pascale, to lighten him up.'

Jude would have been impressed by the accuracy of this assessment, had her attention not been distracted by another framed photograph in the display. This showed a considerably younger Howard and Marie Martin, standing outside an open front door. Howard was less bulky than in later years and almost handsome in his old-fashioned way. Marie looked washed out, but triumphant. In her arms she bore the source of their pride, a tiny, shawl-swaddled baby.

Across the white strip at the bottom of the photograph was handwritten: 'Pascale comes home – 27 May 1974.'

Jude, intrigued by the lack of symmetry in the spaces between the '27' and the 'May' and the 'May' and the '1974', looked more closely.

Chapter Thirty-Three

Carole had done a big Sainsbury's shop that afternoon. On her return to High Tor, Gulliver treated her as though she had been absent for a decade. She told him not to be silly, which rather offended him, because he knew that, as a Labrador, it was his God-given mission in life to be silly.

The answering machine registered a couple of messages, but when Carole played them back, there was just the click of contact and nothing else. She checked 1471 for the last caller. The call had been made from a mobile she did not recognize. Probably a wrong number.

It was unsettling, though.

Jude enjoyed her food. She was not pretentious about it. She could wolf down fish and chips out of the paper or the Crown and Anchor's dish of the day cottage pie with as much relish as a gastronomic menu, but she was a great believer in trying whatever was on offer. So when Gaby said she knew a rather good restaurant in Villeneuve-sur-Lot, Jude was very definitely up for it.

The interior was of stone and felt as though it had once been part of some monastic foundation, an impression which was reinforced by the thick bare wood of the tables and the heavy wrought-iron chandeliers. But any image of gloomy austerity was quickly dispelled when they opened the menu.

Over a convivial *kir royale*, they ran through the gastronomic possibilities. They felt the panic of people with only two days to do justice to the entirety of French *cuisine*. Lunch that day had been a wasted opportunity, a snatched sandwich in transit from the airport. Lunch the next day was doubtful. Gaby had entertained the possibility of taking *Grand'mère* out somewhere with them, but the old lady's frailty precluded that. So really they only had the two evening meals for certain, and then they'd be back in England.

With this in mind, neither stinted herself on the ordering. As a starter, Gaby went for the *Feuilleté d'Escargots au Beurre Vert Bordelaise*, while Jude chose the *Terrine de Foie Gras de Canard Rôti tout Natural Cuit en Terrine* with a *Confiture d'Oignon au Vin Vieux*. Their main courses were, respectively, *Poitrine de Pigeonneau Rôti, les Aiguillettes au Foie Gras, Poêlée de Girolles* and *Filet d'Agneau Rôti à l'Ail Confit, Mongettes de Vendée Facon Cassoulet*. The wine list was familiar territory to Gaby, and she homed in on a white and red Bordeaux from a chateau Jude had never heard of and would never have found unaided. The choice proved excellent.

Jude had things she wanted to say to Gaby, but not on this gourmet's hallowed ground. In deference to the fury of the *patron* when another guest's mobile phone had trilled, she switched hers off, determining to ring Carole when she got back to her hotel room.

She and Gaby settled down to enjoy the meal, and to talk about any subject in the world that didn't involve murder.

The telephone rang as Carole was washing-up after her austere boiled-egg supper.

'Hello?'

The male voice at the other end sounded surprised. 'Who is this?'

'My name's Carole Seddon. Who did you want?'

The man rang off.

Carole stood for a moment by the phone in the hall. This was very stupid. She was getting paranoid. Just a wrong number. And no, the voice hadn't sounded like the one she'd heard on Gaby's mobile outside the Crown and Anchor the previous week.

Still she lingered. Inspector Pollard had given her all his contact numbers. But no, this was no reason to bother him. It was nothing.

Be good to tell Jude about it, though. Jude would advise her whether she should do anything. And Jude might have something to tell about her encounter with Gaby's *Grand'mère*. Yes, call Jude, that was the answer.

But the mobile was switched off. Carole was given

the option of leaving a message, but she couldn't think what to say that wouldn't sound melodramatic or hysterical. And Carole Seddon had always had a great aversion to sounding melodramatic or hysterical.

She replaced the phone and went to wash down the kitchen surfaces. Then she'd have to take Gulliver out to do his business on the bit of rough ground beyond her back garden.

'Gaby,' said Jude, when they reached the landing of their small hotel, 'I want to talk.'

The girl looked at her watch. 'I was just about to call Steve, but we're an hour ahead, he'll be up for a while yet. So, fine.' And she meekly followed Jude through into her bedroom. Her manner suggested that she'd been expecting this, that she'd enjoyed their wonderful meal in the knowledge that it was an oasis in the bleak landscape of reality, and that they could only stay there for a limited time.

She sat on the bed, and looked across as Jude closed the door and lowered herself into a wicker chair.

'What is it then?'

Jude looked her straight in the eyes. 'Gaby, how long have you known that Howard Martin was not your father?'

Gaby put her hands to her face, then swept them back and upwards, as though she were wiping it clean. But she wasn't crying. Her voice was steady as she replied, 'I think I've always had my suspicions.

Particularly growing up with Phil. We were so different physically, apart from anything else. People at school kept saying, "I really can't believe you two are brother and sister." And I always said, "Well, we are." Because then I thought we were.'

'And when did you know for certain that you weren't?'

'Seven, eight years ago.'

'When Howard had the bowel cancer.'

Gaby nodded. 'I was desperately worried about it. You know, cancer. The Big C. I read up quite a lot on the subject, and the evidence was there in black and white. Something called HNPCC, I particularly remember. Stood for Hereditary Non-Polyposis Colonic Cancer. But basically, if there's a family history of bowel cancer, then the chances of getting it go up by some horrendous percentage.'

'So you told your mother about your anxieties?'

'Yes. And she saw the state I was in, and she knew that she could remove my anxieties instantly. So, rather than let me suffer any more, she swore me to secrecy, and divulged the secret she had kept for more than twenty years.'

'And did the knowledge change your attitude to your father – to Howard, that is?'

'No. In a way, it made sense of a lot of things. He had brought me up like his own, and he loved me – in the rather undemonstrative way he had of loving. In many ways, it was good for me to know. I stopped feeling guilty about the lack of instinctive closeness I felt to Howard – and to Phil, come to that.'

'That, of course, was the other thing that told me you weren't Howard's child.'

'What?' asked Gaby.

'It was something Stephen reported to Carole. And then I checked it with you yesterday.'

'Did you? I didn't realize I was being checked out.' But she didn't sound too affronted.

'When your father – or rather Howard's – body was found, there was talk of it needing to be identified by a DNA match.'

'Yes, I remember.'

'And you said that might have been a problem because that night Phil had gone missing. You never even thought that you yourself might be able to supply a sample, because you knew that you and Howard didn't share any DNA.'

'Ah.' Gaby clapped her hand across her mouth in mock-horror. 'What a giveaway. Dear, oh dear. Thank God I'm a theatrical agent, and have no aspirations to be a criminal mastermind. I'd be really crap at that.'

Jude grinned, not so much because the joke was funny, more to put the girl at her ease, before she asked, 'Do you know if Howard knew you were not his?'

Gaby screwed up her lips in doubt. 'I've really no idea. It all goes back such a long way. And the subject wasn't one that was going to spring up spontaneously in that family set-up. You've no idea how uptight my mum can be. It was very rarely that we talked about family matters, and as soon as she'd given me one scrap of information, she'd clam up.

'Still, I have no complaints. Howard Martin was a good man. And, in a way . . . this sounds an awful thing to say, but it's true, so I'll say it.' She looked defiantly at Jude. 'The fact that Howard was not my father has made the last few weeks easier, you know, since his death. I mean, I've felt shock and all that – and pity for what happened to him – but I haven't felt as emotionally bereft as I would if he really was my birth father.' She seemed to have shocked herself by what she'd said. 'Maybe the impact just hasn't hit me yet. I don't know. But, in all the ghastliness that's been going on for the past few weeks, I haven't really missed him.'

Gaby grinned, as if levity could somehow take the seriousness off their conversation. 'Of course, it casts an interesting light on my mother, too, doesn't it? Puts rather a big question mark over her, wouldn't you say?'

'Yes. There is another thing too, Gaby . . .'

'Oh God, I don't know how many more "other things" I can take. I've had a bellyful of "other things" over the last few weeks.'

'You know you were born premature?'

'Yes. Of course I do.'

'Have you ever looked at that photograph on your grandmother's dressing table, of you as a baby with your parents, outside your house in . . . Worcester, I suppose.'

'Well, obviously I've seen it, but it's been part of going to see *Grand'mère* for so long that I can't really say I've ever given it very close scrutiny.'

'When you came to see me about your back, Gaby . . .'

'Yes?'

'. . . you gave me your date of birth.'

'Twenty-fifth of March 1974.'

'Exactly. But that photograph of your grand-mother's says you came home from hospital on the twenty-seventh of May 1974.'

'OK. Two months in the premature baby unit – that'd be about right.'

'Except that wasn't what had originally been written on the photograph.'

'What?'

'A little piece of paper has been stuck over the month after the first two letters – "M" – "A". I'd put money on the fact that under the paper you'd find the "R – C – H" of "March".'

'Oh, my God.'

'Yes. Your grandmother's eyesight's so bad she would never have noticed the change to the date. But what it means is that that photograph was taken two days after your birth.'

'No!' This revelation had been news to Gaby, and she was slowly trying to piece together its implications. 'So . . .?'

'So when you were born, you were a healthy, full-term, baby. The story of you being premature was only put about to explain the length of time between Marie and Howard's wedding and your birth.'

'Just a minute, just a minute. You're going too fast. So what have I got here? Not only was Howard not my father, but also my mother was pregnant by another man when she married him – is that right?'

'Yes, Gaby. That is exactly right.'

Chapter Thirty-Four

It was dark but still warm when Carole took Gulliver out through the back garden gate on to the scrap of rough ground behind her row of cottages. When they went by this route, the dog was always gloomy. He knew that the excitement of lead-rattling was not the precursor of a proper walk, just a quick functional trip out for him to empty his bowels.

This he did with quiet efficiency, and Carole was about to take him back to High Tor when a tall figure stepped out of the shadows between her and her garden gate.

'Sorry to interrupt you.' The voice was rough and unmistakably familiar.

'Excuse me,' said Carole, in a voice of steely gentility. 'Could I please get back to my house?'

'Yes. But only to leave the dog. Then I'm afraid you must come with me.'

Carole just had time to register that she was talking to someone who knew about dogs. If Gulliver was left wandering around outside, his barking would soon raise the alarm. Inside High Tor, he'd just settle down to snuffle in front of the Aga, reconciled to yet another of his mistress's unexplained absences. But then, of course, someone who'd been a gamekeeper would know about dogs.

As she led Gulliver and Michael Brewer through into her kitchen, Carole wondered what she could do to escape her predicament. Rush to the phone? Rush out into the street screaming 'Help!' Such behaviour wasn't her usual style, but she was hardly in a situation to care about style.

As if anticipating her thoughts, Michael Brewer said, 'I do have a gun in my pocket. I don't want to use it, but if that becomes necessary, I won't hesitate.'

'What do you want me to do?'

'You have to come with me.'

'Where?'

He didn't even bother to answer. 'We'll go in your car. You'll drive.'

'Well, can I just put out some food for the dog?'

Michael Brewer allowed her to put out the dog food, then ushered her through into the hall.

'And don't try calling anyone on your mobile phone.'

'I don't have a mobile phone,' said Carole icily, as he escorted her out through the front door.

She had hoped there might be someone on the road, someone to whom she could call out to for help, someone who would rescue her. But no, the good folk of Fethering kept sedate hours. Every curtain along the road was discreetly closed.

And of course there were no lights in Woodside

Cottage. When Carole needed her most, Jude was in another country.

Like an automaton, following the man's instructions, she opened the garage door. Any thoughts of leaping into the Renault and driving off without him had been anticipated. At gunpoint he saw her into the driver's seat; keeping the gun trained on her, he moved round the car and jumped in beside her.

Touching her with the gun to remind her that it was still there, Michael Brewer told her to keep within the speed limit and drive on the Fedborough road out of Fethering.

Doing as she was told, Carole thought back to the modus operandi of the other murders. In the form of the Renault was she conveniently providing her own inflammable coffin?

Chapter Thirty-Five

There was little traffic on the roads. Each sweep of headlights coming towards Carole was a potential rescuer, but she could not think of any way to communicate her plight. In cars people become anonymous; nothing shows the passions, conflicts or dangers of the drivers or passengers. Carole was helpless, all she could do was follow the instructions of the silent man with the gun beside her.

They by-passed Fedborough and joined the main A27 towards Worthing for a short distance. Here there were more cars flashing past, but Carole still had no way of making contact with them. Then Michael Brewer directed her to take a left turn up a small road into the Downs. This snaked its way past a few straggling houses, then deeper into uninhabited countryside. Eventually he ordered her to stop in front of a railed metal gate that gave on to an open field.

He got out of the car, but, while he unlocked the gate, his gun was still pointing at her. Anyway, Carole, almost immobilized by terror, was not contemplating escape. They were in the middle of nowhere. However fast she ran, he would quickly catch her, and her situation was already grim enough; she didn't want to antagonize her captor further.

Michael Brewer ushered her through the gate, and closed it behind the Renault. Once again there was a potential opportunity. Carole could have put her foot down on the accelerator and shot off into the unknown. But she had no idea what lay ahead, and Michael Brewer did. He wouldn't have taken the risk, if he thought there was any way she could get away from him.

Getting back into the car, he told her to switch off the lights and drive along the track ahead. At first Carole demurred, saying she wouldn't be able to see where she was going, but he would not tolerate argument. And, sure enough, her eyes did soon accommodate to the darkness. There was enough watery moonlight to pick up the chalk whiteness of the compacted farm track, dry and hard after the recent hot weather.

After maybe a mile – it was difficult in her distracted state for Carole to judge distance – she was instructed to turn off down a less defined and more overgrown track which led towards a small coppice. At the edge of this she was told to stop. Ahead stood a tangled mass of brambles, briars and other dense undergrowth.

Michael Brewer again got out of the car, and moved to one side of the thicket. Carole couldn't see exactly what he was doing, but she got the impression he was pulling at something, a rope perhaps.

The effect was astonishing. Like a transformation scene in a pantomime of *Sleeping Beauty*, the mass of undergrowth slid to one side, revealing a narrow opening into the wood.

Michael Brewer didn't get back in the car, but motioned her with his gun to drive ahead. There wasn't far to go. Less than ten yards in, she found herself in a small clearing, surrounded by trees. Behind her, she was aware of the masking undergrowth being replaced. Suddenly, the depths of the wood were very dark.

The driver's side door was opened, and Michael Brewer gestured at Carole to get out of the car. She stood in the lightless wood, wondering whether this would be the last place she would see in her life. She had expected dankness, but a soft breeze filled the clearing with the smell of the fields. In spite of its closeness, so far as Carole was concerned, that fragrant open space could have been on another planet.

Michael Brewer reached down behind a tree, and produced a large yellow torch. He switched it on, keeping the beam focused down on the ground. He gave a flick of his head, indicating that Carole should follow him. Since her capture, he had said nothing beyond giving directions.

She did not have to follow him far – the whole coppice was probably no more than fifty yards across – then the torch beam revealed the ragged outlines of an old building. Once perhaps a shepherd's hut, its roof had long ago fallen in, the walls had crumbled, and bricks had been displaced by encroaching trees and their disruptive roots. Little of the remaining structure was more than waist-high.

The beam of light directed Carole to follow Michael Brewer through an old doorway into the space inside. So unworried now was he by the chance of her escaping that he put the gun in his pocket and passed her the torch, as he bent down to shift a couple of rotting but substantial rafters that lay across the floor. Then he kneeled, and seemed to be scrabbling for something in the dirt.

There was a metallic clang as he pulled upwards, rising to his feet as he did so. He took the torch back from Carole and directed its beam. The light showed a battered metal trapdoor lifted back to reveal a brick-walled opening in the floor, and steps leaning downwards.

At last, he said something. 'Not the kind of place you'd imagine to have a cellar. I thought there was a good chance it'd still be here after thirty years. Nobody comes this way.'

And the torch beam flicked across to Carole, showing her the way down. Michael Brewer, staying at ground level, lit the individual steps as she descended, then flashed light across to an old chair. 'Sit there.' Carole did as she was told.

But he didn't follow her down. The cellar smelt musty and damp, and she got no impression of what else was in the space.

'I'll be back soon. Just got to check we've covered our tracks.'

And Michael Brewer slammed the metal trapdoor

down. Carole heard above her the scrape and thud of the massive rafters as they were replaced over the opening.

The darkness in the cellar was total.

Grand'mère looked frailer when Jude and Gaby arrived at the home the following morning. They got there about ten, but were told they should have come earlier. 'I sleep little. I am awake from five.'

She was not on the balcony, but propped up on her bed by a heap of cushions, and she seemed peevish. Maybe she was in pain, suffering from one of the many infirmities of age. She greeted Gaby warmly, but kept Jude at a distance.

The reason soon became clear. 'I had a call from my dear Robert last night. He wanted to see that I was well, and that you had arrived safely. And he was a little cross with me, you know.'

'Why cross, *Grand'mère*?'

'Well, cross with you too. He says it is bad for me to talk of the past, that dreadful time when Janine Buckley died. And he is right. What we spoke of yesterday did make me upset. Last night it is a long time before I got to sleep. And then, as I say, I wake so early. I do not sleep well now. I long to have a proper night's sleep.'

Gaby tried to shift the old lady's mood with talk of her wedding plans, but here again she met with a reproof. 'It is not good that you marry in an Anglican church. You have a duty to your Catholic faith.'

'I lost my faith, *Grand'mère*. A long time ago.'

'That is no good, to say that. You speak of your faith as if it were just a handkerchief or something, that you can lose and it does not matter. If you are brought up a Catholic, you can never properly lose your faith. It is always a part of you.'

'Well, it doesn't feel like a part of me.'

'I do not like you to say that, Pascale. You should have a proper Catholic wedding ceremony. But even if you don't do so, you must give me your word that, if you have children, they will be brought up as good Catholics.'

'I don't think I *can* give you my word about that, *Grand'mère*. Steve and I have talked about these issues in great depth, and it would be hypocritical for us to—'

Seeing the rising fury in the old lady's face, Jude decided that a tactical change of subject might be in order. 'Did Robert say whether the police have recaptured Michael Brewer yet?'

'No. My son does not talk to me of such things. He knows they upset me, and cause me to lose sleep.'

To Jude it seemed that Robert served the same function for his mother as he did for his sister, insulating them both from the unpleasant realities of life.

But Gaby decided that some realities had to be faced. '*Grand'mère*,' she said, 'I know that Howard Martin was not my real father.'

The old lady's reaction was so instinctive that it

could not have been anything but real. 'Don't be ridiculous. Of course he was your father.'

'But—'

'Oh, I know it is common for young girls, when they are in their adolescence, to have fantasies that they were born to something greater than the lives they lead, but, really, Pascale, you are no longer a child. You should no longer be having these silly thoughts.'

'*Grand'mère*, it is important that . . .'

But, cued by a small shake of Jude's head, Gaby did not pursue her argument.

'Howard was your father. There is no question about that.' This was spoken with the unbreakable conviction of someone who totally believed it, or who, a long time ago, had made herself believe it.

If she was going to find out more, Jude knew she had to risk the old lady's displeasure. Her son did not want her to be upset by talk of the early nineteen-seventies, but there were still details Jude needed to find out. And her window of opportunity with Madame Coleman was closing fast.

'I know that Robert does not want you to talk about unhappinesses of the past, but there is one question that I do have to ask you.'

'You may ask. I, however, retain the right not to reply unless I wish to do so.'

'Very well. Knowing what you do of Michael Brewer, do you think he was capable of killing Howard?'

Her reaction was as immediate as the response to

Gaby's doubt about her real parenthood. 'I have no doubt in my mind at all. Michael Brewer is the nearest I have ever encountered in a human being to pure evil.'

Chapter Thirty-Six

There was now a light on in the cellar, and Carole could take in its contents. Michael Brewer kept things tidy, there was a monasticism about the place, or maybe it was an echo of another kind of cell. From hooks on the walls hung old threadbare waterproofs, cartridge belts and rabbit snares, dating from the occupancy of thirty years before. But since his release from prison Michael Brewer had stocked the room with boxes of tinned food, packs of bottled water and Camping Gaz cylinders. He could live out a long siege here. He also had a mobile phone and a modern laptop with a large supply of battery packs. There were also plastic crates filled with cardboard files. Stuck on the wall in front of a makeshift desk were press cuttings covering the murders of Howard Martin and Barry Painter.

He had not left her on her own long. In less than an hour Carole had heard the shifting of the rafters on metal overhead, then the trapdoor had opened and he came in and lit a gas light.

Immediately she had asked him, 'Why have you brought me here?'

'I want to get at Gaby,' he replied. 'You are my way of getting at Gaby.'

'Gaby is in France, visiting her grandmother.'

'Oh.' He scratched his beard, assessing the information for a moment. 'How long is she away for?'

'Just two nights. Back the day after tomorrow.'

'Maybe she will have to come sooner.' He looked at his watch. 'Maybe you will ring her in the morning.' He thought about this, too. 'No, better perhaps to wait till she comes back. We don't want to set any alarm bells ringing.'

'So you are proposing that I should stay here for the next two days?'

He looked straight into her affronted eyes. His were hazel and full of pain. 'I have stayed here for much longer than that.'

'Why? Why do you hide away here?'

'What would be my chances out in the open? What would be my chances if the police caught me?'

'All right, I take your point.' There was a silence. 'So it's Gaby you're really after? I'm just a means to an end.'

'Yes, I need Gaby.' Then he added, chillingly, 'I need her to finish what I've started.'

They said little more that night. Even though he passed her an old sleeping bag, Carole didn't think there was much prospect of her eyes closing. But he said he was about to turn the light out. 'And don't try anything.'

'I won't. Just tell me one thing. Suppose I do manage to lure Gaby to come to you . . .'

'Yes?'

'What would happen if I managed to communicate the danger to her? If she brought the police along with her?'

'Then I would have to kill you,' said Michael Brewer, as though it were the most reasonable answer in the world.

They both felt down after they left the retirement home, Gaby because of the disagreements with her grandmother about Catholicism, and Jude because she had the feeling she had screwed up an opportunity and lost a valuable source of information. Neither felt up to another lavish meal, so they settled down outside a small café in Villeneuve-sur-Lot for a *croque-monsieur* and a glass of wine.

Their jaunt felt as if it was nearly over, and they were both crestfallen by how little they had achieved. Nor had they heard anything from Inspector Pollard. Both had expected a call to say that Michael Brewer was now safely in custody, but there had been nothing. For Gaby, the prospect loomed of returning to England the following day with her life still under threat.

So when Jude's mobile rang and the caller announced himself as Inspector Pollard, she was ecstatic with relief.

But only briefly. 'I was just wondering, Jude,' he said, 'if you have any idea where your friend Carole Seddon might be?'

'So far as I know, she's at home. In Fethering.'

'I tried calling her there, but got no response.'

'Well, she could be out shopping. Or she has a dog. She takes him out for a lot of walks.'

'She's not with the dog.'

'What do you mean?'

'I got one of the local coppers in Fethering to check on her house. The dog was barking, so he gained access. The mess on the kitchen floor suggested that the dog had not been let out at all since yesterday.'

Panic flickered within Jude. 'But Carole would never leave Gulliver that long. Something must have happened to her.'

'That was rather the direction in which my thoughts were beginning to move.'

'Do you think Michael Brewer may have got her?'

'I wouldn't go that far.'

'Are you any nearer to finding him?'

'I can assure you, Jude, that we are making every effort to track him down. We're pretty sure he's gone to ground somewhere in West Sussex. I don't think it'll be long now before we get him.'

'I hope not.'

'Robert Coleman's helping us out. Apparently he was brought up in the same area as Michael Brewer, knew him pretty well. He's down in Worthing now advising the local force. We'll get him,' said the Inspector grimly. 'In the meantime, I'll contact Mrs Seddon's son. He may have some idea where his mother's gone. Or do you think she's likely to have been in touch with her ex-husband?'

'Very unlikely, I would have said.'

'Oh well, it might be worth giving him a call. And how's Gaby bearing up?'

'She's fine. With me right now. Do you want to speak to her?'

'Not necessary. Just give her my good wishes . . . and tell her I think at the moment France is the safest place she could be.'

Gaby had caught the alarm in Jude's responses and looked at her, eyes wide in fear. 'What's happened?'

Jude brought her quickly up to date. 'There's only one thing I can think of to do. We must pay another call on your grandmother.'

He refused to talk, just sat there playing patience. Carole thought she would be driven mad by the intermittent slapping of the cards as he turned them. Michael Brewer was used to waiting. Waiting a little longer, at this stage of his life, was small hardship.

Apart from the silence, he didn't treat her badly. He offered, even cooked, food, and was discreetly unobservant when she had to leave the cellar to relieve herself. There was no way Carole could feel relaxed in the presence of a double murderer, but – apart from holding her as a prisoner at gunpoint in a remote cellar – he did nothing else to add to her stress.

Michael Brewer had the air of a man whose plans were nearing completion.

*

Grand'mère was not pleased to see them again. She might have been happy at another visit from her granddaughter, but not bringing this other woman, this inquisitive other woman, with her.

Jude was too concerned about Carole's safety to be over-sensitive to the old lady's feelings. 'I'm sorry, this is important. A friend of mine is in danger, and you may have the information that could save her.'

'I do not understand this. Why do you wish me to—?'

'Don't worry about the "why"? Just answer my question.'

'But this is very ill-mannered. Pascale, will you let this woman talk to your grandmother in such a way?'

'Please, *Grand'mère*. As Jude says, it is very important.'

The old lady still looked put out, but said grudgingly, 'Very well. What is it you wish to know?'

'It goes back to something you said when you were talking about your husband going shooting with Michael Brewer—'

'Oh no. Why are we always back to this Michael Brewer? It was a terrible time for me and my family. As Robert said, you should not be bringing such memories back to me.'

'Please, Madame Coleman. Please. Just think back to that time once more.'

'Please, *Grand'mère*.'

'Oh very well.'

'You said that, when your husband went out shooting at night-time with Mick Brewer, they used to drink.'

'Yes. I told you this.'

'You mentioned that Mick "always had drink stashed away on the estate".'

'Yes, but this was thirty years ago. Why is it now so important?'

'Just take my word for it, it is. Did you mean that there was a place on the estate where your husband and Mick Brewer used to go to drink.'

'I believe there was. From what my husband said, Mick Brewer had a secret place, somewhere that his employers did not know about, where he kept a supply of drink, where he could hide for a few hours if he felt like it. I believe also –' Madame Coleman's thin lips set in a *moue* of disapproval – 'that Mick Brewer also sometimes took girls there.'

'And did your husband ever say where the place was? Did it have a name?'

The permed head shook with the effort of recollection. 'No, I don't think . . . or was there a name? It is so long ago that . . . Oh, the name was strange, I remember that. Something to do with illness or . . . It had to do with – Oh! Yes. Leper. Leper's something – Leper's Copse. Yes, that was the name. Leper's Copse.'

Chapter Thirty-Seven

In the hire car outside the home, Jude rang the number Inspector Pollard had given her. She tried again and again, but it was resolutely engaged.

'Don't worry.' Gaby took out her mobile. 'Pollard said Uncle Robert was working with the West Sussex police. I'll see if I can get through to him.'

She called a number from the phone's memory. 'Uncle Robert, hi. It's Gaby. No, I'm fine. Listen, we've been talking to *Grand'mère*, and she may have given us a lead on where to look for Michael Brewer. It's something she remembered from ages ago when Grandpa used to go shooting with him. I think it's somewhere on the estate – or near the estate where Michael Brewer used to work. And it's called Leper's Copse.'

She listened to her uncle's response, said goodbye and turned to Jude, her eyes gleaming. 'I think we're nearly there. Robert's going to check with the local police. If anyone knows Leper's Copse, or if it's on any map of the area, then I think everything's going to be all right.'

*

There is a finite time that one can stay at a pitch of total panic, and Carole had found she was, if not relaxing in the cellar, at least occasionally thinking of subjects other than her own imminent demise. It was after six in the evening. Another night of enforced proximity to the murderer approached. Then, the next day, Gaby and Jude would be back. That would be the time of danger, when Michael Brewer required something of her. Until then, in spite of her discomfort, frustration and sheer boredom, Carole reckoned she would be relatively safe.

He had left the cellar again, on another unexplained mission. He took the mobile phone with him. If he was going to use it, Carole deduced, then it must be to call someone who represented no threat. The police, she knew, had means of pinpointing the exact location from which a mobile call had been made. Which must mean that Michael Brewer had some friends out there, at least one person who he knew would not betray him.

Because she was on her own, and bored, Carole felt empowered to check out her enforced environment. She looked at the laptop first. A sudden spark of hope glowed within her. Maybe he'd linked it up to the internet. Maybe she could send out an email for help.

But such optimism was soon crushed. Even with her limited knowledge of computers, Carole knew that an internet connection required a phone line of some kind. Maybe he could hook the laptop up to his mobile, but he had that with him. And, anyway, she had to admit to herself, she'd never sent an email in her life. She wished she hadn't been such a Luddite when it came to new technology.

She tried summoning something up to the laptop's screen, but it remained blank. A password was needed to access Michael Brewer's computer files.

But his other files – the cardboard ones in the plastic boxes – there was nothing to stop her from accessing those.

For a moment she was assailed by middle-class doubt. After all, the files were his private stuff. She shouldn't really be snooping at the personal documents of—

Carole quickly realized the stupidity of that knee-jerk reaction; after the way Michael Brewer had treated her, she owed him nothing. She picked up a cardboard folder and opened it.

The contents were computer printouts, newspaper cuttings and handwritten notes. From a quick glance it was clear that all the material related to the murder of Janine Buckley.

Carole heard the scrape of the rafters above, and went quickly to replace the file in its box. Too quickly. In her haste she dislodged the whole box from its shelf. Files and their contents scattered over the cellar floor.

Carole looked up guiltily towards the oncoming torch beam.

'What the hell do you think you're doing?' asked

Michael Brewer harshly. 'Have you been looking at that lot?'

In his hand was the gun, and in his eye a look of murderous intent.

Chapter Thirty-Eight

'Time you moved,' said Michael Brewer. He stepped back into the outside world. Even though dappled through the trees, the early evening June light dazzled Carole as she climbed the steps out of the cellar.

'Get in the car.'

'No, I don't want—'

'Get in the car!' His voice snapped out like a whip-crack. The gun was still following her every movement.

Trembling, she inched towards the Renault, which had not been moved since she left it the previous evening. Instinctively, she went towards the driver's door. But was that right? The bodies of the other strangled victims had been found on the back seats.

It seemed ridiculous even to be thinking of such niceties, but Carole found herself asking, 'Do you want me to sit in the back or the front?'

Michael Brewer opened his mouth, but the reply never came. Suddenly he hurtled forward, as a body burst through the trees and cannoned into his back.

The gun went flying. As Brewer scrabbled forward

to recapture it, the other man leapt on to his back. With huge relief, Carole recognized the white hair of Robert Coleman.

'I've got you now, Mick,' he shouted. 'Give yourself up. The police are on their way!'

Brewer was the bigger man. And the stronger. He'd kept himself in shape – perhaps he'd had to keep himself in shape – in prison, and kept tough during the past few weeks of living rough. He lifted himself off the ground, and turned around at speed, shaking off the lighter Robert Coleman, who crashed to the ground.

Ignoring the gun, Brewer pounced on his winded opponent. Grabbing hold of his lapels, he dragged the man up off the ground. But Robert was not completely out of commission, and managed to thump a punch into Brewer's midriff.

The taller man recoiled, but did not lose his grip. 'You bastard, Robert!' he gasped. 'Don't worry, though, now you're going to get what's coming to you!'

Keeping one hand tight on the lapel, he drew the other one back for a punch, but Robert was quick enough to butt his head hard forward. He was too short to catch Brewer's chin, but the thud into the base of the throat made the man choke and release the jacket.

Surprised by his sudden freedom, Robert Coleman swayed, and at that moment Michael Brewer's bunched fist caught him hard on the mouth. He flew backwards into the undergrowth. Brewer moved forward to tower over him.

Carole Seddon had never hit anyone over the head with a gun before, but since she had picked the thing up, she thought she might as well have a go. She'd never have a better opportunity – or a more important one. Holding the gun's barrel tightly, she reached upwards, and brought the butt crashing down on to the back of Michael Brewer's neck.

The effect was very satisfying. He tottered for a moment, then crumpled to the ground, emitting a sound like the air being forced out of a paper bag, and lay immobile.

'Thank you very much, Carole,' said Robert Coleman through his bleeding lips. 'You really helped me out there.'

'My pleasure.' She waved the gun ineffectually in her hand. 'I'm afraid I'm not used to handling these.'

'No reason why you should be. I'll take it.'

She handed the weapon across, and looked down at the recumbent figure of the ex-prisoner. 'So what do we do with him? Wait till the police arrive?'

'We could do that,' said Robert Coleman, 'but we might have a long wait.'

'What do you mean? What are you going to do with him then?'

'I think he might suffer an accident. Get caught in the blaze when he torches your car.'

'What are you talking about? Why would he want to torch my car?'

'He wouldn't. But to the police that would look like what he'd been trying to do.'

'But, Robert, why should my car be torched?'

'Because it will have your body in the back of it, Carole. Strangled. Just like all the others.'

Chapter Thirty-Nine

The shock was so great that Carole could hardly get her thoughts together. 'You mean the police aren't coming?' she asked feebly.

'No. I was told where to look for him, and it was expected I would pass that information on to the police. And I will. But not yet. I'm afraid the police will arrive here in Leper's Copse too late to find evidence of the last act of Mick Brewer's murderous career.'

'So you killed Howard?'

'Had to. He was going to meet up with Mick. I couldn't risk Howard hearing what Mick had to tell him.'

'And it was you who set up the car to take Howard from the hotel?'

'Phil did it, actually. But I knew Bazza would do what I told him. He owed me a few favours for the lenient treatment I'd arranged for him when he came up before me as a magistrate. But, once I knew the police were after him – well, he'd become a security risk.'

'A security risk who conveniently came down to Fethering to see you?'

'Yes, disposing of him was easy. Bazza would always do exactly what I told him.'

'And that business of the DNA link to Michael Brewer – you left the playing cards at the crime scene?'

'Of course. A pack of his I'd had since before he was arrested for Janine Buckley's murder.'

'So what about that murder?'

'What about it?'

'Did you do that too?'

Robert Coleman smiled a crooked smile. But it wasn't just his bruised lips that made it crooked, and triumphant. 'You'd never find any proof linking me to that. Whereas there was lots of proof linking Mick. Fingerprints on the stolen car, fingerprints on the petrol can.'

'How did you arrange for that to happen, Robert?'

'It's amazing what people will do when they aren't on their guard. I stole the car, having previously fixed to meet Mick. Siphoned out a lot of fuel, so that it ran out. Got Mick to fill it up from the can in the boot. Then took him off to get drunk, just the two of us, back at his place. I put something in his drink, so he was soon out cold. Then I spilled a bit of petrol on his clothes, and left him. I was the only alibi he had – he thought I'd stayed with him overnight, but no, I'd left about nine. I'd already arranged another alibi for myself for the rest of the evening, so when the police questioned Mick, it sounded like he was lying. Anyway, he was too drunk and drugged to have a very clear recollection of that night.'

'Then you picked up Janine Buckley, drove into the estate where Mick Brewer worked, strangled her and torched the car?'

He shrugged. 'It had to be done. *Maman* would not have survived the shame.'

'What shame? Oh, my God! Are you saying that the baby Janine Buckley was carrying was not Michael Brewer's? It was yours?'

His cocksure silence was quite as articulate as a spoken confirmation.

'So that night – the party at your parents' house in 1973, when Janine Buckley and Michael Brewer went upstairs, when you were supposed to be with Diana Milton . . .'

'Sorry about that. I couldn't resist it when you mentioned Diana Milton at lunch at my club. I saw a chance of putting you off the scent. If I was screwing Diana all night, there was no way I could have been with Janine.'

'So it was you and Janine who were the couple?'

'One couple.'

'What do you mean?' The realization came to Carole like a thunderclap. 'Marie and Michael Brewer? Michael Brewer is Gaby's father!'

Robert Coleman didn't confirm this either, but Carole knew she had hit on the truth. All kinds of potential ramifications spread from this one revelation, but she wasn't really in a position at that time to pursue them through to their logical conclusions.

'But why, Robert? Why did you do all this?'

'To protect *Maman*. She was so frail emotionally,

and her Catholic faith was so strong. She could not have coped with the knowledge that I had got a girl pregnant. She could certainly not have coped with the knowledge that Marie was pregnant. *Maman* had very high standards.'

'You mean she couldn't have condoned an unwanted pregnancy, but she would have condoned murder?'

'Of course not.' He was shocked by the suggestion. 'She never knew about the murder, or never knew of any family involvement in it. Whereas there was no way she could have remained ignorant of the pregnancy.'

'Or the two pregnancies. It was your idea that Howard Martin should marry Marie?'

'Yes. He wanted that more than anything, so he was happy. To me the marriage seemed a good way of covering up her lapse. Everything was confused round that time, with my father dying and *Maman* having her breakdown. I was afraid Marie might have a breakdown too, so I told her that she would be safe with Howard. They married quickly, and moved away to Worcester. Then I encouraged them to announce that Gabs had been born prematurely. It all made sense.'

'But did your killing Janine Buckley also make sense?'

'Of course. I was about to start my career in the police force. The last thing I needed at that stage of my life was a woman and child in tow.'

He spoke with the logic of the criminal. Anything was justified, so long as it served his ultimate purpose.

'But how did you get Marie to agree to marry Howard?'

'She was in shock after Janine's death. And,' he said with the confidence of an arch-manipulator, 'Marie has always done what I told her to.'

Carole began to understand the full scale of the trauma which had changed Marie from the bright and lively schoolgirl to the frightened neurotic of her later life.

'So did Marie know that you killed her friend? And that you had framed the father of her child for the murder?'

Robert Coleman smiled another irritatingly complacent smile. 'Marie has always been very good at shutting certain things out of her mind. And I have always seen it as my duty to protect her from the . . . nasty things of life.'

The strength of Robert Coleman's control over his sister was becoming clear. Marie might even have worked out that it was he who had killed her husband. But that was one of the areas where she would not have allowed her mind to go.

'Just as you always protected your mother from the unpleasantnesses of life.'

'Yes. I could never have done anything to upset *Maman*.'

'Or never have allowed her to know about things that might upset her?'

'Precisely.' He smiled again, then said abruptly,

'Still, enough of this. I'm afraid it's time to stage Michael Brewer's final murder. Sorry you've got involved, Carole – though it is, it has to be said, completely your own fault. If you and your chubby friend had not stuck your noses into other people's business, then your quiet little life in Fethering could have continued uninterrupted. But, as it is, I'm afraid you have got involved, and there's no way I can allow you to live to tell the tale.'

Carole made a sudden dash for the entrance to the copse, but it was pathetic how short a distance she had travelled before Robert brought her down in a rugby tackle. 'No. Sorry. You're not going to get away.'

Trying another escape seemed pointless. She looked hopefully at Michael Brewer's prone form. He was breathing, but showed no sign of consciousness. My own bloody fault, thought Carole savagely. Why did I have to hit him so hard?

'Do you have a petrol can in the car? I have my own supplies, but . . .'

There was no point in denial. Robert Coleman would find the can in the boot, anyway. So much for prudence, thought Carole. Though she'd never had cause to use it, she'd always carried a spare can of fuel in the Renault. In case of emergency. Now it was going to be the cause of an emergency.

The keys were still in the ignition. Robert Coleman ripped them out and opened the boot. Then he opened the two doors on the driver's side of the car. He unscrewed the top off the petrol can, and began to pour.

'No,' said Carole instinctively. 'Not over the upholstery.'

He laughed at the incongruity of that, but she couldn't see the joke.

Robert Coleman splashed some more petrol over the Renault's bodywork, then cruelly over Carole's front. He trickled a trail across the ground to where Michael Brewer lay, and upended the remains of the can over the unconscious man. The drenching did nothing to bring the victim round. Brewer lay there, unmoving except for his shallow breathing.

Robert Coleman took a disposable gas lighter out of his jacket pocket. 'After I've set fire to the car, I'll leave this beside dear old Mick. Serve him right, the police will say. Hoist with his own petard.'

He faced Carole. 'Get in the car.'

Numbly, she moved towards the open driver's door.

'No, in the back.' They were the most chilling words she had ever heard.

The petrol fumes were disgusting, burning the back of her throat as she slid inside the Renault. She felt the slime of the fuel penetrating her skirt. In her mind the fatuous thought formed that she'd never get the upholstery properly clean again.

Robert Coleman slammed the front door shut. She looked up at him through the other door, the only opening in her private crematorium.

'Aren't you going to strangle me?' she asked. 'Like the others?'

He chuckled. 'Only if you try to escape. Otherwise, I don't think I need bother.'

He slammed the remaining door shut. The petrol fumes were so intense that Carole could hardly breathe.

Through the car window, she could see Robert Coleman hold up the lighter as he backed away towards Michael Brewer's body.

'I'll light it from the edge,' she could just hear him saying with a silly giggle. 'Don't want to get my fingers burned, do I?'

Robert Coleman had already destroyed Michael Brewer's life once. And now, as he stood beside the man's prone body, he prepared to do it a second, more permanent, time. He flicked the lighter flame into life.

Carole Seddon held her breath, not only to shut out the fumes, but also as though in some way that might lessen the inevitable agony.

What happened next was so fast as to be almost a blur. Michael Brewer's body jerked into action. From the ground his legs scissored and slammed against Robert Coleman's knees, sending him flying away from the petrol-soaked area.

Immediately, Michael Brewer was on his feet, grabbing his quarry once again by the lapels, lifting him up like a rag doll and slamming his back against the broad trunk of a tree. As Robert Coleman sank dazed to the ground, Brewer reached in and removed the gun from his pocket.

Keeping the gun trained on his enemy, he backed towards the Renault and opened the back door.

Carole Seddon burst out of her malodorous prison, and in sheer relief pressed herself against her rescuer. Fumes of petrol rose around the two of them.

Chapter Forty

Robert Coleman's eyes opened, and took a moment to focus on the tall man with a gun who faced him. 'What are you going to do, Mick? Kill me?' The question was almost a sneer.

'Don't think I haven't thought of it. Often, over the last thirty years. And don't think I'm not tempted now.'

He pointed the gun at the heart of the crumpled man on the woodland floor. Carole saw the finger whiten as it tensed against the trigger, and she could feel Michael Brewer's desire for the purgation that this death would bring.

A long moment elapsed. Then, his inner demon vanquished, he lowered the gun. 'But no. I want you to be punished as I was punished.'

Half an hour later, Carole and Michael Brewer stood in the petrol-reeking clearing. Robert Coleman was safely tied up in the old cellar, with the metal lid firmly closed on him. It was nearly dark. Through the gaps in the trees they could see the daylight dwindling over the Downs.

'So what do we do now?' asked Carole. 'Call the police?'

His response was an automatic and distinctive 'No!'

'But this is a police matter. We're both witnesses to what Robert tried to do to us. He should be in custody.'

'I'm not questioning that, but I'm not going to let a policeman get near me.'

Carole tried to soothe the paranoia she saw in his eyes. 'Michael – Mick, it's all right now. Your nightmare's over. We know the truth. And we can tell the truth. At last justice can be done.'

'I'm still not going near the police,' he insisted doggedly.

'Mick, the police are on your side. On the side of justice.'

He barked out a bitter laugh. 'You dare tell me that? I had my bellyful of the police thirty years ago. On the side of justice? They didn't listen to me. They believed what was easiest to believe. The police stitched me up.'

'It was Robert Coleman who stitched you up.'

'The police helped. They wanted me sent down. They were part of the conspiracy with all the other authorities: the judges and barristers who convicted me; the judges who rejected my appeals; the prison officers who made my life hell. I'm never again going to get close enough to the police for them to arrest me. Because experience has taught me that, with my record, that's the first thing they would do.'

Carole wanted to argue, but she knew that the long build-up of distrust would not easily be shifted. And, in some ways, she could not help feeling sympathy for his view. Given what had happened in his life – spending thirty years under a brutal prison regime for a crime he did not commit – Michael Brewer was entitled to be paranoid.

'That's presumably why you didn't approach the police after Howard's murder? You must have known Robert had done it.'

'Of course I did, but there was no way I was going to put myself at risk. Robert's framed me once, and he's quite capable of framing me again. Come on, if it came to a choice between him and me, who would the police go for? Ex-copper and bloody Justice of the Peace? Or the lag who's just done a thirty-year stretch for murder?'

Carole could see his logic, and part of the reason for his instinct to hide himself away. She felt enormous pity for the man, the way his trust in everything had been destroyed. 'Listen,' she said, 'what you need is legal representation.'

'Oh yes? A fat lot of good that's done me in the past. The lawyers are all part of it. They're all in it together.'

'Mick, I used to work for the Home Office—'

'So you're part of the conspiracy too, are you?'

'No. But I did make some useful contacts while I was there. In particular, a solicitor called Jerome Clancy. Have you heard of him?'

An abrupt shake of the head.

'Well, he's got quite a reputation for taking on cases of miscarriage of justice. Given what we've now got on

Robert Coleman, I'm sure he'd take you on. With Jerome Clancy behind you, you wouldn't need to worry about the police.'

'I'm still afraid. If they get me alone in a police station, they'll charge me with something. I'll never get out of there.' The eyes flickered with fear.

'You will, Mick. I know you've had a lousy deal in the past. But believe me, your life is about to change.'

'Huh.'

He did, however, finally agree that she should ring Jerome Clancy in the morning, and try to arrange a meeting. And Carole agreed that she would stay another night in Leper's Copse, because the police were probably on the lookout for her too, and might force her to lead them to Michael Brewer.

'All right,' she said. 'I'll stay. But I have to make one phone call first.'

'Not to the police?'

'Nothing to do with the police, I promise. In fact, it might well take the police pressure off, stop them searching for me as well as you. I've just got to call a friend to tell her I'm all right.'

Jude was in the hotel in Villeneuve-sur-Lot, just getting ready for bed, when her mobile rang.

'Carole! Thank God. I've been so worried about you.'

'Well, this is just to say I'm fine.'

'Where are you?'

'I can't tell you that. All be clear tomorrow, I promise.'

'But, Carole . . .'

'I can't tell you anything else.'

'Oh. All right, I'm sure you know what you're doing. Listen, shall I ring Inspector Pollard? He said I should get in touch the minute I heard anything from you.'

'No. Under no circumstances tell Inspector Pollard you've heard from me.'

'What about Gaby and Stephen? They're desperately worried about you too.'

Which was rather gratifying, really, Carole thought. 'Tell them I'm OK, but don't tell them anything else.'

'I can't tell them anything else, you're being so cagey. Ooh, and what about David?'

'What about David?'

'Stephen says he's been terribly worried about you. Can Stephen tell him you're all right?'

'Yes,' said Carole, somewhat surprised, 'I suppose he can. One other thing . . .'

'What?'

'Gulliver. That poor dog has been stuck in High Tor since—'

'No, he hasn't.'

'What?'

'A local policeman checked on your house because Inspector Pollard was worried about you. Gulliver is apparently living it up as a guest of Fethering Police Station.'

After she finished the call, Carole grinned at Michael Brewer. 'Probably as well I'm lying low.

Apparently the police have taken my dog in for questioning.'

Their next task was to try to clean themselves up and get out of their petrol-soaked clothes. Michael Brewer proved to have quite sophisticated domestic arrangements in his primitive hideaway. He had a tank of water for washing in, and an array of soaps and detergents.

He also found some clean clothes. 'Be a bit big for you, I'm afraid. And perhaps a bit masculine. I've only got one dress' – he looked wistful – 'and that's been here for over thirty years.'

'Marie's?'

He nodded. 'Little disco dress she wore. Her mother didn't know about it. I'd pick her up in some sedate little number her mother approved of, then bring her out here to change.'

'Did Marie often come here?'

He nodded briefly, as if the recollection were painful. 'Marie and I loved each other,' he said.

Carole had had some prudish qualms about washing and changing down in the cellar with Robert Coleman there, but he appeared to be asleep, trussed up against his chair. Perhaps he was concussed after Michael Brewer's smashing him into the tree. Anyway, his eyes were closed, and he twitched and mumbled, as though in troubled dreams. And given what he'd done, Carole thought tartly, his dreams deserved to be troubled.

She managed a fairly effective basic toilette. Keeping on her underwear, to which the petrol did not seem to have penetrated, she dressed in the T-shirt, knitted jumper and jeans Michael Brewer had looked out for her. The jeans needed a lot of rolling up, giving her the look of an American bobbysoxer. Very definitely not Carole Seddon's usual style.

In spite of assiduous washing and fresh clothes, the smell of petrol still lingered around her. She didn't think she'd ever be free of the smell of petrol. And, as for the Renault . . .

She vacated the cellar for Michael Brewer to do his own cleaning-up process, and went for a little walk around Leper's Copse as she tried to settle her mind. In the hollow of a field a little way away, she found a small blue Peugeot, presumably the car in which Robert Coleman had arrived.

When Michael Brewer emerged in his change of clothes, he suggested cooking a meal for them. To her surprise, Carole realized that she was suddenly very hungry, and accepted the offer.

Neither of them wanted to eat down in the cellar. The space felt contaminated by the presence of Robert Coleman. So Michael Brewer brought plates of hot sausages and beans out into Leper's Copse. He said he'd offered food to Robert, who hadn't wanted any. 'Have to be humane to prisoners,' said Brewer with a trace of humour. 'At least I know all about that.'

They ate their food on the edge of the copse, as far away from the smell of petrol as possible. As on the previous evening – which to Carole now seemed a lifetime away – her eyes soon adjusted to the darkness and she was aware of the greying contours of the surrounding Downs. It was a beautiful area, which kept its secrets.

Among his stores, Michael Brewer had managed to find a bottle of wine, and their little dinner à deux – the Home Office retiree and the former lifer – felt surprisingly cosy.

After they had finished eating, Carole asked, 'How long have you known that Gaby was your daughter?'

He sighed. 'I suppose I always suspected it . . . hoped it was true – hoped that there might be one positive thing salvaged from the wreck of my life. But I didn't know for sure until Marie wrote to me in Parkhurst.'

'When was that?'

'Seven, eight years ago.'

Just round the time of Gaby's panic about bowel cancer, thought Carole, and Michael Brewer's next words confirmed her conjecture.

'Marie said she had wanted to keep the truth from Gaby all her life, but for some reason she'd had to tell her that Howard wasn't her real father. She hadn't told Gaby who her father was, but there was a lot of stuff in the press around that time about adopted children tracing their birth parents. Marie was worried Gaby might have a go at that. And I had been around at the right time, so, in case Gaby made the connection, Marie thought I should be prepared for some kind of contact from her.'

'And did Gaby contact you?'

He shook his head. 'I doubt if it ever occurred to her that I might be involved. Doubt if she even knew of my existence. But, obviously, once I knew for certain she was my daughter, I wanted to make contact with her. But I couldn't write or anything, because I didn't know what the set-up was with Howard. I didn't want to put Marie in an impossible situation inside her family, so . . . I knew I'd have to wait till I was released.'

'Why did you vanish when you were released? Why didn't you go to your appointments with your probation officer?'

'I've told you!' The light of paranoia was back in his eye. 'I had to get away from authority. I knew that lot would re-arrest me as easy as blinking.'

'I'm sure you're wrong.'

'Well, I'm not. And I've had a lot more experience of that kind of world than you have, Carole.'

That was unarguable. 'So what Gaby interpreted as you stalking her was just you trying to make contact?'

'Yes. But it was difficult. I needed to see her on her own. I needed to find out whether she knew anything about me.'

'Which was why you broke into her flat . . . Was it her birth certificate you wanted to see?'

'Yes, that kind of thing. Just to check whether there was any acknowledgement of my existence in my daughter's life.'

'And was there?'

He shook his head bitterly. 'Nothing. Father's name on the birth certificate was Howard Martin.'

'And abducting me? What was all that about?'

'It was a way of getting to Gaby. She wouldn't respond if I contacted her, but if you did . . .'

'Well, why on earth didn't you tell me that? Why did you have to go through all the strong-arm routine?'

'In my experience, violence – or the threat of violence – is the only way you can get anything done.'

Carole was about to argue with this, and then she thought about what his recent experience had been. In a prison environment, the principle he had just outlined might well be the only viable one. Michael Brewer's faith in his fellow human beings was not going to be easily re-established. So she contented herself with saying, somewhat huffily, 'I still don't see why you had to take me away from High Tor.'

'The police were looking for me – are looking for me. I had to get both of us somewhere safe.'

'Huh. Well, you could have said.'

There was a silence. It was much darker now. Carole could sense rather than see the curves of the Downs in front of her.

'There's one thing, Mick . . .'

'Hm?'

'You had a lot of information. I know some of it you got from Gaby's flat – like her mobile number, for instance. But there's other stuff you couldn't have known unless someone told you. For example, how did you know where Gaby's flat was?'

He was silent for so long that she didn't think she was going to get an answer. Then, slowly, he said, 'Marie.'

'You talked to Marie?'

'Yes. After she wrote to me that first time in Parkhurst, we wrote quite a lot of letters. Couldn't say much in them, of course, because of the prison authorities my end, and Howard at her end. But . . . we re-established contact. And then, when I was released . . . I got her phone number and rang a few times. We found it easy to talk. Marie and I always found it easy to talk.'

'But weren't you worried about Howard answering the phone?'

'He never did. His deafness made using the phone difficult for him. He could use it, but he preferred not to.'

'So was it Marie who set up the meeting you were going to have with Howard – you know, the day after he died?'

'No. I didn't want her to know about that. I rang Howard to fix it at a time I knew Marie would be out.'

'And of course the meeting never happened.'

'No. Wouldn't have happened even if Howard hadn't been killed. As soon as I discovered that Robert knew about it, there was no way I was going to turn up.'

'But how did you discover that Robert knew about it?'

'Marie told me. I rang her that night after the engagement party.'

'You did? Where did you ring her from? Were you in Essex?'

'No. I was planning to go up the following morning. I was down here.'

Carole's eyes sparkled in the gloom. 'Mick, do you realize what that means?'

'What?'

'It means you've got an alibi for the time of Howard's murder. Your call to Marie in Harlow. The police can trace where the mobile was being used from. If you were down here talking on the phone, there's no way you could have been in Epping Forest, strangling Howard Martin.'

'I hadn't thought of that,' he said softly.

'And if Marie had told the police about your call, then that would have removed the suspicion from you straightaway. Why didn't she?'

'I think she wanted to protect me. She thought that if the police knew I'd been in touch with her, it would make it easier for them to track me down.'

Carole wondered if that was the real reason. She reckoned that Marie Martin's secretive nature, encouraged by her control-freak of a brother, had stopped her from saying a lot of important things over the years. Some of which would definitely have prevented murders.

Neither of them slept much that night. The weather was so mild that they didn't feel the need to go back down to the cellar. They talked intermittently, half-dozing through long silences. And, as the June dawn rose over the Downs, Carole Seddon realized that she had spent the night talking to the father of her prospective daughter-in-law.

And they hadn't discussed wedding plans at all.

Michael Brewer made them some breakfast, and Robert ate a little too. Then, at nine o'clock, the time when Jerome Clancy always arrived at his office, Carole rang through to him. Like so many from her Home Office days, his number was etched into the address book of her brain.

Jerome Clancy remembered her well, and was very interested in the story she had to tell about the miscarriage of justice against Michael Brewer. More than interested, excited. He asked how soon they could get up to his office in High Holborn.

They went all the way up to London in Robert's Peugeot, Carole driving. On public transport there was still a risk of Michael Brewer being recognized.

Jerome Clancy was delighted to see them. They talked for two hours, and he took copious notes. As the conversation developed, he grew increasingly gleeful. This was exactly the sort of case he relished.

That afternoon, acting on information received, the police arrived at Leper's Copse, and arrested Robert Coleman.

Chapter Forty-One

On that August evening outside the Crown and Anchor, Fethering felt more like the South of France than the South Coast of England. Global warming, the locals tutted, but they couldn't help loving the warm weather.

Gita Millington had come down to stay at Woodside Cottage for the weekend, and had insisted on treating Carole and Jude to dinner at the pub as a thank-you.

'What for?' Jude had asked.

'I'll tell you when you're there.'

So after they'd loaded up with drinks, heard Ted Crisp's latest joke about the difference between a fish-monger and a footballer, all ordered his recommendation of Fethering Crispy Fish Pie, and found a table outside, Jude said, 'All right, Gita. Enough of this mystery. What are you thanking us for?'

'I'm thanking you for putting me on to the Michael Brewer story.'

'Well, thank you for all the research you did,' said Carole. 'It really helped. And now, thank God, Michael Brewer has a chance of living the remainder of his life in peace.'

'In peace, and in some luxury, I would imagine.'

'What do you mean, Gita?'

'Compensation. I know no amount of money can actually make up for thirty years in prison, but he will be getting a pretty substantial sum.'

'Yes, I hadn't thought of that.'

'Come on,' Jude urged. 'Why are you thanking us for getting you to do our research for us?'

'I'm thanking you, because, the more I got into the story, the better I realized it was. So I put together a proposal for it and—'

'What, a proposal for a magazine feature?'

'Better than that. A proposal for a book. A true crime book, following the whole story through from 1973 right up to the present day. And the great news is – I've got a publisher! It's been commissioned! With, I may say, a very substantial advance.'

Jude leant across to hug her friend. 'That's absolutely brilliant!'

'I know, it's great. Because, not only is it terrific to have got the commission, it's also a new direction for my career. For a long time I've been wanting to get away from the grind of journalism – I told you – to write something that lasts more than the shelf-life of a magazine. And the book will achieve that. I'm going to write most of it in the next six months,' Gita bubbled on with excitement. 'Then I'll sit in all the way through Robert Coleman's trial, add the finishing touches and the publishers will have it in the bookshops within a week of the verdict!'

Jude grinned at Carole, who knew she was being

judged. Did she still resent Gita having been included in their investigation? She didn't. Such worries seemed to belong to a very distant time. She smiled graciously back at Jude.

'And the good thing is,' Gita continued, 'that Jerome Clancy's also going to help me on the book. Obviously there are things he can't talk about for professional reasons, but he'll give me any assistance he can.'

'Which might mean,' Jude suggested slyly, 'that you'll have to have quite a few meetings with him.'

'I suppose I might.'

'Or has that process of consultation already started?'

Gita Millington looked coy. 'Well, we have had the odd dinner . . .'

They caught each other's eye and burst out laughing. And as she looked at her friend, beautifully dressed, beautifully made-up, glowing with professional and emotional confidence, Jude felt that the rehabilitation of Gita Millington was well under way.

Embarrassed now, the journalist wanted to move the conversation on. 'But tell me, Carole, how are preparations going for the wedding of the century?'

'Absolutely brilliant.'

'And how's the blushing bride?'

'Wonderful.'

'Except, of course,' said Jude with a little smile, 'that she's been coming to see me for a few sessions. She's got trouble with her back again.'

*

The wedding was one of the most splendid that Fedborough Church had ever witnessed. The fourteenth of September proved to be a glorious late-summer day, contributing to the general feeling that nothing would be allowed to spoil the happy couple's good fortune.

The bride looked gorgeous, in a Victorian-style cream dress. Though her bridesmaids were two beautiful and well-known actresses (and, incidentally, clients of her agency), there was no doubt who was the star of the show.

The bride's mother and the groom's mother were both transformed from their usual conventional (Carole wouldn't have like the word 'dowdy') style of dress. Both had been taken shopping individually by the bride, who had pushed them to much greater daring than they would have demonstrated on their own. Marie Martin was in a simple suit of Burgundy silk, and Carole Seddon in a light wool dress and jacket in purple (a colour she would never have expected to see herself in this side of the grave). But, then again, she would never have expected to have had such girlish fun as she had had touring the boutiques with Gaby as her guide. Both mothers looked stunning and glowed with pride.

Jude also looked magnificent, a galleon of full-length yellow cotton in full sail. The straw-based hat she wore could have provided perching space for a whole aviary of birds.

But an older generation was represented too. Phil Martin had volunteered to drive down to Villeneuve-sur-Lot and collect *Grand'mère* for the wedding. She was very frail and in a wheelchair, but looked splendid in a suit of pearl-grey silk. Though honour bound to keep saying how much better the service would have been in a Catholic church, and though continually correcting everyone who didn't call Gaby Pascale, she could not hide the fact that she was enjoying every minute of the day.

Phil had another duty too. He had tidied up his act, had his hair cut and looked very handsome in his morning dress. Part of his transformation was due to a new girlfriend, who was present, resplendent in pale green linen. She was a strong-willed nurse, who was generally agreed to be 'a good thing for Phil'. Jokes at the reception about her and Phil being 'the next ones up the aisle' were not denied with quite the vehemence that they once would have been.

Phil's other duty was to give his sister away. There had been much discussion about this. After Howard's death, it had been assumed that the bride's uncle, Robert, would take on the task. But that was no longer possible – and indeed Uncle Robert's name was not mentioned once during the wedding day. His trial had not yet taken place, but Jerome Clancy was confident the case against him was so strong that he would spend the rest of his life experiencing the fate to which he had condemned his former friend.

Marie had suggested to Michael Brewer that the job of giving Gaby away was rightly his, but he had demurred. Still shy about social occasions, he did not wish to draw attention to himself. Though his relationships with both Marie and Gaby were developing wonderfully, he was as yet unwilling to make them public. Nor did he want Howard Martin's memory to be sullied; the old man deserved respect and gratitude for the way that he had brought up the girl he believed to be his daughter. So Michael Brewer was happy that Phil should give his sister away. For himself, all Gaby's father wanted to do was to be one of the signatories of the register, to be a witness at the wedding.

He stood proudly in the church, clean-shaven and immaculate in morning dress.

Everyone said the service was wonderful. The hymns had been carefully selected, and the solos were sung by more of Gaby's clients (and friends), whose understudies had taken over their matinees in West End musicals. The only slight criticism was that the Vicar of Fedborough, the Rev. Philip Trigwell, had gone on a bit. It was fine that he thought the institution of marriage was a good thing, but had he needed to point out that it didn't necessarily suit everyone? And while endorsing the Anglican faith, had it been necessary for him to list all the other faiths which were equally viable alternatives?

But such cavils were quickly forgotten in the excitement of the photographs and the magnificent tithe-barn reception. The meal was brilliant and the speeches excellent. The chief partner of Gaby's agency spoke with wit and deep affection, but Stephen was not upstaged. Knowing the limitations of his oratorical talent, he had really worked on his lines, and the sincerity of his adoration for Gaby had the audience eating out of his hand. The best man, one of his work colleagues, was another professional whose anticipated string of jokes brought the house down.

Then there was dancing. Gaby and Stephen led off, as was very right and proper, but then almost everyone joined in. Carole was surprised to find herself whisked away by Michael Brewer, and Phil Martin even took *Grand'mère* for a spin in her wheelchair. David, who was rather drunk, danced extravagantly with his daughter-in-law. To Carole's surprise, everyone seemed to find this endearingly amusing rather than embarrassing.

She and her ex-husband did, it must be said, behave impeccably. No one, who did not already know of the divorce, would have guessed there had been any rift between them.

But Carole could not pretend that she found it easy. And as she looked around the tithe barn, witnessing the unqualified love between Stephen and Gaby, the burgeoning rapprochement between Marie Martin and Michael Brewer, the fresh glow of happiness between Phil and his nurse, she felt a little wistful in the knowledge that nothing of that sort lay ahead for herself and David.

Still, three out of four happy endings wasn't bad.

THE STABBING IN THE STABLES

When healer Jude pays a visit to Long Bamber Stables one evening – to meet her new equine patient and his owner, Sonia Dalrymple – she does not expect to stumble across a man lying in the darkness. Co-owner of the stables Walter Fleet has been viciously stabbed to death.

Unable to resist a mystery, friends Jude and Carole begin to make discreet enquiries, quickly discovering that Walter's cynical widow shows no desire to mourn his departure, Sonia Dalrymple is concealing a deeply troubling secret, a stubborn teenager is curiously desperate to spend time at the stables and a horse hand appears to be more of a danger than a help.

It soon becomes clear that Long Bamber Stables are a hotbed of dangerous passions, murderous rivalries and sinister secrets . . . and this equine community will do anything to conceal the truth about their deceptive lives . . .

The Stabbing in the Stables, the delightful new mystery by Simon Brett, is out now in Macmillan hardback.

The opening scenes follow here.

Chapter One

'A horse?' Carole Seddon echoed with distaste. 'You're planning to heal a horse?'

'Well, to have a go,' said Jude.

'But I don't see how it can possibly work. Horses don't have human understanding. A horse won't know it's being healed, so how can it be healed?'

Jude chuckled, and her bird's nest of blonde hair rippled before resettling around her plump face. 'What you're saying, Carole, is that because a horse doesn't know it's being healed, it's not going to fall for the idea that it *is* being healed – as a human being might. You're saying horses aren't that gullible.'

'Well . . .'

'Yes, you are.'

'Maybe.'

'I know you don't believe in healing.'

Carole tried to find some form of denial, but all she could come up with was, 'Let's say I don't understand it.'

'I don't understand it either. I just know that it sometimes works.'

'Yes, but not with animals.'

'There are many authenticated reports of animals' ailments having been cured by healing.'

'Huh!' That was Carole Seddon's customary response to the world of alternative therapy, and to many other things that challenged the security of her sensible life.

They were sitting in a part of that security, the kitchen of her house High Tor in the West Sussex seaside village of Fethering. The tidiness of the room, the gleaming surfaces, the neatly aligned pots and pans, the rack of spice jars whose labels had been dragooned into facing the front, all conspired to cancel out the cosiness that the Aga should have imparted. In front of the stove, Carole's Labrador Gulliver, satisfied by his late-afternoon walk on Fethering Beach, snuffled in a contented dream of saving the world from killer seaweed.

'So whose horse is it?'

'Woman called Sonia Dalrymple.'

'Do I know her?'

'No. She's a client.' Jude always used that word to describe the people who took advantage of her occasional healing and balancing services. 'Patient' never sounded right to her.

'Oh.' Carole managed to fill the monosyllable with exactly the same ration of scepticism that she had put into the 'Huh'. Her attitude to Jude's 'clients' was that they were slightly flaky people with insufficient self-control – and probably more money than sense. Carole's view was that when you were genuinely ill,

2

you went to your GP, and when you weren't genuinely ill, you put up and shut up.

Carole Seddon suffered from the innate puritanism of a middle-class southerner in her fifties, a system of values that had been dinned into her by timid parents in the post-war austerity of her upbringing. She was suspicious of the foreign, the unknown and, most of all, anything with the slightest whiff of mysticism. She hated herself for her hidebound world view, but it was too much part of her personality to yield to major change.

That personality was, she liked to think, reflected in her appearance. Her grey hair was cut sensibly short, and her pale blue eyes were assisted by sensible rimless glasses. Bright colours and patterns were eschewed, and the only part of her wardrobe aspiring beyond Marks & Spencer was a well-kept, though now ageing, Burberry raincoat.

But over the previous few years chinks had appeared in the carapace of correctness with which Carole Seddon had deliberately surrounded herself. As she grew further away from the trauma of divorce from her husband David, as she became more reconciled to her unwarrantably early retirement from the Home Office, she had not exactly mellowed – indeed, the idea of 'mellowing' would have been anathema to her – but she had entertained the possibility that there might exist valid attitudes other than those with which she had been brought up. This process had been partly assisted by a rapprochement with her son Stephen, engineered by Gaby, the girl to whom he was now married.

But the greatest change in Carole Seddon had been effected by the serendipitous arrival of Jude in Woodside Cottage next door. Carole would never have admitted it, because she was not an advocate of any kind of sentimentality, but her friendship with Jude was the most potent agent in the recent thawing of her character's permafrost.

The attraction between the two women was unlikely. In spite of the fact that Carole wanted to organize every moment of the future to within an inch of its life while Jude was comfortably content to let events come to her, their relationship survived remarkably well. And the detail that from time to time that relationship had incorporated murder investigations was regarded by both women as an inestimable bonus.

'So for what imagined ills does this Sonia come to you?' Carole continued sniffily.

Jude smiled an easy smile. 'There is such a thing as client confidentiality.'

'Yes, I suppose there is' – the temptation to add – '. . . in your kind of world,' proved irresistible. 'And it's her horse?'

'As I said. He's called Chieftain.'

'She must be rich.' There were certain triggers within Carole that resulted in this knee-jerk reaction, and all of them came from her childhood when her parents had made sacrifices to put her through private education. Anyone who had a horse must be rich; equally anyone who had a boat. The same went for anyone who went skiing – and certainly anyone who went waterskiing. The fact that all these indulgences had now become widely available to the general public did not change Carole's views. In the ineluctable way of prejudices, they stuck.

'As a matter of fact, Sonia is quite well heeled.'

'I thought so,' said Carole, prejudice vindicated.

'But that's not important.'

Oh no, of course not. Owns a horse, and can afford to splash out on alternative therapies, but the money's not important. Carole kept such reactions to herself.

Jude's grin suggested she had read the thoughts without their being voiced. She sat at the kitchen table, swathed in her customary layers of fabric – more of them at this time of year to fend off the February chill. Jude didn't always wear the same clothes, but they always gave the same impression. She dressed in a profusion of floaty shirts, skirts and scarves, which never seemed to define where one garment ended and the other started. The outline around her plump body was always imprecise, but it generated a feeling of comfort – and, to men, an undoubted sexual allure. People were always at their ease around Jude – something that could never be said of Carole.

'Anyway, what's wrong with the horse?'

'Chieftain's lame. Trouble with his knee.'

'Do horses have knees?'

'Of course they do. Their legs are hinged in the middle, you know.'

'Yes, I know they are, Jude. But "knee" sounds a

rather prosaic word for a horse. I thought they were all "fetlocks" and "withers" and . . .' Carole's repertoire of equine anatomy ran out.

'I can assure you they have knees, as well as fetlocks and withers.'

'Ah.' She still needed something with which to come back at Jude. 'I thought, if horses were ill, they were taken to vets.'

'And if a horse is taken to the vet, and the vet can't find anything wrong . . .?'

'Oh, I see. Then their owners resort to alternative remedies.' Carole couldn't stop herself from adding, 'Just like gullible humans.'

Jude grinned again. In anyone else, such a grin would have been infuriating, with her, somehow it wasn't. 'Except, you've already established that horses can't be gullible.'

'No. Well, maybe not,' Carole conceded. 'Anyway, when you came in, some time ago, you asked if I could do you a favour. So far as I can recollect, you haven't yet said what that favour is.'

'No, I haven't.'

'What is it then?'

'I wondered if you'd mind giving me a lift to the stables, so that I can have a look at Chieftain.'

Carole's first reaction was to refuse. It was late afternoon, nearly time for a television chat show to which she was becoming secretly addicted. But her puritan instinct told her that wasn't really an excuse and, if she used it as such, she'd have to admit to Jude

6

that she actually watched the thing. So she said yes, she'd love to give her friend a lift to the stables.

As they drove along in Carole's sensible, recently vacuumed Renault, Jude provided a skimpy background to their destination. Long Bamber Stables were on the Fedborough road, maybe a mile up the River Fether from Fethering. They advertised regularly in the *Fethering Observer*, offering DIY full/part livery, an indoor school, hacking, riding lessons and other services.

Though Jude had not been there before, she had heard from Sonia Dalrymple that the stables were owned by a married couple, Walter and Lucinda Fleet. In riding circles, Walter Fleet had apparently once been known as a promising eventer (whatever that might be, Carole inevitably interpolated) whose career had been cut short by a serious fall from a horse. Jude had also got the impression that Lucinda Fleet was not Sonia Dalrymple's favourite person.

But that was all she knew. Except for the fact that Sonia had agreed to meet her outside the stables at six that Tuesday evening.

'And how would you have got here if I hadn't given you a lift?'

'I knew you would give me a lift.'

Carole saw Jude's teasing smile, illuminated by the headlights of an oncoming car, and seethed quietly.

The parking at Long Bamber Stables was some way from the main gates, and when she switched off the engine, Carole insisted on staying in the Renault. She'd even brought a book with her – and there was always a torch in the glove compartment, because she had a paranoid fear of running down the car's battery.

Jude didn't argue, although she knew Carole's decision to stay arose from her unwillingness to meet Sonia Dalrymple, someone new, someone who believed in alternative therapy, someone who was rich enough to own a horse. Saying she wouldn't be more than half an hour, Jude walked across the tarmac to the stable gates. She checked the large watch, fixed by a broad ribbon to her wrist. Three minutes to six.

The buildings appeared to make up a timber-clad square, no doubt with loose boxes lining the inside and paddocks behind. There was no roof over the yard onto which the gates opened, though somewhere inside there must be a covered indoor school and storage barns. A little way away from the stables stood a modest red-brick house, presumably the home of Walter and Lucinda Fleet. Although she couldn't see it, Jude could hear the swishing flow of the River Fether which ran alongside the site.

To her surprise, there was no light over the gates, nor could she see any evidence of lights inside the yard. There was no sign of Sonia Dalrymple either.

It was cold. Jude waited for a few minutes, stamping her feet to maintain circulation but no other vehicle appeared to join the Renault in the car park.

A thin February moon cast a watery light over the scene. Jude could see that the double gates were closed, and she looked in vain for a bell-push or knocker. Apart from the underscoring of the river, the only sounds were distant rustlings and clompings, presumably from the horses within.

Jude checked her watch again. Nearly quarter past six. Though she didn't know Sonia Dalrymple that well, her client had always been punctual for her appointments at Woodside Cottage.

Surely Sonia had said to meet *outside* the stables. She must have been held up somewhere. Sonia had twin teenage daughters, so no doubt she'd been delayed by some crisis in ferrying them somewhere. Or maybe Jude had got it wrong, and the arrangement had been to meet *inside* the stables, near Chieftain's box. Worth trying. If the gates were locked, Jude would know she hadn't got it wrong.

Just as she had the thought, there was a sudden outburst of neighing and heavy-footed stamping from the horses within. Something had disturbed them. More likely, someone had disturbed them. Sonia Dalrymple must be inside the yard. Odd that she hadn't put any lights on, though. If the stables were locked, Jude would hammer on the gates to attract attention.

But when she turned the heavy metal ring, they readily gave inward, letting out a grudging creak of timber. Jude pushed through into the hay- and dung-scented yard, where near-silence had reasserted itself. As she did so, from the far side of the square courtyard she heard the sharp impact of wood on wood. A gate closing?

Jude moved into the centre of the square where the moonlight was strongest. She'd been right about the loose boxes, forming the walls of the yard. Unseen horses shifted uneasily. One whinnied, troubled by the presence of an intruder. There was no sign of human life.

On the other hand, there was a sign of human death.

In the middle of the courtyard lay the body of a man. The pale moonlight glistened on the blood that had only recently ceased to flow from his face, throat and chest.

Chapter Two

Jude's plump body moved with surprising speed back across the tarmac to the Renault. Carole took a moment or two to interpret her friend's excited gabble, but once she understood was quickly out of the car. With her torch.

Its beam did not improve the look of the body. The man had been the object of a frenzied assault. A trail of bright blood spots suggested he had been backing away from his attacker. Deep gashes on his hands showed he had tried to protect himself, until he had tripped over backwards or collapsed from his injuries.

The horses in the stalls shifted nervously, some snorting with unease at this new invasion of their domain.

Carole looked back along the trail of blood. A few feet beyond where the broken line stopped – or in fact where the spillage had started – the door to a wooden two-storey building hung open. A solid door, not divided in the middle like those on the loose boxes. Hinged metal bars and heavy padlocks hung from rings on the frame. From inside there was a slight glow from a hidden light source.

'What's that, Jude?'

'I've no idea. First time I've been here. Saddle room, tack room maybe . . .? Mind you, the blood spots suggest that the victim and his attacker came out from there and—'

'It's not our place to make that kind of conjecture,' said Carole, suddenly all sniffy. 'We should ring the police. You've got your mobile, haven't you?'

'Yes.' Jude reached reluctantly into the pocket of her coat. 'I wouldn't mind having a quick look around before we—'

Carole's Home Office background would not allow the sentence to be finished. 'This is a crime scene. It would be deeply irresponsible for us to disturb anything.'

'Just a quick look?' Jude wheedled.

'No.' A hand was held out for the mobile. 'If you won't do it, then I will.'

After a short hesitation, Jude said, 'I think we should tell the Fleets first.'

'What?'

'The people who own the place. They must live in the house next door. They should know what's happened on their premises before the police arrive.'

Carole wavered just long enough for Jude to say, 'I'll tell them,' and set off towards the gates.

'Do you want the torch?'

'No, I can see. Besides, I don't want to leave you alone in the dark with the body.'

'We must call the police as soon as the Fleets have been informed,' Carole called after her friend's retreating outline. 'We must be very careful we don't tamper with a crime scene.'

She stood still for a moment, then let the torch beam explore the space around her. Not onto the body – she had seen quite enough of that for its image to haunt her dreams for months to come.

Most of the loose-box top-halves were open, but the moving ray of light did not reveal any of their inmates. The horses lurked in the recesses of their stalls, snuffling and stamping their continuing disquiet.

A complete circuit of the yard revealed double gates at the far end, offering access to the paddocks beyond, and other gates leading to barns, tack rooms and the indoor school. The torch beam ended up once again fixed on the open door. Carole felt a sudden, over-whelming temptation.

She shouldn't do it. Everything she had ever learnt during her extensive dealings with the police told her she should touch nothing, explore nothing. Jude's foot-prints and her own might already have destroyed important evidence. To investigate further would be the height of irresponsibility. Her duty as a citizen dictated she should stay stock still where she was until the police arrived. Or, perhaps even better, go back to the Renault and wait there.

On the other hand . . . how were the police to know she wasn't just another incompetent, invisible woman in late-middle age? In most recent dealings she'd had with them, that's how she had been treated. There could be any number of reasons why an incompetent, invisible woman in late-middle age might go through that open door. She might be looking for bandages, cloth, something to staunch the wounds of the victim, unaware that her ministrations would come too late. She might be looking inside the wooden building for someone to help. She might go there to hide from the homicidal maniac who had just committed one crime and was about to commit another. She might . . .

Almost involuntarily, Carole felt her footsteps following the torch beam towards the open door.

The lack of lights in the Fleets' house was a discouraging omen, and repeated ringing of the bell confirmed that no one was at home.

For a second, Jude contemplated ringing the police from their doorstep, but quickly decided not to. Maybe, after all, Carole could be persuaded into a little preliminary private investigation before the call was made?

But the walk back from house to stables was interrupted by the beam of high headlights turning into the car park. Jude stopped, thinking the Fleets might have returned, but quickly recognized the black Range Rover as it drew up beside her and the driver-side window was lowered.

'Jude – so sorry. Have you been waiting hours? I got horribly delayed.'

Even though flushed and flustered, Sonia Dalrymple's face was still beautiful. She was a tall, leggy blonde in her early forties, with a fabulous figure toned by riding and a metabolism that helped her never put on an ounce. Her voice had the upper-class ease of someone who had never doubted her own position in society. No one meeting her would ever be able to associate such a goddess with the deep insecurities which had brought her to Jude in search of healing.

'No, don't worry, there's no problem.' As her client doused the headlights and got out of the car, Jude realized how inappropriate, in the circumstances, her words were.

Sonia Dalrymple was wearing cowboy boots and the kind of designer jeans which had been so gentrified as to lose any connection with their origins as working clothes. She had a white roll-neck sweater under a blue and white striped body-warmer. The blonde hair was scrunched back into an untidy ponytail.

'I'm really terribly sorry. Come on, let's see how old Chieftain—'

'Sonia, something's happened.'

'What?'

'I was just trying to tell the Fleets . . . at least I assume they live in that house.'

'Yes, they do.'

'There's no one in. There's . . . Sonia, there's been an accident in the stables.'

The woman's face paled. 'Oh, God. Is Chieftain all right?'

'Yes. All the horses are fine.'

Sonia's reaction of relief seemed excessive to Jude, but then she wasn't a horse owner.

'No, I'm afraid it's a human being who's suffered the . . . accident.'

15

'Who?' The anxiety was at least as great as it had been for Chieftain.

'No idea. It's a man.'

'What's happened to him?'

'He's dead.'

'Oh! But . . . how?'

'It looks very much as if he's been stabbed to death.'

'You mean murder?'

Jude nodded grimly. 'Come and have a look.'

Inside the stables Carole stood exactly where Jude had left her, torch modestly pointing downwards. Sonia was hastily introduced, and Carole moved the torch beam to spotlight the dead man.

'Oh, my God!' A deep sob shuddered through Sonia's body.

'You recognize him?' asked Jude.

'Yes. This is – or was – Walter Fleet.'

www.panmacmillan.com